A TOUCH OF SOMETHING DIFFERENT

Maryellen choked over her glass of milk and had to put it down. "I can't believe this is happening! I can't believe you're real. You're so much like a nightmare specifically designed to humiliate me—coming in here and telling me I'm having thoughts about having sex with you! I could be in a hospital someplace with amnesia and hallucinations after . . . after an automobile wreck, and all this happened to me days ago! You could be a doctor or nurse in some expensive private pavilion Felicia's committed me to, and I'm being taken care of in wonderfully luxurious accommodations—any minute now they're going to bring me dinner from outside, catered by Le Cirque!" She glared at him. Then suddenly she said, "I want to touch you."

His cobalt blue eyes blinked. "Touch me?"

"Yes." She had finally taken him by surprise. "You claim you aren't a hallucination or a glob of intergalactic Jell-O, so I want to find out just what you are. If you're really real, you won't mind my touching you."

"I didn't say I *minded* your touching me." He paused. "It just depends on what touching it is. What part do you, er, have in mind?"

KATHERINE DEAUXVILLE

OUT of the BLUE

LOVE SPELL NEW YORK CITY

*With all my thanks to Ashley, Brooke, Chris, Fidencia,
Kate, Katy, and Leah*

*Once upon a time not so long ago,
when we had a lot less to worry about . . .*

A LOVE SPELL BOOK®

February 2002

Published by

Dorchester Publishing Co., Inc.
276 Fifth Avenue
New York, NY 10001

ISBN 0-505-52469-4

The name "Love Spell" and its logo are trademarks of Dorchester
Publishing Co., Inc.

Printed in the United States of America.

Visit us on the web at www.dorchesterpub.com.

OUT of the BLUE

Chapter One

When Maryellen Caswell woke she was aware something out of the ordinary was happening. She seemed to be cursing—at least it sounded like cursing—in a moderately deep, but not unpleasant baritone in words she couldn't understand.

At the same time, she knew the source of the voice. It was *inside* her. She could feel her lips move, yet the deep, telltale vibrations in her chest were too resonant to be her own. It was rather horrifying. When she tried to open her eyes, she found they wouldn't work—like someone or something was holding down her eyelids.

Maryellen was still too foggy with sleep to give over to total panic, but even so, she knew that this was not her voice. She had a rather charming speaking voice and, when she chose to use it, a particularly seductive purr that had been known to drive a few men crazy.

But this angry sound was not female. Even though it seemed to be coming from right inside of her.

Mercy, she thought groggily, what was going on? If it was a dream, it was a strange one, complete with infuriated words in a language that was not like anything Maryellen had heard before.

Then, quite suddenly, the voice said in perfect English, "Damn, I'm in this squalid place again! And if there's anything I hate in this rotten backwater solar system, it's planet Styrex Three. Those clowns in the transport system ought to be chained to the rocks of a K-403 moon for screwing me up like this!"

At this point Maryellen was horrified to feel what was obviously her own hand, although just as obviously not under her control, move down her arm and across her chest, exploring.

"Eeeeek," she whispered as it investigated her left breast thoroughly. She hardly dared breathe.

There was a pause. Then the voice burst out, "Hell, it's a WOMAN! of all the—I've landed in a *woman's* body!"

Maryellen heard what sounded like a snarl of exasperation. Then the plainly masculine voice burst out, "Court martial! I'll have every damned one of them up on charges for this! You can't convince me this is just another sloppy mistake by that crowd in Intergalactic Travel. It has all the earmarks of deliberate sabotage!" To Maryellen it said, "Stop squirming. I have to find out what your body is like while I assess the situation."

Assess the situation? Maryellen tried to take a deep breath, in spite of the insistent probing of her thumb and forefinger around her nipple.

It was some sort of early-morning nightmare, she told herself shakily. A nightmare that didn't seem to want to go away. *Aaagh!* Now her hand was exploring places she definitely didn't want explored!

"Stop that!" she cried. She was determined to break free from this ghastly dream and open her eyes. "Take my hand off my—uh, down there!" She struggled to lift her eyelids. "I mean, what's going on? Why am I doing this?" She gritted her teeth, willing herself to lift her arm, with little success. "I'm taking my hand back, do you hear me?"

"Go right ahead," the voice said, "I'm through, anyway."

Released from the strange power, Maryellen's arm flew up, smacking her on the forehead.

"Relax, I'm not interested in Styrex Three's cultural emphasis," the voice continued rather blandly, "on female virginity. Just put it down to a little—ah, personal curiosity."

Maryellen's eyes suddenly flew open.

Whatever nightmarish power that had held her had now relaxed its grip. She could make out the normal surroundings of her bedroom, her four-poster bed, the pale sun of midtown Manhattan streaming through window blinds that disguised the apartment's view of the air shaft.

It took a long moment before she could get her wits about her to think *What a terrible way to start the day! What a really stupid nightmare!* On the other hand, she consoled herself, everything was all right. There was, after all, nothing so reassuring as to find oneself in familiar, undisturbed surroundings. It had just been an extremely bad dream, that was all.

"No, it wasn't," the voice said. "This is no dream; it's one hell of a mess. At least for me. Your situation, if you cooperate and don't lose your head, is a purely passive one."

Maryellen screamed.

She threw back the covers, jumped out of bed, and ran for the bathroom. There she grabbed the door and slammed and locked it.

The mirrored wall behind the bathroom sink reflected a wild-eyed young woman with curly brown hair literally standing on end. She was gasping for air like a stranded goldfish.

It occurred to Maryellen that if she didn't stop gasping she'd probably hyperventilate, perhaps even pass out on the floor of the bathroom. But she couldn't stop. She grabbed her hair wildly with both hands. The image in the mirror did the same.

It wasn't possible that there was something inside of her that had taken possession of her body, was it? Something that spoke in a deep, macho male voice about transportation systems and intergalactic travel? Or was she having some sudden, terrible psychosis that had just

this minute attacked her, and that would ultimately ruin her life and destroy her career?

People in advertising, she told herself, were
always having nervous breakdowns. It was sort
of an occupational disease. Just last year the art
director at the Robinson Foote Agency had
flipped out right at his desk, yelling that he was
a pigeon and was quitting his job to go live with
the rest of his family in the park behind the New
York Library. The art director had tried to jump
out of his office on the forty-fourth floor, but of
course all the windows in skyscrapers were
sealed. Everybody in the ad business knew that.

Maryellen leaned up against the cabinet, despairing sobs welling up inside her. In her case,
going bonkers and thinking there was some
voice or something inside her was even worse
than wanting to join the New York Library pi-
geons! Ad agencies already regarded commercial artists as pretty flaky. She could just hear
them now. *Poor Maryellen Caswell. Just woke up
one morning in the middle of work on a four-color
layout of Calvin Klein underwear and went all to
pieces. Right in the bathroom. Flat on the floor.*

"This is very interesting," the voice inside her
said. "All these mirrors in a place essentially for
sanitary functions. And do you always sleep in
the nude?"

Maryellen clutched at herself. Her face in the
mirror wall looked as though she were seeing a
ghost.

"Aaagh!" she cried. She lunged for the bathroom door, unlocked it, and hurled herself back
into the bedroom. She took a flying leap into the

bed, screaming, and pulled the sheets over her head.

The voice was right there under the covers with her. It immediately said, "Don't act like an idiot. You have a very nice Styrex Three–type body. I fail to see why you're running around making terrified noises just because I happened to view it without any wrappings."

Maryellen pulled the sheet back from her face. "I don't think I can stand this! A nervous breakdown at my age! I'm only twenty-six, and I have a brilliant career ahead of me—everybody on Madison Avenue says so." Her voice rose to a wail. "Now I'll end up living in doorways, eating out of Dumpsters, taking free medication every week where they line up at the Bellevue psychiatric outpatient clinic!"

"Preposterous," the voice inside her said irritably. "You're not having a nervous breakdown, which is not a valid medical term, anyway, even on this benighted planet. Now, I'll explain the situation if you'll give me half a chance."

"I don't want to hear it," Maryellen cried, pulling the sheets back over her head. "I'm going crazy, I'm—I'm—having *hallucinations*, I wish you'd stop talking to me!"

Her own hands pulled the covers away. "Now listen," the voice ordered. "Are you listening? It's difficult enough when we're both trying to talk at the same time. I am Ur Targon, sub commander of—" He stopped abruptly. "Actually there's no need to go into all that, let's just say I come from a place you've never heard of. I landed here by mistake, or so my cohorts would

12

have me believe," he added ominously. "And in a woman's body, which may be somebody's idea of a joke. But I've been effectively put out of commission for a few Styrex Three days." The voice paused, thoughtfully. "Frankly, it looks as though I've been set up. My work doesn't exactly generate a lot of close friends."

"Your work?" Maryellen asked in spite of herself.

"I'm chief investigator of potentially subversive government agencies." There was a note of satisfaction in his voice. "I track down burgeoning treason in bureaucracies and eliminate them. In your culture, something like the secret police."

"In our culture," Maryellen felt obliged to say, "we don't have secret police."

He snorted. "Of course you do. Every government has them. My division is an elite cadre renowned all over the—" He stopped again. "Never mind that, either. Let's get down to the business at hand. I need to find myself a more suitable host body and you, I take it, need to do the things you usually do in the morning. Naturally you'll need some measure of privacy. Just hold still for a moment while I temporarily detach myself from you."

Before Maryellen could say or do anything she felt a slight tugging all over her body, as if her skin were shifting, then a deeper, even more disturbing sensation of something inside her stirring and slipping away. She gasped.

She gasped again when she saw him. Her nightmare had materialized in a sitting position

13

on her wicker slipper chair, his legs and arms crossed, looking very comfortable in spite of the fact that he was big and the slipper chair was small.

His size was not the important thing. He was shaped like a human being, she saw with a rush of relief. It could have been something far worse.

Maryellen had to strain to see because he was covered in a luminous aura, rather like gold-colored Day-glo paint. Under it—or rather, through it—he seemed to be wearing skintight clothes like a spandex jumpsuit. The face was hardest of all to see, it projected so much of the golden glow, but Maryellyn thought he had fairly even, not unattractive features. And shoulder length, glowing gold hair.

Still, the whole effect was rather insubstantial, as though she could put her hand through all that pulsing bright shimmer and see it come out the other side.

No doubt about it, whatever was happening, it was something out of a science-fiction movie. One of the better, high-budget special-effects ones.

Maryellen got to her knees, dragging the sheet from the bed and wrapping it around her. She lurched off to the bathroom. She was thinking as she closed the door that if she didn't look at him her hallucination might go away. Because it *was* an hallucination, she kept telling herself. When she started seeing golden hunky bodies that looked like something out of old fifties movies she knew it was her brain that was malfunctioning, not reality.

Maryellen took the telephone extension off the bathroom wall and dialed her sister's condo number on the East Side. There was a moment of uproar in the background before the maid could get Felicia to come to the phone.

"Maryellen?" Her sister's voice projected loudly over the mayhem. "My God, it's not seven o'clock yet. Get down, Damian, sweet, and don't climb on mommy, you're getting oatmeal all over me! Mel, can't you call me back later?"

"Felicia," Maryellen cried, not even sure she could be heard on the other end. "You've got to help me! I've got an alien in my bedroom."

There were howls as Felicia apparently handed the baby to Juana, the maid. "Of course I'll help you, sweetie," her sister said, "but I hope it's really, really important. This is not a good time to call, you know? I'm still trying to get the kids off to school and Stephen's being a bear because he can't find his notes for some damned director's meeting, and of course the baby's just smeared me with what's left of his breakfast. What kind of alien is it?"

"Felicia," Maryellen almost shrieked, "will you listen to me very carefully? I have an emergency; I think I'm having a nervous breakdown. In fact, I'm sure of it! I woke up this morning and there was an alien in my body talking about how much he hated being on this planet and that somebody had messed him up by sending him here! He was really very nasty about it. Felicia, he was talking right inside of me, and now he's sitting in the bedroom in my wicker slipper chair waiting for me to get through in here!"

"He?" the voice on the other end of the line said almost before Maryellen finished speaking. "Melly, you didn't go out last night to a bar or anything like that and let a man buy you a drink, did you? They've got this drug that men put in girls' drinks that sends them out of their minds. These sex fiends can do anything to them, then. Haven't you been watching Ricki Lake? Listen, is this rapist bastard still in your bedroom? Hang up right away, I'll call 911—"

"Felicia," Maryellen screamed back, "I don't need you to call 911! I haven't been to any bars, I'm too busy working for that, and there's no rapist in my bedroom! I'm just having an ordinary nervous breakdown like people who wake up hearing God telling them that they ought to take off all their clothes and make a speech in front of the United Nations. Remember the art director who wanted to be a pigeon in the park behind the public library?" She hesitated, envisioning her older sister, indestructibly chic and beautiful in spite of the early-morning chaos in Felicia's Crump Tower condominium, and how all this must sound. In fact, there was a prolonged silence, now, on the other end.

"Felicia?" she said weakly.

"Honey, I'm still here," her sister's voice reassured her. "I don't know what's wrong, but you're not the type to wake up in the morning claiming there are aliens in your bed. I'm taking all this very seriously. Frankly. I think you've been working much too hard, you hardly stick your nose out of that studio, and God knows you don't have any social life since you broke up with

George Parker. You know what I think about these three-year engagements where you live together and are always planning the wedding, and then the guy decides he doesn't want to get married after all. But okay—if you say you think you're having a nervous breakdown, I believe you. What we need to do is look up a good shrink. I'll call around and ask the girls and see who's being recommended this week."

"Do you really think I ought to see a shrink?" Maryellen asked forlornly. "I mean, there's only been this one episode. Maybe it's an hallucination that's already gone away."

"First, lunch," her sister said. "You'll feel better after that. We'll do lunch at 21—it's old and quiet, and I'll tell the maître d' to put us in a corner at the back. And I'll make an appointment for you with the psychiatrist, and you can spend all afternoon telling him about your alien. If you ask me, Mel, I don't think it's going to amount to anything more than some sort of fatigue syndrome that hit you when you weren't expecting it."

Maryellen clung to the bathroom telephone. Felicia had a marvelous way of reducing problems to reasonable proportions. It did make her feel better when her sister talked about a civilized lunch at 21, then spending an afternoon with a psychiatrist, telling him all the details of her problem.

"Honey, do me a favor." Felicia's voice came crisply over the wire. "Are you on the bathroom extension? Okay, open the door very, very carefully, and look into the bedroom and tell me if the alien is still there."

Maryellen hesitated. It was an eminently practical suggestion. She cracked the bathroom door and put her eye to it.

Her slipper chair was empty. She quickly searched the rest of the room, opening the bathroom door a little wider. The bedroom was empty unless Sub Commander Targon was hiding under the bed. And Maryellen didn't think he would do that.

"I can't see him," she whispered into the receiver. "Felicia, can you hear me? The alien or the hallucination or nervous breakdown or whatever it is, is gone!"

"I still think we should have lunch," her sister responded. "And let me make an emergency appointment for you with some good West Side shrink. Don't say no—suppose you wake up and find the thing is there in bed with you tomorrow morning? Let's make it 21 at noon. Promise?"

"I promise," Maryellen said, and hung up.

"I thought you'd never get off the phone," the all-too-familiar voice said inside her.

Chapter Two

"I think we should have soup," Maryellen's sister said as she picked up 21's menu. "All those doctors who did research on it said chicken soup really does work. Why don't you try some of 21's lobster bisque—that has to be better than chicken."

Felicia was looking dazzling—as she could almost on a moment's notice, a legacy of her modeling days. Even Maryellen, who in her distraught state was not up to noticing much of anything, couldn't ignore her sister's blazing red Ralph Lauren wool dress and matching long shirt-coat that set off her blond hair. Felicia looked a lot like Jerry Hall, Mick Jagger's former wife. Her looks were one reason her multimillionaire husband, Stephen, had fallen in love with and married her.

"I don't know that I need soup to comfort me," Maryellen muttered. Having lunch with her sister was not really such a good idea, after all. The popular New York restaurant was making her even more nervous, although her alien visitor hadn't spoken since she'd arrived. Maybe he was no longer with her. She'd been ignoring him, hoping he'd disappear. Maryellen didn't think she could be so lucky. "If I'm going crazy," she said out loud, "I need something more powerful than soup. Like a glass of wine. Or a gin martini."

Felicia shuddered. "Oh, really, Mel, you people who don't drink can make the most horrible choices! Believe me, a martini would kill you. I'd have to call old George, the waiter, to carry you out of here."

"I wouldn't mind a martini right now," the voice inside Maryellen said.

At the sound of Sub Commander Targon's words, which apparently no one else could hear, Maryellen dropped her menu on the table, overturning her water glass. "Oh, God, he's back!" she cried. "Felicia, the alien is really here!"

"Martinis are one of the few good things Styrex Three has to offer," the baritone voice observed. "Make that vodka with a twist of lemon, not gin."

George the waiter hurried up with linen napkins to mop up the mess. "Oh no, miss," he murmured as he hastily surveyed the clientele of 21's upstairs dining room. "We don't have such people in here. As far as I know, everyone having lunch today is a U.S. citizen—with the exception of the Japanese gentlemen from the Mitsubishi corporation."

"Not that kind of alien, George," Felicia corrected him gently. "But thank you, anyway. Give my sister another glass of water, and we'll both have the lobster bisque."

"What about the damned martini?" Targon demanded. "Do you always let your sister order you around like this?"

That was too much. Maryellen hissed, "Will you *shut up?*"

Her sister looked startled, then quickly compassionate.

"Sweetie, I have a feeling I'm just making things worse," she murmured, putting her hand reassuringly over Maryellen's violently trembling one. "I really hate to see you in this state. Do you want me to stop talking? I mean, I won't mention a thing about the you-know-what; we can just have a nice, silent lunch together. Just tell me what to do."

Before Maryellen could reply, her sister opened her Hermes purse, withdrew a pill bottle, and shook a little white tablet into her palm.

"Melly, I wouldn't advise a martini, not in your present—ummm, over-stimulated condition. And especially since you're going to see Dr. Dzhugashvili right after lunch. He's a bit odd, but I hear he's all the rage right now. It certainly wouldn't do to come into your first meeting with him all boozed-up, not after asking for an emergency appointment—that wouldn't make the right impression, and it would only confuse the issue. I have a better idea."

"I don't trust your sister," Sub Commander Targon interrupted. "She looks great, but she's a wacko. Don't take any pill she gives you. Stick with the martini."

Maryellen wanted to scream for Targon to be quiet. But crying out right in the middle of one of New York's most elegant restaurants was not the way to handle a nervous breakdown. Still, her hand was wobbling as she took the tablet her sister handed her, and lifted her glass of water.

"Don't take that pill," Targon warned. "You don't even know what she's giving you."

"It's not as strong as Prozac, sweetie," Felicia was saying, almost as if she'd heard him. "But it will calm you down. It works wonders for my migraines."

Desperate, Maryellen popped the tablet in her mouth and washed it down just as ancient George rolled up the cart with a silver soup tureen and proceeded to serve their lobster bisque.

They ate in silence for a while. George followed the lobster bisque with a light pasta jardin. Maryellen hardly tasted the food. She was beginning to feel the effect of the little white tablet her sister had given her and Felicia was right—it was quite calming. So much so, in fact, that there was an ominous inactivity inside her where Sub Commander Targon usually made his presence known.

Felicia suddenly put down her fork and stared intently at Maryellen.

"Are you all right?" she whispered. "You look

strange. I mean, I'm reacting, too. It's definitely traumatic when your own sister calls you up and tells you she's having a nervous breakdown because an alien has taken possession of her body. There's something positively spooky about it." She looked around the restaurant. "And then here we are, having lunch at 21."

"It's unreal, all right," Maryellen said with difficulty. "Thanks to that pill you gave me I'm getting so ironed out I can hardly see my plate."

She put her hand to her head. She felt strange, all right. The tips of her fingers were a little numb. The warmth of the lobster bisque seemed to be contributing to the effect of her sister's medication, whatever it was.

"What was in that pill?" she wanted to know. "I think it even put Sub Commander Targon to sleep."

Felicia frowned. "That's exactly what I mean. It's so . . . well, *convincing* when you talk like that. I almost believe that thing has taken up residence in your body. Ugh, what a disgusting thought! It sounds like being pregnant."

George was hovering over them with a silver coffeepot saying something about regular or decaffeinated. Since Felicia wasn't paying any attention, Maryellen motioned for him to pour her a cup. She was feeling she needed the caffeine.

"There's definitely a sensation," Maryellen said hesitantly, "although I can't exactly describe it. If I said, well . . . sensuous . . . you'd laugh. But I feel it through my whole body when he decides to materialize someplace outside it."

Her sister stared at her. "Oh, sweetie, this

comes from working day and night and not dating, or taking any interest in men except those commercial artists you hang out with. There are all sorts of dynamic, success-oriented men in advertising, men who would be attracted to someone as basically good-looking as you, if you'd just give them a chance. Don't tell me none of them has even tried to chat you up?"

"I'm not interested in advertising types," Maryellen told her. "I spend enough of my time trying to sell them my art. And yes, they do try to hit on me. I've turned down my share of invitations to the company's suite at the Carlysle Hotel for a heart-to-heart chat after lunch."

"Well, then, there are models," her sister insisted. "Some of the best-looking men in the world pose for Ralph Lauren and designers like that. You'd be surprised how many of my friends have really interesting encounters with male models. Not to mention those hunks who act on soap operas. They tell me you can't get a job on daytime TV unless you look like a combination of Pierce Brosnan and Mr. Universe."

"Felicia, I work for a living," Maryellen protested. The coffee George had poured was beginning to revive her. "I'm not rich like you, remember? I don't get to chase male models and soap opera actors; I'm too busy trying to make it in a crazy business! Besides, after three years of George Parker, believe me, I've kicked the habit."

"I didn't say anything about chasing them," Felicia replied a little huffily. "But when you start having sensuous feelings about some alien you think has taken over your body, I think that's a teeny bit indicative of some sort of sexual frustration, don't you? It's overwork, Melly, overwork and all sorts of lifestyle deprivation that's caused you to hallucinate."

"Felicia, please," Maryellen began.

Her sister shook her head. "No, listen to me. You've cut men out of your life so much that your psyche has given you one here, practically sitting on your ovaries so you can't ignore him!"

Maryellen started to reply to her sister's version of her problems, but she was distracted by a humming sound. Not a mechanical noise that might have originated, for instance, in 21's air conditioning system, but a vocal undertone like someone trying to carry a tune. It was coming from inside her, Maryellen realized. And this time quite a few people heard it.

Felicia raised a beautiful eyebrow. "What is that noise? Are you doing that?"

"I think he's woken up!" Maryellen blurted. The humming grew louder; it was definitely some kind of song in a baritone voice. "I think your pill put him to sleep, Felicia, and the coffee I drank to wake me up woke him up, too!"

Felicia gave a little cry of dismay. "Do you know what you look like when you tell me things like this? It gives me the creeps, Melly. An alien waking up inside you? Dear God, forgive me, I keep forgetting you may be seriously ill. You've got me so confused about this damned thing. How are you *doing* that? Can't you make him shut up? People are staring!"

It was true. At nearby tables people were look-

ing around them, trying to locate the hidden vo-
calist.

George had rushed up. "Ladies," he whispered. "No singing in the main dining room,
please! Wouldn't you like to do it downstairs in
the bar?"

But Felicia had gathered her coat and purse
and was already out of her chair. "Mel," she
cried slapping down money for the check, "since
you can't make that thing shut up, we're going
to have to get out of here. Before they throw us
out! I mean, I come here all the time. What will
people think?"

"I told you it was an hallucination but you can
see and hear it," Maryellen explained, following
her. "Don't blame me, I can't do anything about
it!"

"Hum hum de dum," Sub Commander Targon
rendered loudly as they reached the top of 21's
stairs. Old George followed closely behind, looking anxious. "Mum har de dar lum dar!"

It was strange music, totally foreign to Maryellen, who had taken advanced piano at Ben-
nington. She tried to put her hand over her
mouth, then her abdomen, but neither did any
good.

"Am I confusing you?" the voice of Targon
said cheerfully. "Roger then, I'll sing some popular Styrex Three thing. A little Al Jolson? No?
Frank Sinatra? OK, I've got it!" He broke into an
old Tina Turner song, "What's Love Got to Do
With It" in full voice.

The downstairs part of the restaurant containing the bar and lounge was filled with people.

Most of them put down their drinks and looked around, startled, trying to locate the source of the singing.

Maryellen bypassed the bar and ran for 21's front door, Felicia close behind. "Mel, where are you going?" her sister cried when they reached the sidewalk. She tried to grab her arm.

"You can hear it, can't you?" Maryellen was distraught. "Everybody can. Look how the people on the street turn around and stare!" Her voice broke on a sob. "Or is this an hallucination, too?"

"No, people are looking," Felicia assured her. "Oh, Melly, what in the hell has happened? How are you making those strange noises?"

"He's drunk!" Maryellen screamed. "Can't you tell a drunk when you hear one? It's that pill you made me take! First it put him to sleep, then he woke up drunk and started humming." Targon had switched to a Beatles tune, which suited his not-unpleasant baritone better than the Tina Turner number, except that he was obviously slurring his words. "Now he's singing Golden Oldies," she cried.

"We've got to get you to Dr. Dzhugashvili right away," Felicia said. "The doctor won't mind if you're a little bit early. This is serious. I need the 21 doorman to get us a cab."

But Maryellen couldn't hold still. Some strong force, Targon, of course, was hurrying her down Fifty-seventh Street, away from Felicia and 21. And embarrassingly, she was staggering. When Targon was high on Felicia's pill, it appeared that she was, too.

27

"I've got to be at the psychiatrist's by three o'clock," Maryellen said.

"Not a moment too soon, baby," a passing street person in a dirty raincoat and combat boots called to her. "Give your shrink my regards."

Maryellen swept past him. Targon had stopped singing. Now he wanted to dance. Arms spread, she moved out into Fifth Avenue traffic.

Of course there was a very clear danger of getting run down by a bus or a taxicab. Maryellen found herself in her plum velvet Donna Karan suit with miniskirt attempting something that must have looked to the New York lunch crowds who stopped to stare like a Russian Cossack dance, complete with dazzling high kicks.

"Will you stop this?" she screamed. She whirled, bounced off the hood of a limousine that screeched to a halt just in time, and wheeled away. There were raucous whistles from the cabbies at the cab stand on the corner. "You're drunk," she wailed. "And now you're trying to kill me!"

A couple had stopped to watch Maryellen, her hair flying and her long legs showing to good effect in Targon's exuberant dance.

"They're shooting some movie," one man observed knowledgeably. "They're all over Manhattan these days."

Targon allowed Maryellen to throw herself on a blue-painted U.S. Postal Service mailbox and hang on to it.

"I'm not trying to kill you," he managed to say huskily. "I told you not to take that pill."

Maryellen was choking back tears. If he continued to make her sing and dance in the middle of Fifth Avenue, the police would show up eventually. And she wasn't at all sure that the NYPD would listen to her explanation that she was already on her way to an emergency appointment with a psychiatrist.

"Listen," she cried as Targon tried to pry her away from the mailbox, "If you don't sober up the police are going to come and take me to jail. With what's going on, we'll never get out!"

Targon thought it over for a moment. "New York City jail is not, I gather, a particularly wonderful environment."

"It's the pits!" she cried. "It's where all the poor crazies go that the police pick up off the streets. Now if you don't want me to start screaming right here in the middle of Fifth Avenue, then you'll let me catch a cab so I can go to my appointment with Dr. Dzhugashvili!"

"Be calm," he assured her. "You can see the head doctor. I have no objection to that. It's what you Styrex Three people spend most of your time doing, anyway."

Maryellen didn't have time to respond to Targon's latest slur. After a few tries she flagged down a cab and gave the cabbie the psychiatrist's address on the upper West Side.

Then as she threw herself into the backseat and the cab took off with a head-shaking jolt, Maryellyn did what she'd been longing to do all day.

She burst into tears.

Chapter Three

"I don't want to go through anything like this ever—*ever*—again," Maryellen said, wiping her reddened eyes with a Kleenex that Dr. Dzhugashvili's receptionist had provided. The bout of weeping that had lasted all the way across midtown and through Central Park had finally worn itself out, leaving her drained. "You could have killed me, you and your crazy dance and all that wild singing!"

"It's an ancient battle song and accompanying footwork," Targon said, "intended to intimidate the enemy. I wouldn't expect anybody on this sorry little planet to appreciate it."

"You were drunk!" she told him, furious. "Let's not try to fancy it up with a lot of stuff about battle songs and dancing. The truth of the matter is, you could have killed me! I bounced off the hood of that limousine on Fifth Avenue when, luckily, the chauffeur stopped just in time!"

Hearing the sound of voices, Dr. Dzhugash-vili's receptionist came out to check and saw Maryellen angrily addressing an empty waiting room. Shaking her head, she went back in again.

"Lower your voice," Targon said. "I've got the mother goddess of all headaches stomping around in my skull."

"*My* skull, you mean," Maryellen said. "I can't tell you how sick I am, making a spectacle of myself in the middle of Fifth Avenue! All I can say is, I hope nobody in advertising was around to see it. Oh, please God," she added. "Let Dr. Dzhugashvili do some good—I can't wait to get rid of you!"

"Don't be nasty," Targon warned her. "And it isn't going to be that easy."

He made Maryellen's hand reach for a stack of the reception room's magazines and selected an issue of *Time*. The cover story announced in big red letters: FBI AND CIA; AMERICA'S HIDDEN EMPIRES?

"I have to," he said, flipping through the pages, "look for a suitable host body. That's top priority. I've been surveying the Styrex Three males we've encountered since we left your apartment, and they're the usual substandard lot. I'd hate to confine myself to one of those bodies for even a couple of days. On the other hand, it's obvious I can't stay with you. The situation is ludicrous. I've landed in a Styrex Three

31

female body, thanks to some malevolent bastards in my solar system, and it's been an annoyance, to say the least."

"An *annoyance?*" Maryellen spluttered. "You mean trying to kill me, humiliating me in 21 and driving me into the arms of a psychiatrist *annoyed* you? Listen you—you—outer space—p-poltergeist—if I didn't have a rich sister, I couldn't even pay for all this!"

Targon ignored her outburst. He was studying *Time* magazine's article on the "secret empires" of the FBI and CIA. "While I respect your right to see this head doctor, there's a slight logistical problem involved. We should be hanging around hospitals looking for bodies, not wasting our time in a psychiatrist's office."

"Hospitals?" Maryellen tried to put the magazine down, as she was hardly interested in articles on the FBI, but he wouldn't let her. "Good heavens, why would you want to do that?"

"The most efficient way to pick up a host body is to claim it just as the—er, donor expires," he explained. "When done promptly, with no extended time lag, it's one hundred percent effective. Not like 'accidentally' falling into some sleeping Styrex Three woman's body. I assure you, heads are going to roll over that one when I get back."

"You mean you want to find someone who's dying and steal his body just as he . . . passes on?" Maryellen exclaimed, horrified. "Is that what you're talking about?"

"Somebody acceptable, naturally. I can't tell you how much I hate to select out of the New

York body pool—good specimens are rare. And I want to match myself as closely as possible. I was thinking, actually, of Brad Pitt. Or perhaps Keanu Reeves."

"They're not dying," Maryellen cried. "Oh, God, at least I hope not! You wouldn't think of killing anybody, would you? Oh, I refuse to be a part of anything that would eliminate Keanu Reeves or Brad Pitt in the prime of their lives!"

"Stop yelling," Targon said. "Nothing's being killed except my head when you screech like that. We haven't got time to go out to California so Reeves and Pitt are quite safe—you can stop worrying about them. But we'd better put a midtown Manhattan hospital on our schedule right away. I have some urgent business to attend to. See this article? I may have landed in the right place after all."

Maryellen tried to resist as her own hand waved the *Time* magazine in front of her face. "What urgent business?" she asked, trying to push the magazine away. "You don't know anything about the FBI!"

At that moment the door opened and the receptionist beckoned. "The doctor will see you now," she told them.

"I'm not going to do any talking," Targon said as she got up, "so don't ask me to."

Dr. Dzhugashvili's office was located in an old Central Park West building similar to its neighbor, the Dakota, which had been made famous as the place where the movie *Rosemary's Baby* was filmed. It had the same National Guard Armory architecture, and spacious, somewhat rambling apartments built for the lifestyles of another era. The elevators were antique brass cages, and the corridors were tobacco brown where the gloom was broken by fixtures of hand-blown amber glass in the shape of tulips.

Even the psychiatrist's waiting room reflected the glory of the past with oil portraits that Maryellen guessed were of Dr. Sigmund Freud and Dr. Carl Jung and other gentlemen with beards.

The inner office of what her sister had termed "New York's currently hottest shrink," was more of the same: a heavily curtained room with bookcases filled with leather-bound books, paintings of castles on peaks above Germany's Rhine River and stags at bay about to be torn to pieces by packs of hunting dogs.

Maryellen was greeted by a little man in a short brown beard who jumped up from behind his desk and rushed forward to meet her.

"Ah, dear young Ms. Caswell," he boomed in a surprisingly deep voice, "whose very socially prominent sister, Mrs. J. Stephen Crump, has already informed me that you are possessed by intergalactic-traveling aliens. Did they arrive," he asked, pumping her hand, "by UFO?"

Maryellen couldn't find her voice for a moment. Dr. Dzhugashvili was something of a surprise, more like an energetic little teddy bear than what one would expect of an eminent Manhattan psychiatrist.

"Only one alien." She couldn't suppress a slight shudder. "Believe me; one is enough."

"One alien," the doctor repeated. "And it is inside you now?"

"He," she corrected him, looking around. Maryellen felt somewhat embarrassed. "I'm sure it's an hallucination, doctor. My sister's probably told you I've been working much too hard and . . . and not getting out as much as I should," she added nervously. "But it's definitely a 'he.' Sub Commander Targon from someplace in another solar system."

Dr. Dzhugashvili waved her forward, looking slightly disappointed. "No UFO? Ah, what a pity. UFOs are very interesting; I am fascinated when patients tell me about them. You might say it's my specialty." He shrugged. "Well, let us not mind; we will get to the bottom of the matter. Will you stand up as you tell me all that has happened, sit in the chair, or lie down on the couch?"

Maryellen knew that lying down on Dr. Dzhugashvili's leather-covered couch was probably the accepted way of doing things, but she was exhausted after her bout of crying in the taxicab and wanted to get her breakdown, or whatever it was, diagnosed as quickly as possible. Face-to-face seemed better. "I'll sit down, if you don't mind."

The doctor nodded, then returned to his seat behind his big mahogany desk. He pulled a yellow legal pad to him and began writing rapidly. "Now, I am putting down some notes," he explained. "You have a space-traveling alien who identifies himself as—" He looked up.

"Targon," she told him after a moment's hesitation. "Sub Commander Targon."

"One moment, dear young lady," Dr. Dzhugashvili responded, writing that down. "Sub Commander Targon from an unnamed solar system, having taken possession, according to subject, of her body. Transportation did not involve UFO."

Maryellen wished they could drop UFOs as a topic, but she felt compelled to say, "Well, actually, I only know what he told me. You have to realize I woke up in bed this morning and I was speaking in a man's voice! It was a terrible shock. But this man's voice was raving on and on about how his enemies in the transportation system had done this deliberately, sent him to Earth when he should have gone somewhere else to investigate crooked bureaucracies. He seemed to think they put him in a woman's body—my body—for a joke!"

"It was no joke," Targon said inside her. "Those bastards wanted to sabotage me."

Maryellen started. "There, you see? He just said something, and he vowed he wouldn't open his mouth! But he's so unbelievably paranoid, I knew he couldn't keep quiet. He believes he landed on Earth because his enemies wanted to get rid of him!"

Dr. Dzhugashvili looked excited. "My dear young miss, you are telling me the alien is talking to you right now? At this moment? Wonderful, wonderful! Tell me, does he sometimes speak out loud? Would it be possible that he would speak to *me*?"

"This guy's a nut," Targon said. "He sounds like a UFO fanatic to me. There are tons of them on this planet."

Dr. Dzhugashvili had been watching Maryellen intently. "He's talking to you again, is he not? What a tragedy I cannot hear him! What a tragedy I cannot *see* him! Tell me, has he by chance appeared to you? It would be the most excessive luck if he has, but dear Ms. Caswell, I dare not hope that you have had an actual visual manifestion!"

"Oh, I've gotten a good look at him, if that's what you mean." Maryellen was beginning to sense that Targon was right when he said that the psychiatrist might be, well . . . eccentric. Certainly Dr. Dzhugashvili didn't seem at all concerned that his patient might be having a dangerous mental breakdown. Instead, he was talking about wanting to see and hear the sub commander—as if he'd immediately believed that the alien existed.

"Dr. Dzhugashvili," she began. "I hope you understand that my sister arranged an emergency appointment with you because I have never— *never*—had hallucinations about aliens or anything else. In fact, we think this whole episode is due to overwork. I'm a freelance commercial artist for several well-respected advertising companies, and the competition and stress in my line of work is pretty terrific. If you don't mind, I think I'd like to lie down on your couch, now, because I'm not really feeling very well."

"You must tell me in detail," the doctor interrupted, "about this wonderful visual manifestation of the alien. You didn't take any photos, did you? Polaroids? Videotape?"

"Why don't you draw him a picture?" Targon snapped. "That's your business, isn't it? Show him I look like a bowl of Wheaties."

Maryellen didn't want to make the mistake of yelling for Targon to shut up. Nor did she want to deal with this somewhat eccentric psychiatrist. Seeing no alternative, she decided to stick with the shrink for just a few minutes more.

"Well," she said, trying to go on. "He appeared sitting on my bedroom chair so I could go take a shower. But I don't think he can do it for very long, materialize like that, because he keeps talking about finding another host body. That's another thing—"

"What did the alien look like, please, Ms. Caswell?" the doctor prompted her.

"Oh," she said, blushing. "Well, you know—kind of interesting if you're into exotic types. But I mean, he's not ugly or gruesome-looking with tentacles all over his body and one eye, thank goodness!"

"That's a Medusian," Targon inserted, "or something close to it."

Maryellen tried to ignore that. "He glows all over," she told the doctor. "A gold color that sort of shimmers, and he has matching hair and skin. And he has a very well-muscled, well-proportioned body. I'd say he's about six feet one or two, and 175 to 180 pounds, and he seems about thirty years old."

"Thanks," Targon said. "I'm thirty-seven by your way of reckoning things."

Maryellen said more loudly and somewhat resentfully, "He's certainly better looking than anything Stephen Spielberg put together. If he didn't glow so much I guess he really would look like Brad Pitt."

"Marvelous, marvelous," the doctor murmured. "We must pursue this, you and I in future sessions, dear Ms. Caswell. That is, why your psyche reacts to an apparent lack of sexual stimuli due to overwork by creating a beautiful glowing gold male creature that must exist only in your body."

"I didn't say that," Maryellen protested. "In fact, he's looking for another body right now. Except it involves visiting hospitals looking for dying men who are as good-looking as he is."

Dr. Dzhugashvili, nodding and smiling, was writing on a prescription pad. "Yes, yes, that is understandable. Especially if he really does exist." The doctor gave her an odd look. "Perhaps this is not an hallucination, young Ms. Caswell. Perhaps you are really harboring a lost visitor from outer space. If this is true, think of what extraordinary data it could provide—the papers of controversy it would engender in the *American Journal of Psychiatry*! Not to mention the formidable technical publications of NASA, and *Aviation Week*. And the SFWA, and Arthur C. Clarke! But we must not get carried away," he finished, tearing off the prescription form from his pad and handing it to her. "First we must explore traditional avenues of inquiry. I wish you to attend a special therapy group. It is meeting this very evening at seven-thirty at the address I have given you. When you mingle with this group, perhaps you will be able to learn which it is—whether you are suffering from delusions caused by lack of sexual stimuli or whether you are the host body of a true extraterrestrial."

Maryellen was experiencing decidedly mixed feelings. She really didn't think this was anxiety caused by working too hard—but that meant it had to be the latter, which was worse.

"Was that a prescription he gave you?" Targon wanted to know. "Listen. No more pills! When I get snoggered there's dancing in the middle of the street, remember?"

That was the last straw. Maryellen was sick of having this voice inside her that others could sometimes hear—but only when it wanted. She jumped to her feet, gathering up her things. "Oh, you're such a smartass," she burst out. "Dr. Dzhugashvili half-believes you exist. He's dying to have you say something to him! Why don't you get me out of this fix and just open your mouth and talk?"

She suddenly felt herself being propelled toward the psychiatrist's desk, then pushed over to lean on it. Her face was right in the doctor's.

"Boo!" the baritone voice of Targon bellowed. "How's that?"

The sudden assault of sound right in his face made Dr. Dzhugashvili recoil in shock. But he instantly recovered. He lifted his hands to his face, his eyes closing in sheer ecstasy. *Mein Gott*," he whispered. "It has happened! Please,

40

please, I beg you, could you do it just once more?"

"Oh, hell!" Targon said, propelling Maryellen rapidly toward the door. "Let's get out of here before I make you do something to *really* embarrass us."

"Why do you do things like that?" Maryellen exploded as the taxi took the Eighty-sixth Street crosstown through Central Park. "Talk about sabotage—you deliberately did that when I begged you to say something to Dr. Dzhugashvili to help him decide whether this whole thing is one big hallucination. Instead you decide to yell 'Boo!' right in his face! What good do you think that does?"

"It got us out of there," Targon said grimly. "That shrink was wasting your time and mine, too. Right now I've got more important things to do. I have to warn the President of the United States of the danger from his subversive bureaucracies. But not until I've made at least a preliminary personal investigation of the FBI. According to the magazine I read in the doctor's office there are several official investigations of the FBI going on that have already amassed a good bit of evidence, but it's not the kind of evidence that's important. Bungling, incompetance, and cover-ups are irrelevant. What we really need to look for in this sort of situation are elite cadres of conspirators dedicated to overthrowing the government. Assassination is part of it, too. Before he died, J. Edgar Hoover was planning to do all of that. And he especially disliked Lyndon Johnson."

Maryellen stared at the back of their cabbie's head. Targon was talking out loud, and the cabbie was obviously listening. "Will you keep your voice down?" she hissed. "I don't know how you know all this about J. Edgar Hoover if you come from another galaxy. Why don't you concentrate on how to steal a body from the nearest hospital?"

The cabbie must have overheard her, for the taxi swerved coming out of Central Park and nearly sideswiped another automobile. While the drivers exchanged shouts and curses, Targon said loudly, "I got my information on J. Edgar Hoover from the exposé I just read in *Time* magazine. It was a complete history of the agency. It's my own conclusion that if Hoover hadn't died when he did, he would have launched a joint FBI-CIA coup, and taken over the White House."

"That's the most preposterous thing I've ever heard!" Maryellen cried. "Now I know you have to be an hallucination!"

"It's not preposterous," Targon shot back. "Dammit, I know my profession; I've been practicing it with top honors for years. While I'm on this planet I intend to warn your president of his danger—the whole *country's* danger. Hoover was only a milestone, a charismatic leader. The same crowd will try to do it again."

Maryellen had been keeping track of the cabbie, who'd been rather frantically watching her in the rearview mirror. The cabbie was hearing two distinct voices but seeing only one passenger. He likely was as confused as she.

She tried to warn Targon to be quiet, again, but it was too late: as the cabbie turned the corner into Lexington Avenue he was too distracted to see a NYPD police car double-parked. The cab hit the rear end of the police cruiser with a loud crash.

For a moment there was an eerie silence. People passing by on the sidewalk stopped and stared as if they could not believe what they saw.

Upon impact, Maryellen slid to the floor of the cab, landing on her knees. The taxi driver, too, seemed stunned. He sat for a long moment with his eyes fixed on the rearview mirror as if still searching for the phantom voice. Then he threw open the door of the taxicab and jumped out to meet the police officer who came running up, service revolver drawn, and his partner, who sprang out of the driver's seat of the cruiser.

"This should be interesting," Targon said. "Now we get a chance to see your *federales* in action."

Maryellen hauled herself up onto the backseat. "They're not *federales*," she said finally. "That's the wrong word, wrong country. They're the NYPD. And yes, we're going to see them in action. Our cabbie is going to get lots of tickets for having smashed into the back of a police car, which was a really stupid thing to do. And I hope you have lots of fun, because I think right now he's trying to tell those two officers the weird reason it happened."

Chapter Four

Their cabdriver was an Indian gentleman, Mr. Sajit Patel of Queens, according to the license displayed in the glass partition separating the front seat from the rear of the taxicab. And his ability to explain to the police about the accident was greatly hampered by his horror over having rear-ended a New York police cruiser on Lexington Avenue.

"Oh, my God," Mr. Patel kept saying in his precise Indian accent. "Oh, my God, this is the result of a baleful extraterrestrial influence sitting there in the backseat of my taxi, but invisible, so that you could not see him! Officers, I tell you, I was hearing the alien and looking for him when I turned the corner, although all I could see was the young lady. Thus this terrible accident occurred, which smashed the back of your vehicle!"

"An alien made you do it." The officer who was writing up the first ticket shook his head admiringly. "I've heard a lot of things, man, but this is the first time I've heard that one."

"Actually," his partner said, leaning against the shattered V of the taxicab's hood, "we pick up a lot of DUI's in Brooklyn who are into aliens, especially on the Long Island Expressway. When you pull them over that's what they say— 'An alien from outer space was chasing me.' Sometimes it's a spaceship. You know, like in *Close Encounters of the Third Kind*. They go on and on like how it made a big circle over Greenpoint and came straight at them."

"No kidding," the other said. "We don't get that here in Manhattan. Everything else, but not UFOs—at least not in Traffic." He shrugged. "Maybe in Vice. I'll have to ask the guys over there." He flipped to another page of his summons book, then laughed. "Okay, Mr. Patel, under 'cause of accident,' I'm going to put down what you told me, that is, you had an 'alien in the backseat.' And the name and address of the witness, the young lady who was back there with him." He started on the second summons. "You'll go to court, anyway, so you can explain it to the judge."

The taxi driver wrung his hands. "Now I go to court," he cried in anguish. "Oh, how could this dreadful thing be happening to me? I have done nothing in my life to become the target of space aliens! Officer, I wish you to put down in your report that this alien was saying he was looking for a hospital where he could steal dead bodies. My God, but it was very upsetting! No wonder I was so distracted from my driving!"

Maryellen had been watching a tow truck arrive and attach a chain to the back of the taxicab. She'd given her name and address and an account of the accident to the police officers, and she was free to go, but she lingered. She couldn't help feeling terribly sorry for Mr. Patel; he was bound to have a horrendous bill for the damage to his taxi and the police cruiser. She was feeling it was all her fault.

The cabbie *was* telling the truth, of course, about an alien in the backseat. Hadn't she tried to warn Targon to keep his voice down? There was no doubt his shouting had unnerved the poor man, who was trying to locate the invisible passenger in the rearview mirror when they hit the police car.

Maryellen wished there was some way to help the cabbie, but it looked as though the damage would be very expensive. From the state of her checking account, she knew she couldn't afford to offer anything. Maybe her sister . . .

"Don't worry about it," Targon told her. "Insurance will cover the cab, as well as the *federales'* vehicle."

Maryellen didn't bother to answer. Targon made her angry, and nervous when she stood so close to the police and the overwrought cabbie.

"If you don't mind," she told the officers as they all stepped back to allow the tow truck to pull the taxicab out and away down Lexington

Avenue, "I have to go home now. I have an appointment this evening. I have to leave. You have my telephone number and address and everything."

None of them seemed to be listening. They'd turned their attention to the police cruiser. Another NYPD police car had arrived on the scene, lights flashing.

Maryellen left in search of a bus stop. She'd decided she wasn't going to get in a taxi again with Targon, even if she had to walk all the way to her apartment. Fortunately Targon had nothing else to say. They boarded the downtown bus in silence.

Forty-five minutes later she entered her loft apartment with a sigh of relief, even though the little red light of the telephone answering machine blinked from across the room with an overload of urgent messages.

Maryellen knew they were urgent even before she pressed the button to play them. She had several deadlines for artwork for two big agencies, and they'd be checking in. As the machine played back the first voice—Carson Shott, the art director for Bloom, Heinewitz, and De Mano—she went to the refrigerator, found a package of bologna, mayonnaise, and a loaf of bread and put it out on the counter to make herself a sandwich. The next instant she felt the peculiar sensual tugging inside her body, and soon Targon materialized, taking a seat in one of the living area's leather-and-chrome chairs.

47

Targon had been quiet for so long Maryellen blurted, "What happened to you?"

"I took a nap," he said, stretching and yawning. "After the automobile accident, I'd had about as much as I could take."

Maryellen stared at him. He'd had as much as *he* could take? She was a bundle of nerves from the most terrible day she'd spent in her whole life, she was missing important work deadlines because of it, and it wasn't over yet. The incarnation of her possibly deranged mind was sitting in one of the chairs in her living room, blandly complaining about *their* predicament.

She put two slices of bologna on bread, smeared it with mayonnaise, and angrily slammed the sandwich together. She was so ravenous she didn't even take time to get milk out of the refrigerator and pour herself a glass.

As she ate, she listened to the voice of yet another art director on the answering machine, this time the Jerry DeLuna Agency, reminding her that she had promised to call him the very first thing that morning, as the agency had wanted the client to view her layout at lunch.

She groaned aloud. She had forgotten all about it! That error had probably cost her the DeLuna account, she thought, glowering at Sub Commander Targon, who was lounging in her chair, one booted leg crossed over the other, while he turned the pages of an art magazine.

When he looked up, she realized his eyes were a dazzling cobalt blue. And they certainly had a peculiar effect on her. "I—I suppose you want something to eat," she said, her mouth full.

Blue fire shot her way. "No, I don't really eat or drink when I'm in this mode. It's a little complicated to explain. But thanks, anyway." He paused and looked at her keenly. "What's the matter?"

Maryellen stared, the sandwich in her hand forgotten. She had been wondering about other things he *could* do in that golden, gleaming manifestation. She had identified the feeling when he entered and exited her body, and it was definitely sexual. It made her shiver even now, thinking about it.

On the other hand, she told herself, still staring, he might have other forms. Maybe back on his home planet Targon was something with blue eyes and gold hair embedded in a large glob of purple Jell-O.

He put down the art magazine. "What's purple Jell-O?" he wanted to know.

Maryellen jumped. "How long have you been able to do that?" she shrieked.

"Do what?"

"Read my mind! You bastard, have you known what I was thinking all along and kept it a big secret?" Maryellen jerked open the refrigerator door and got out the carton of milk. "I don't know what they do where you come from, but here reading someone's mind is a dirty, sneaky rotten trick!"

"Don't yell, I get the idea. Although I would have thought by now that you'd have discovered the inadvertent intimacy of sharing your body with me was bound to have certain side effects. Did you ever consider there are some things you

49

practically force on my conscious mental levels? Like constantly speculating what my nude body is really like? Or if I even have one?" Before Maryellen could respond he said, "I hope I can relieve your curiosity by saying that I am *not* made of purple Jell-O. Whatever that is."

"Hah! I thought you knew everything," she flung back at him. "You're an expert on the FBI and J. Edgar Hoover after reading one *Time* magazine in a doctor's office. And you certainly claim to know everything about psychiatry, although I don't know how you managed to take a course in that since you despise my culture so much. Besides, I did not 'speculate' about your nude body. That's disgusting!"

"No, it was very interesting," he said calmly. "In my present physical manifestation—which incidentally is an almost exact replica of what I am when I'm in my own solar system, except for some carbon-based life-form fuel needs—I can do the maneuver you were thinking about quite satisfactorily. Although I have to admit I have only tried it once—with a Styrex Three female when I last visited Chicago."

Maryellen choked over her glass of milk and had to put it down. "I can't believe this is happening! I can't believe you're real. You're so much like a nightmare specifically designed to humiliate me! You read my mind and say I have sexual thoughts about you, then you talk about playing around with Chicago hookers!"

"That isn't what I said at all," Targon responded. "And what makes you assume she was a hooker? As I understood the situation, she was a postulate in the Sisters of the Little Flower. The order thought she was having a religious experience."

"A nun!" Maryellen cried, genuinely horrified.

"Not quite. Besides, she changed her mind. She's a game girl now on MTV."

"Oh!" Maryellen cried. "You—you—you're impossible! I should have given you a glass of milk with poison in it and made you drink it!"

She hurried into the living area while he said, "You don't have any poison, I did a quick, if perfunctory check, and you have only one large bottle of laundry bleach under the kitchen sink. Which wouldn't affect me one way or the other, externally or internally."

"I wish I knew," Maryellen wailed, "whether you are really *real!* I could be in a hospital someplace with amnesia and hallucinations after—after an automobile wreck, and all this happened to me days ago. You could be a doctor or nurse in some expensive private pavilion Felicia's committed me to, and I'm being taken care of in wonderfully luxurious accommodations. And any minute now they're going to bring me dinner from outside, catered by Le Cirque!"

"Interesting theory," Targon observed. "But to go back and clear up one point, your mental images of sex are intriguingly frank and earthy, if you'll excuse the pun, and certainly—ah, stimulating."

She glared at him. Then she suddenly said, "I want to touch you."

The cobalt-blue eyes blinked. "Touch me?"

"Yes." She had finally taken him by surprise.

"You claim you aren't an hallucination or a glob of intergalactic Jell-O, so I want to find out just what you are. I want to *touch* you."

He looked cautious. "Yes, well, maybe that's not a great idea. I don't think you're going to clarify anything by doing that. Tell me," he said, hesitant but obviously curious. "What does your idea of 'touching' consist of? And why do you want to do it?"

Maryellen realized she had the upper hand, for a change. "Remember," she said. "Dr. Dzhugashvili claimed my psyche might be reacting to a lack of sexual stimuli due to working night and day without any time off for a social life. So that means I've created a beautiful glowing gold male creature that existed only in my subconscious."

He grimaced. "It seems a fairly standard Styrex Three theory. Of that type."

"Well, then, if you're really *real* you won't mind my touching you."

"I didn't say I *minded* your touching me." He paused. "It just depends on what touching is. What part do you—er, have in mind?"

She started to say "your hand" but decided against it. "A—arm—*arm*," she decided. "Just stick out your . . . uh . . . elbow."

He considered it. Then he stuck out his left arm, elbow lifted. "All right, but proceed with some reasonable caution, will you?"

Maryellen jerked her hand back quickly. "Why? What's the matter? You're not poisonous or radioactive, are you?"

He made an irritated noise. "I never can be quite sure—conditions in another solar system can be unpredictable. Look, use just one finger. When you get past the aura you should connect with what you feel is solid flesh."

Maryellen was no coward. And she *was* burningly curious. She'd wanted to touch Targon from the moment she'd seen him materialize in her slipper chair.

With a shaking hand, she let her finger penetrate the pulsing gold light that encased him. He was right. The finger found what appeared to be the solid, warm flesh of his arm underneath. Not only that, there was even a tingling sensation that was indescribable but very pleasant.

He'd been watching her. "Not so bad, then?"

"Oh, no, not at all. It's like warm ginger ale." She let her finger wander down his arm to the wrist. She could see a trail of sparkling gold specks following it. "Mmmmm. Are you like this all over?"

He frowned. "Well, champagne is the usual comparison, not warm ginger ale. And reactions seem to vary, depending on the life-form."

She thought of the woman in Chicago. Maybe she *had* been a nun. Or an almost-nun. Now she was regularly seen on MTV.

Good grief, Maryellen told herself, she was buying into the whole thing! Yet what she was touching seemed very real. She was using only one finger, but the sensation made her wonder what it would be like to be pressed against this Targon full length. As in bed. Would the tingling gold glow seep into her, too, light up her whole body? Had that happened to the nun?

"She said it was a very transporting experience," Targon volunteered, reading her mind again. "In her words, 'out of this world.'"

"Stop it!" Maryellen cried. "You know what you're doing, don't you? I find that particularly revolting, reading my mind, digging into my private thoughts. Don't you have any sense of decency?"

"Hah, decency hardly has anything to do with it when you're thinking so graphically." He gave her a pointed look. "Your thoughts contrast so interestingly with what Styrex Three refers to as an all-American-girl exterior."

Maryellen jerked her finger away. "I don't have an all-American-girl exterior! Oh, I'm so confused, I almost wish I *had* woken up in a psychiatric ward someplace among kind, caring nurses and doctors."

He snorted. "You mean after all that poking and prodding you still think I'm a bad dream? Even for an inhabitant of Styrex Three you take a lot of convincing."

"It's my sanity we're dealing with here, and I'll think what I please! Especially when you start accusing me of wanting to have sex with you!" She jumped up and started back to the kitchen. "And furthermore—stay out of my body!"

He stood up, too. "I can't do that. There are certain complications that will result if I stay out of a host body too long. I don't want to go into the details right here, but getting a satisfactory alternate body is my top priority right now."

Maryellen put the mayonnaise and bologna away and slammed the refrigerator door. "You seem to do as you please, landing in my body when I'm asleep, coming and going at will! What do *I* have to say about it?"

"The first thing you can do is get busy and arrange to visit the local hospital emergency rooms. A little preliminary research shows that ten P.M. to one A.M. is the best time—that's when they're the busiest."

Maryellen started for the bedroom. "I'm not going to look up any emergency rooms for you tonight. I'm busy. I have to go to Dr. Dzhugashvili's therapy group."

He followed her. "We haven't got time to do that. I need a body. Then I need to get started on a preliminary investigation of your treasonous bureaucracy, the FBI, as soon as possible. Remember, warning your president about the danger he's in from the so-called J. Edgar Hoover conspiracy is the only reason I've decided to extend my stay here on this backwater outpost."

Maryellen yanked a black turtleneck two-piece out of the closet. "The J. Edgar Hoover conspiracy? I never heard such a stupid thing! Let me give you a piece of advice. The president of the United States doesn't need any crackpot warnings about the FBI from some radioactive hallucination from outer space. Besides, the Secret Service would probably shoot you before you could get through the White House front gates."

"You're not making any sense."

Maryellen stripped off her Donna Karan velvet suit, not caring that Targon was appraising her body in bra and bikini panties with obvious interest. She put on the black outfit. "Me? I'm not making any sense? Besides, I don't have to make any sense, not where I'm going tonight. Look at it this way, if I say anything in this therapy group that *isn't* crazy, they'll throw me out!"

Targon blocked her way to the door. "Didn't I just say it was imperative we go to the nearest hospital ER? Pay attention—we may have to go as far out as Long Island to find the sort of body I want."

"Right now I've got the only body around," Maryellen cried, "and I'll say where it goes! You can do what you please, but my body and I are going to Dr. Dzhugashvili's therapy group in the Bronx!"

She rushed across the living room. "You can stay here. Turn on the television, or play movies on the VCR. How about Arnold Schwarzenegger in *The Terminator*. Be my guest!"

He caught her at the front door. "It's bad enough I've got to sit through some damned therapy group," he growled, "after landing on a planet I'd usually avoid at all cost. Now I have to endure your hostile lack of cooperation. All when what I'm trying to do is expose the subversive activities of your own country's FBI." There was the familiar sensuous rush as he settled back into Maryellen's body. "The fact that you're attractive isn't much of a consolation, frankly."

"Oh, shut up!" Maryellen said as she went out and slammed and locked her front door. "I'm just as sick of you as you are of me!"

"I didn't say that," Targon said.

Chapter Five

"I thought I had seen the worst parts of Styrex Three," Targon said, "but apparently I was mistaken. What did you say the name of this place was?"

Maryellen didn't answer, as she wasn't in a very good mood. She thought she had made herself perfectly clear in their last exchange about how much they obviously wanted to get rid of each other. At that moment she had to pay attention to her driving. The exits on Bruckner Boulevard were not easy to see until you came right up on them. In addition, the borrowed Jaguar she was driving made her nervous. Since she'd vowed never to get into a taxi again, at least not until she'd gotten rid of Targon, and couldn't chance the subway for the same reasons, she'd asked for one of her sister's cars to make the trip to the therapy group in the Bronx.

Along with her fear of not returning it in one piece, another trouble with borrowing her sister's car was that there wasn't an ordinary, inconspicuous automobile in the whole Crump family.

Stephen, Felicia's husband, preferred his Rolls Royce and uniformed chauffeur, at least for city travel. Felicia used the bright red Jag and a silver-toned Mercedes when she wasn't taking taxis, and the two nursemaids drove the kids in a customized Dodge van complete with snack bar and VCR for playing Disney videos.

Which really left Maryellen with a choice between Felicia's red car or the gleaming silver one, knowing full well it was not a good idea to be driving a $60,000 fire-engine red sportscar at night in New York City. But was the Mercedes any better?

More than once she'd considered she shouldn't be making this trip at all, especially after a day overloaded with traumatic events. But, she argued with herself, Dr. Dzhugashvili's therapy group was probably her last chance for help. If she could just meet someone else who'd experienced feeling that an alien from outer space had entered his or her body it would be a great relief! Goodness, just to have the opportunity to compare notes would be such a relief! And maybe she could even get a few tips on what others were doing to get rid of it, whatever *it* was—mental infirmity, or real, certifiable extraterrestrial.

"I wish you'd stop going back over all this," Targon said, intruding on her thoughts. "It's making you drive all over the road. Did you see that truck you just cut off back there? Styrex Three citizens have a nasty habit of shooting one another over little things like that."

"Whatever you've heard has been grossly exaggerated," Maryellen muttered, switching lanes again. "Nobody's been shot down on Bruckner Boulevard in a long time."

But even she had to admit they were traveling through a very dark and uninviting part of the Bronx. Just at that moment she found the exit she was looking for and swiftly crossed two lanes to the accompaniment of horn blasts from a semi-tractor rig and assorted screams in Spanish, making it just in time.

As the Jaguar careened down the off-ramp Targon said, "I hope you are aware that if you have a wreck and manage to kill yourself and a few others, I will have to make several emergency host-body choices here on Bruckner Boulevard. And I want to say I don't look forward to having to learn Puerto Rican or Cuban for the rest of my stay on this planet. Styrex Three American jargon took me long enough to learn on my first trip here."

"Oh, shut up," Maryellen snapped.

She slowed the Jaguar, surveying an intersection with a dimly lit candy store on the corner, wondering if she should stop for directions.

"Of course," Targon said in a different tone of voice, "it would be very inconvenient to have anything happen to you, as actually you would represent a severe loss to this mediocre environment. There's no doubt about it. You're much more beautiful than your sister."

Maryellen slammed on the brakes. They were at the curb before the candy store. "Attractive? *Beautiful?*" She could hardly believe what he'd said. "What's going on? Are you trying to get me to turn around and go to the nearest hospital emergency room? Is that what you want?"

"I want you to get off this corner," he responded. "Those adolescent males wearing jackets with 'Knights of Blood' on the back appear extremely interested in both you and this damned red car."

Maryellen took one look and quickly slid the Jaguar away from the curb. It was almost seven-thirty; they were sure to be late. Targon was saying again: "I'm not going to do any talking. So don't ask me to."

"Huh," Maryellen sneered. "No one's going to ask you to make a speech. Really."

"Don't be too sure," Targon told her. "Just don't be too sure."

Sixteen-twenty Harvildson Avenue was a very ordinary-looking Bronx house with a wooden front porch painted beige and brown. After putting the Jaguar in what was hopefully a safe spot under a streetlight, Maryellen rang the doorbell and a tall, middle-aged gentleman with a gray beard opened the door.

"Ah, Ms. Caswell," he greeted her, pumping her hand. "I am Hector Consalvos, your leader and guide. We have a large group tonight, all eager to hear about your wonderful extraterrestrial manifestation."

Maryellen stepped inside. "I don't want to get anybody's hopes up," she said uncertainly. "You see, I don't know whether it's an extraterrestrial manifestation yet, or just an ordinary nervous breakdown. That's why I'm here."

Mr. Consalvos took her by the elbow and steered her past a large statue of an Egyptian sphinx and a larger-than-life-size figure of the Indian deity Krishna. The rest of the vestibule was swathed in iridescent plastic sheets such as one could buy by the yard in hardware stores, dazzlingly lit by strings of winking tiny lights. Maryellen couldn't help staring. It was an exotic setting. She'd expected a group of people sitting on folding chairs in a rather stark room while they vented their innermost anxieties.

"To be perfectly truthful," she said, ducking under a loop of blue plastic, "this . . . hallucination . . . never claimed to be intergalactic, only that he was from another solar system. There *is* a distinction, isn't there?"

"Of course," the therapy leader said. "Although I am happy to say our group has had experiences with both."

"They have?" Maryellen stopped short. She was confused. So far, she couldn't help thinking that what she was seeing and hearing didn't seem to match up with what she'd expect from a therapy group of a prominent New York psychiatrist.

Mr. Consalvos smiled. "Be calm, Ms. Caswell; you are in the right place—although I admit our anticipation has been high since Dr. Dzhugash-vili's call. Frankly, we can't wait." He pushed open a door. "If you don't mind—be so kind as to get down on your hands and knees."

Maryellen stepped back, bumping into the image of Krishna. *"Do what?"*

"Hands and knees," Mr. Consalvos repeated, smoothly. "You'll find the entrance to the pyramid is quite low, in order to contain its cosmic energy."

At that moment, several miles away in the Manhattan Nineteenth Precinct of the NYPD, Officer Slikowitz was doing the necessary paperwork for the citations he'd issued that day before routing them to the office secretary for processing. Finally finished with the time-consuming job all policemen hated, he was about to put the papers in the outbox when his eye fell on the name of Sajit Patel, the cab driver from Queens.

Jeez, Slikowitz couldn't help thinking, it would be a long time before he forgot that particular arrest. *Failure to yield right of way, rear-end-collision with a police vehicle, no injuries.* On top of it all, the Indian cabbie insisted he had a non-paying passenger from outer space in the back of his cab. Slikowitz didn't want to read through the citations and police report again. After all, who was interested in some crackpot account of yet another freaky incident involving a New York City taxi driver?

But his hand hesitated. He reached out and slowly lifted the citation from the top of the pile in the out basket. He had just remembered a memo from the New York district attorney's office asking the cooperation of all levels of the judiciary and law enforcement with the Feds—the FBI, in this case—who were checking out potentially suspicious aliens. Some bigwig was coming to town. The Korean premier, or the president of the Congo—Slikowitz couldn't remember which.

Nobody in the New York police department loved the spooks in the FBI. This was especially true if one had ever been unlucky enough to work with them. However, Slikowitz reminded himself, if the FBI wanted to chase space visitors and UFOs, that was not his problem.

OK, here comes *Star Wars*, Slikowitz told himself as he underlined Mr. Patel's "cause of accident" paragraph about an alien in the backseat. Adding a department form routing it to the Feds, he dropped it again into his out box.

Meanwhile, Maryellen was finding, there actually *was* a pyramid. It took up most of the space in the next large room, and appeared to be a replica of the real thing, right down to its fake stone sides made of painted Styrofoam blocks.

"Please enter," Mr. Consalvos told her. "You'll find the floor is as smooth as Khafre's own tomb. And not as hard on the knees."

Maryellen gingerly dropped to all fours and crawled up the ramp. When she paused, uncertain, at the top, the group leader said, "Courage, dear young lady, don't falter. We are all friends here. Once under the shelter of Khafre's pyramid you will feel a focused cosmic force reaching out to cleanse and strengthen you."

Maryellen didn't know about the "cleanse and strengthen" part. She looked inside where she could see a large group of people seated on the floor.

"I'm not sure I'm ready for this, Mr. Consalvos," she told him. "Actually, I expected a therapy group like the ones my sisters' friends go to. You know, where people sit around and cry and hug one another, and talk about when they were a kid accidentally seeing their mother and father making love. . . ."

Just at that moment, Maryellen was greeted by a burst of applause from the people inside. Whereupon Mr. Consalvos gave her a no-nonsense shove, and she half-slid into the space under the pyramid's apex. Applause and a few cheers continued as a woman in the front row reached out and seized Maryellen's ankle in a firm but friendly grip.

"I, too, was kidnapped," the woman cried emotionally. "And then I was taken to a UFO off Rockaway Beach where I was raped by all the crew members, and bore their child five months later." In her free hand the woman held up a photograph that looked vaguely like the main character from the movie *E.T.* "This is what he looked like—the alien baby I gave birth to looked just like this!"

"Well, I . . . I wasn't abducted." Maryellen was visibly flustered, knowing Targon was listening to all this. "Actually, I woke up in bed and—"

"Maudie has had a very unique experience," Mr. Consalvos interrupted, detaching the woman's grip from Maryellen's foot. "Maudie is a very brave person. Few of us can say we've met extraterrestrials face-to-face."

"Not face-to-face," the woman cried. "Aliens don't have sex like we do."

Maryellen goggled. "They *don't?*"

"Later," the leader said, waving Maryellen to move directly under the pyramids apex. "Let's not go into it now. Maudie will supply you with the details of her experience later. She's not the only victim here of alien kidnapping; we have several."

"Mine wasn't like that at all," Maryellen protested. "I woke up in my own bed and he—Sub Commander Targon from this planet he hasn't gotten around to telling me what the name of it is yet—just started talking. I can't tell you what a terrible shock it was. I thought I had gone, er . . ." She looked around, apologetically. "Well, you know, *crazy.*"

No one seemed to be listening. An argument had broken out among members of a group near the back, people who were dressed in *Star Trek* outfits. Someone had apparently written Leonard Nimoy to ask for permission to make public appearances in shopping malls as his character, Mr. Spock. Several others were maintaining no one could imitate Spock except the authentic Mr. Spock, Leonard Nimoy. They were very vehement. In fact, it looked like they were on the verge of coming to blows.

Maryellen watched, amazed. This therapy group didn't resemble any she'd ever heard of. In addition to the Trekkies, there were people dressed as characters from *Star Wars* including two Darth Vaders. Several women to the right held up blurry photographs of aliens they claimed they'd encountered. The photos seemed to be mainly of infants with bald heads and enormous black eyes that took up most of their faces.

"They took the baby away," Maudie said, trying to drown out the wanna-be Mr. Spock. "Back to their UFO. They told me that was the whole purpose of kidnapping earthlings like me. To breed with us so they can infuse their races with stronger genes!"

Targon laughed sarcastically. "A likely story. The truth is, it's a tough trip from the M-17 galaxy. The poor bastards must have had a hard time getting here and were pretty worn out to grab the first thing they saw—which was, apparently, this Maudie."

Maryellen jumped in surprise. She might have known Targon couldn't keep quiet!

"Don't start anything," she warned him. "You said you weren't going to say anything, remember?

"You're in the wrong place," he told her. "These people are so far out of their tree they wouldn't know a real alien if they saw one." He gave a sudden, violent twitch that almost knocked Maryellen over. "Sweet quarks! I'm in trouble! If I don't get out from under this pyramid I'm going to have *big* problems of my own."

Maryellen frowned. "What do you mean?"

At that moment the discussion group's Trekkies were having a fistfight with a *Stars* creature over the credibility of the astrolines in the Peruvian desert that were supposed to be navigational aids for travelers from outer space.

The non-Leonard Nimoy Mr. Spock tried to separate them, shouting, "Cut the crap, will ya? We don't want to hear about any extraterrestrial staying in somebody's body, no matter who this woman thinks she is, until we've finished hearing Charlie's paper on the time frame for UFOs landing in Peru!"

The others didn't seem to agree. In the uproar that followed, Maryellen couldn't believe what was happening. But it didn't take much to figure out things weren't working out well at all as far as interactive therapy went, she thought, looking around her.

"Sit still," the voice of Targon said. "I want to get out of here as much as you do, even though these cuckoos have finally hit on something. Those transecting lines down there in the desert in Peru are still used by M-17 ships, because their navigational systems are still pretty primitive."

Maryellen hadn't the slightest idea what Targon was talking about. Not that it seemed to matter—Dr. Dzhugashvili's clients were crawling about on their hands and knees in the close space, shouting and taking pokes at one another.

On the other hand, she couldn't ignore the fact that something seemed to be wrong with Targon. He couldn't seem to be quiet, his presence kept shifting restlessly around inside of her, a sensation that was new and unsettling.

"What *are* you doing?" Maryellen hissed. "It's making people stare!"

He snorted. "They can't see anything. Besides, it serves them right for fiddling around with pyramids. 'Cosmic energy' hell! This damned Styrofoam thing is generating pi-meson mega-units through that hole in the peak!"

"I can't believe it. You mean," Maryellen whispered, wide-eyed, "there really *is* something cosmic to sitting under this dratted thing?"

"Cosmic?" Now Targon was speaking out loud. "These are compressed quarks, dammit—" His voice rose, irritably. "And they're making me *itch!*"

"Shhhhh," she tried to tell him. "Don't make so much noise. Can't you see these weird people are looking at me?"

But he went on even more loudly. "Listen, a pi-meson bombardment is an anti-matter attack. It's serious, dammit! I can't take much more of this pyramid, I'll go critical!"

The group under the pyramid had quieted, listening. Now Mr. Consalvos cried, excitedly, "Dear lady, the therapy group is hearing two voices, a most exciting experience! Is this conversation between you and your intergalactic traveler?"

"It's a Vulcan," a Trekkie burst out. He threw himself down on his knees before Maryellen, his face ecstatic. "I know it is! The real Spock! Oh, my God, listen to it—can't you *tell?*"

Maryellen hastily scrambled to her feet, even though she instantly found she couldn't stand up straight inside the Styrofoam pyramid.

Anyone could see the evening was a total loss. She hadn't had a chance to tell her story or get any helpful feedback from the group, and now Targon's peculiar twitching was getting worse. It was very embarrassing and uncomfortable. "I think it's time for me to go," she announced over the uproar.

Then an amazing thing happened.

Maryellen had seen Targon materialize before, so she knew what to expect. But as he separated himself from her now, crouching on his hands and knees because he was too tall to be upright, instantly recognizable as a six-foot-two, iridescent, shimmering figure in space suit and gold hair, a stunned silence settled on the therapy group.

Only for a moment. Then, as Targon would say, all hell broke loose.

Chapter Six

By eight o'clock the overhead light in the mid-town Manhattan office of the Federal Bureau of Investigation had been dimmed, leaving only a few pools of brightness where late-working agents were still busy in their cubicles.

From her seat at the reception desk by the elevators, Candace Ruggiero could hear the soft clicking of computer keyboards as the FBI agents downloaded the day's files and sent them on to the giant mainframe computers in Washington. A few were still making all-important telephone calls.

As she watched the lights on her telephone console click on and off with busy traffic, Candace smiled. She loved the late-evening activity of the midtown Manhattan office. It was silly to feel so sentimental about a huge organization like the FBI, but she'd been raised by a very patriotic Italian-American family on New York City's Staten Island, and believed in the romance of action-filled movies and television films about Eliott Ness and J. Edgar Hoover. She particularly loved Tommy Lee Jones in *Men in Black*.

She'd never had any reason to change her opinion that the department was the most exciting, patriotic arm of the federal government. With the possible exception of the U.S. Marine Corps.

Now Candace surveyed the office with a warm, satisfied feeling. She loved the hours from eight until midnight when things were quiet, and those agents still working at their desks were the smartest and most dedicated. Like the dark-haired, broodingly attractive Wolf Madder.

From where she sat she couldn't see Agent Madder; his cubicle was in the back near an expanse of windows. But she could make out the distinctive sound of his keyboard. Wolf hit the keys pretty hard. That was probably because he wrote the longest, most complicated reports of anyone in the midtown office. Candace had to proof some of his reports, so she knew.

In spite of his impressive writing, Agent Madder, the youngest in age and experience, was assigned to routine low-level work. At this late hour, Candy knew, he was probably reviewing police reports and passing them on from his computer terminal to other, more senior agents.

Soon would come the one moment in her

workday that Candace looked forward to most eagerly, the one where Wolf Madder passed her desk on his way out. With the usual preoccupied look in his green eyes, she could tell he really wasn't aware of her, but he always remembered to say "Good night, Miss Ruggiero," on his way to the elevators.

Candy had decided there was something mysterious about Agent Madder, something that obviously set him apart from the other agents. For one thing, he was fiercely solitary and hardworking. And terribly sexy. In fact, there were times when she could barely restrain herself. He was enough to make any woman want to grab him as he passed by and throw him down on the floor and kiss him senseless.

The thought was so overpowering that for a moment Candy couldn't get her breath. Goodness, she didn't know what made her imagination run wild like that! Then she heard the pounding on Agent Madder's keyboard pause. The silence went on. He was, she knew, probably studying something on the computer screen.

Candy Ruggiero wondered what he had found.

Wolf Madder had been scrolling through what the New York FBI office usually referred to as "the daily garbage from the NYPD" when he glimpsed something out of the ordinary. Then it disappeared.

With a frown, he scrolled back.

Several traffic citations? The police report from a car accident? What in the devil were these doing being forwarded to the FBI?

As he ran the cursor down the NYPD document, the cabbie's account of the cause of the wreck caught his eye. The report was all about the distracting presence of an alien in the backseat of the cabbie's taxi.

As he stared at the words, Wolf remembered a message from the Department of Defense a few months back asking the cooperation of all law enforcement agencies in the surveillance of illegal aliens now in the United States. The notification had obviously meant foreigners, though—aliens wading across the Rio Grande at night, Cubans and Haitians paddling sinking rafts toward Miami, and Chinese hustled out of rusty freighters in the shadow of the Golden Gate Bridge—and not what the NYPD traffic cop who'd written out this accident report thought it did.

However, after a few minutes studying the computer screen, Wolf came to the conclusion that the report was real. That he had not been picked out as the object of some sort of office joke.

Still, *aliens?*

Despite his skepticism, he felt a surge of excitement. He had waited years for something like this. From the taxi driver's description, the backseat of his cab had been occupied by a disembodied voice carrying on a conversation with a lone woman passenger.

The cabbie had made it plain that the voice was no hungry Mexican fugitive, half-drown Haitian, or dehydrated Chinese. The cabbie had heard an *alien*, an extraterrestrial type that caused him to be so momentarily distracted he had run his taxi into the back of a police car.

But could Wolf believe such a report? Agent instinct told him he must. He abruptly swiveled his chair to stare out the window at the glittering night towers of Manhattan. The vista before him was a long way from the wheat fields of eastern Colorado and the strange journey that had brought him to New York. The city spread out before him like a scattering of diamonds, hard-edged and challenging. He had often wondered what his long and mysterious odyssey here had been about.

He had a feeling that soon he was going to find out.

The therapy group gathered under the pyramid shot to their feet as Sub Commander Targon suddenly materialized. After a joyous burst of gasps and cries, they surged toward him, arms outstretched.

Unfortunately, their joy quickly turned to horror. As the crowd sprang to their feet, their heads came into contact with the slanting ceiling of the pyramid's Styrofoam shell. The sudden upheaval of a massed bodies was too much: the replica of Khafre's tomb cracked. Then the bottom parted from the foundation.

The fractured pyramid's walls wobbled. Hands went up to support them, but they came too late. Large sections broke off and fell to the floor, shooting clouds of plaster of paris dust. The topmost point, like some expiring umbrella, collapsed slowly onto the heads of those still standing.

Targon had had the presence of mind to seize Maryellen and drag her toward what was left of the pyramid's exit. Her ears rang with the dismayed shrieks of Dr. Dzhughashvili's therapy patients still stuck under the collapsing structure. She skidded, landed on her bottom, and slid down the length of the ramp. Mr. Consalvos, Maudie, and one of the Darth Vaders had freed themselves and were in hot pursuit. Targon was the catch of a lifetime. They weren't going to let him escape if they could manage it.

"Run!" Targon shouted over the noise.

Maryellen stumbled through the room with the sphinx and the dancing Shiva. The trio pursuing them was gaining. As Targon ran he pulled down festoons of blue plastic drapery and wrapped it around himself.

"What are you doing?" she screamed.

The blue lights had come down with the plastic sheets, and wires entangled their legs as they stumbled for the front door.

"Plasma, I'm losing plasma!" Targon's voice was strangled. "Got to get covered up!"

Maryellen unwound an electrical cord from her arm. "Are you hurt?" she cried.

They burst into the street.

"Sick—I'm as sick as a Nyrockian dog!" he yelled. "I never know what this damned planet will do to me!"

Luckily, the street was deserted. Otherwise, Targon in his blue plastic draperies and dangling blue lights would have attracted attention.

As it was, spots of gold from his glowing skin still showed through.

They sprinted toward the Jaguar, still miraculously unharmed under the streetlight. Hector Consalvos and Maudie and the Darth Vader burst through the door behind them.

"Stop them!" Maudie screeched.

The hefty woman raced down the street in pursuit and came even with the Jaguar. In an attempt to keep Targon and Maryellen from escaping, she threw herself on the hood with a crash that made the sports car shudder. Meanwhile, Maryellen wrenched frantically at the door on the driver's side to get it open.

Hugging the Jag's windshield with her massive arms, Maudie pressed her face against the glass. "Baby stealers! Aliens!" she howled. "You won't escape!"

On Targon's side, Hector Consalvos was pounding on the window, promising that no one would be harmed; the group only wanted them to stay. But the giant Darth Vader had already seized the windshield wipers, crunching them into a tangle of steel and rubber.

"Stop that," Maryellen shrieked as Vader tore the wipers out of their sockets. "You ape! This is my sister's car!"

Furious, she put the Jag into gear, tires screeching. Maudie rolled off the hood and sat down in the street with an audible thump. As they sped away, a larger delegation of the therapy group burst out of the house and ran screaming down toward the curb. Darth Vader threw what was left of the windshield wipers after the speeding Jag.

Maryellen turned back onto Bruckner Boulevard on two wheels. She squeezed the Jag between a Metro Transit Authority bus and a fire hydrant, briefly mounting the curb.

Targon held a ragged piece of blue plastic up before his face and groaned. Maryellen thought he was being sick again, but he only growled, "Blessed pearls of the Mother Goddess! I never thought I'd be glad to have you driving again!"

The trip back across the Bronx via Bruckner Boulevard, the Cross-Bronx Expressway, and finally West Side Drive to Maryellen's apartment was not a happy one. Targon was ominously silent. Once or twice she thought he moaned. When she took her eyes from the road for a second to look at him, slumped against the passengers side of the car, it seemed to her his glowing gold aura was considerably dimmed. His features looked pinched and drawn—almost what would be, in an Earth person, deathly pale. Curiously, the tangle of Christmas lights in the blue plastic he had wrapped himself in winked rapidly.

"Good grief, are *you* doing that?" she cried. "What are you doing now? Are you making those lights go on and off like that?"

She knew she sounded unnecessarily irritable, but she was pretty sure there could be no batteries or other power sources he could have dragged out of the house on Harvildson Avenue when he pulled down Shiva's plastic draperies.

Yet the strings of lights were blinking madly. They lit up the whole inside of the car.

"It's a side effect." His voice was hoarse and decidedly weary. "I can't help it, I'm leaking magnetic flux. I told you, that damned pyramid knocked my adjustment to this miserable Styrex Three planet all to hell." He made a noise that was unmistakably a wheeze. "Only the Great Mother Goddess knows what's going to happen if you don't get me back to your place quick."

Maryellen glanced at him, more than a little alarmed. "Good heavens, don't *do* anything! I mean, hang on!" She stepped on the gas to go through a light that had turned red a few seconds earlier. They heard the screech of brakes and a few angry shouts as they shot through the intersection. "I'll try to get there as fast as possible!"

Targon groaned again. "That's what I'm afraid of."

He didn't complain, though, when Maryellen helped him from the car in the basement parking lot half an hour later, and practically held him upright as they got into the elevator. Unfortunately, the elevator stopped at the lobby level, and a woman and a little boy about six years old, dragging a scooter, got on.

The child stared at Targon slumped in the corner, wrapped in blue plastic and festoons of blinking lights, with fascination. As the elevator doors closed and they started up, he announced in a loud, solemn voice, "It isn't Christmas yet, you know."

"Shhhh," his mother told him. But she, too, was staring.

Maryellen couldn't help staring back at them. *These people could see Targon*, she realized. *These people could actually see her visitor from out of the blue!*

Of course, in the chaos of the meeting with Dr. Dzhugashvili's therapy group, that very realization hadn't really sunk in—there had been too much going on under the pyramid with all the arguing and brawling. Then there had been the mad chase to escape the leader, Mr. Consalvos, Maudie, and the monstrous Darth Vader. She just hadn't had the time to react to the fact that Targon was certainly visible. And good grief—visible to perfectly ordinary people! Well . . . mostly ordinary. The knowledge made her a little giddy.

She fixed her gaze on the small boy, who was stealthily trying to jerk loose a loop of Targon's winking lights.

Targon was no figment of her imagination! She couldn't express how relieved she was about that. The weight of the world was off her shoulders with the proof that the glowing figure was no nightmare specter manufactured by her overworked psyche. Targon was—whatever he was—really there! In fact, he was standing in the corner of the elevator in her apartment building, wound in sheets of blue plastic and mini Christmas lights. Although frankly, he was not looking so good at that moment. His golden glow had faded to practically a fifteen-watt ghost of itself.

But he was real. He was unquestionably real

if other people could see him, too! "Don't pull at those lights," Maryellen said quickly to the child. "Don't touch, it's important. You don't want to . . . *disconnect* him, do you?"

The six-year-old considered that, then shrugged. "Hey, it's not Christmas," he piped. "It's only June. This is dumb! What's he dressed up like that for?"

"Halloween," Maryellen said firmly as the elevator reached her floor and the doors opened. "He's trying out a Halloween costume. It's very high-tech; I designed it myself."

"No, it's *not* Halloween, either," the kid screeched. "It's only Ju—"

But the elevator doors closed, cutting off his words.

"Thank goodness," Maryellen said, breathing heavily. She propped Targon against the wall with one arm as she turned the key in the lock and opened her front door.

That was as far as she got. The apparition in plastic and winking blue lights could hardly wait for her to get the door open. Suddenly galvanized, he lurched forward to brush past her, wafting sheets of plastic and electrical cord, nearly knocking her against the wall in his hurry, and made for the kitchen.

"Oh, really!" Maryellen muttered, watching the blue glow of Christmas lights reflecting on the kitchen door. "Trample me, why don't you? And not even a thank-you! After I did all that crazy driving through the Bronx—not to mention passing you off as a Halloween decoration to my neighbors."

She heard the refrigerator door open and the contents rattling as Targon searched for something. She didn't bother to call out to ask what he wanted; she was too tired. With another sigh, she made her way into the living room. Even before she turned on the lamp on her desk she could see the lights on her answering machine signaling that once again she had a busy store of messages. By the looks of it, people had been trying to get in touch with her since she'd left. Probably wanting to know where she'd been earlier, as she obviously hadn't kept any of the appointments.

Maryellen stared at the lights. Targon was ruining her life. Her business as a freelance commercial artist was piling up while she was trying to deal with the problems he'd caused. There was completed artwork in her studio waiting to be delivered to ad agencies. Then there was contracted work on a deadline to be finished. Work that she needed at least to telephone reports on to art directors and account executives, explaining the delay.

What a mess.

The obvious excuse, that she'd had to make an emergency appointment with a psychiatrist, wasn't exactly going to increase confidence in her with her clients, either. Probably the worst part was that now she knew Targon was real. It sure didn't help matters any. Telling the truth would be about as bad as saying she'd had to make an emergency appointment with the shrink. Sure, Targon was real—but who was going to believe it? It might have been better, actually, to have had a breakdown.

On the other hand, she thought with a shudder, some people didn't need convincing. Like the group out in the east Bronx with their Styrofoam pyramid. *They* believed in Targon. They had to, because he'd actually materialized in front of them. But fat lot of help they'd be! The Darth Vader was a violent nut who'd shredded the Jag's windshield wipers with his bare hands. And the others, arguing and attacking one another under the pyramid, were no better. Plus, it didn't take a genius to know she couldn't trust Maudie or Mr. Consalvos.

Of course, there was Dr. Dzhugashvili. But from all indications, it was possible—likely, even—that the psychiatrist was as much of a space-alien-Trekkie freak as his Bronx therapy group.

Maryellen threw herself into a chair and stared at the calls on her answering machine. *Why did this have to happen to me?* she wondered, almost on the verge of tears.

She was a perfectly law-abiding, tax-paying citizen who had led a fairly boring life. Who had just woken up one morning in her own bed to find that she was sharing her body with a galaxy-traveling alien! Worse, he'd turned out to be arrogant and argumentative and was convinced he'd landed on Earth because of a trick by his coworkers. That they, according to him, had wanted to get rid of him—*hah, who wouldn't?* she couldn't help thinking—in a manner as inconvenient and embarrassing as possible.

So back on his home planet his fellow aliens who hated him had sent him to a place he detested: the planet Earth. In fact, according to him they had vengefully landed him in a woman's body.

It was such a weird, totally improbable story. But the longer Maryellen was around him, the more believable it became. In fact, she was coming to the conclusion that she would give almost anything to send him to another planet—any planet—just to get him out of her hair! She could sympathize with his enemies.

With a sigh, she reached over and pushed the play button on the answering machine. Then she sat in the darkened living room, hearing the sounds of Targon doing whatever it was he was doing in the kitchen with a lot of clattering glassware, while the art editors at the advertising agencies—her precious money-making clients—demanded to know where the hell she was and why she hadn't returned their calls. And in two cases, wanting to know where their overdue ad artwork was.

Then, after a message from an account executive at Sharpe, Cone, and Belding, a new voice came on.

Maryellen sat up in her chair as the voice identified itself as Special Agent Wolf Madder of the Manhattan office of the Federal Bureau of Investigation. Agent Madder was anxious to get in touch with her as he wanted to check out a traffic accident report involving a taxicab forwarded to him from the NYPD. Would she get in touch with him at the earliest possible opportunity?

The voice of Special Agent Wolf Madder gave the New York FBI office hours, nine to five, then repeated a telephone number slowly. Twice. Then it said, "Thanks," and there was a click as he hung up.

The FBI?

Maryellen stared at her answering machine with a sort of horror as questions raced through her head. What did the taxi's crash with an NYPD police car have to do with the Feds? Of course, she *did* remember the driver, Mr. Patel, had been screaming about another person, supposedly invisible, in the backseat of his cab when he rammed the patrol car. That was what he'd shouted to anybody who would listen that his invisible passenger had so distracted him that he had smashed into the police vehicle. Otherwise nobody in his right mind would do a thing like that.

Now that she thought about it, Maryellen remembered that the overwrought cabbie had also yelled something about an alien once or twice. She hoped they thought he meant illegal alien— like the people who tried to sneak into the country without going through I.N.S.

But . . . hadn't people got into a lot of trouble hiring illegals to do housework, not paying withholding tax, that sort of thing? She was sort of hazy on the subject, but it seemed there had been political nominees on television confessing how they had broken the law when they hired illegal aliens to be their housekeepers. And how they lost their appointments to federal government cabinet jobs as a result. The same problems could happen to a lot of people in New York.

Good grief, Maryellen realized with a surge of alarm; she didn't need the FBI prowling around thinking she was hiring an illegal alien housemaid! She was really hiding something much worse! She was harboring space-traveling Sub Commander Ur Targon!

At that moment, the source of all her woes appeared in the doorway of the kitchen still wearing his blue plastic sheets, which were now somewhat the worse for wear, and looped strings of lightbulbs. The little Christmas minilights were still flashing, but visibly dimmer. Targon had a half-filled glass in his hand. In the other he held one of her plastic refrigerator jugs that dripped a fine stream of gold-colored liquid onto the floor. He actually looked, Maryellen thought, as wan as his lightbulbs.

"What have you been doing in my kitchen? And hold that thing up," she cried. "You're spilling it all over the rug!"

He said, "Orange juice. I have been ingesting orange juice from the supply in your primitive cooling unit because of the effects of that damned pyramid in the Bronx. Styrex Three orange juice contains a mirror-image isomer of ascorbic acid, which fortunately occurs in minute amounts in the natural environment of your planet. The mirror image isomer acts as a chelating agent binding to pi-mesons and rendering them inactive and thus harmless." He added, "I expel them when I belch."

Her mouth dropped open. "When you *belch*?"

He raised an eyebrow. "Consider the alternatives. Frankly, I have to tell you the quality of what was in the cardboard container is much better than that frozen stuff in the freezer compartment."

"Orange juice?" Looking past him, Maryellen could see empty frozen orange juice cans littering the kitchen counters. "Hold up that pitcher. You're ruining my carpet!"

He gave her an annoyed look. "You should be happy I found your supply of orange juice in the nick of time. After I drink this"—he held up the plastic pitcher—"and mommabulate for about six hours, I will be adequately repaired."

Maryellen got out of her chair. She'd been thinking of the FBI, and how much she desperately needed a plan to get rid of Targon. "You're going to do *what* for six hours?"

"Rest and recharge." He motioned with the empty orange juice pitcher. "See you later."

"Wait!" she cried. But he had already disappeared through the bedroom doorway. "Oh drat!" Maryellen moaned, sinking back down into the chair.

She hadn't had anything to eat since the sandwich earlier, and it was past suppertime, but she was too tired to go into the kitchen and fix anything. Besides, the thought of cleaning up the mess Targon had made with orange juice concentrate from the freezer was not exactly enticing.

I have to do something, she told herself.

But what?

In her heart of hearts she knew she would like

nothing better than to call her sister and just scream for help. God knows she needed help, and that was what sisters did; in a pinch she knew she could count on Felicia. She could convince Felicia the alien was *real*, and she could probably make Targon materialize to prove it. Why, she could even appeal to Felicia's millionaire husband, the all-powerfull J. Stephen Crump. Throw herself on his mercy and have him turn the whole thing over to his ingenious lawyers. Or as a last resort, she thought somewhat wildly, she could call her mother in Connecticut. It would be so wonderful just to turn the problem of Targon over to *somebody*.

A second later she calmed down enough to remember she could always call the FBI. She could return the agent's telephone call and arrange to meet him somewhere to ask him if he ever watched the television show the *X-files*, Because she had a situation just like that on her hands.

Oh, she thought, sighing, it would be so wonderful just to put out a loud call for *help*. Throw up her hands and give in!

The next instant Maryellen put her head in her hands. Who was she kidding? If she did any of those things—called her sister, or asked for help from Felicia's superrich husband Stephen, or called her mother, or arranged to meet the FBI—any moron could see it would only make the situation worse.

She wasn't exactly a rocket scientist, but she knew she would have to prove, for starters, that she was *not* crazy if she hoped to convince anybody to help her. That Targon was *not* a symptom of her alleged mental illness.

It might have been easier if her sister didn't know that she'd already seen a shrink about her problem, but Felicia had arranged the appointment. Before anything else could happen, Maryellen knew she'd have to fight her way past everybody's skepticism—and worse, patronizing *sympathy*—before she could persuade them of anything.

And to be perfectly honest, on top of all that was the possibility that Targon probably wouldn't cooperate. He was very difficult to handle; he'd already demonstrated that. Judging from past experience, he *wouldn't* help. He materialized only when he wanted to.

Maryellen stared into the dark of the living room, trying to concentrate. Trying to think. There had to be a plan, a way out, if not a clearcut solution.

She groaned again, even as she acknowledged that she could stew over it for hours, but there *was* no alternate solution to having to deal with an alien from outer space who said he'd landed in your apartment, in bed with you, because of some trick his conniving coworkers had played on him. If there was any answer to any of this, it was with Targon himself. What he'd tried to tell her from the very beginning. He needed a real human body.

Of course. That was it! To solve the problem of Targon, one had to give the alien creep what he needed. Then he could take care of himself. Once he was an operating human being—or at least an alien in human form—he would no longer be her responsibility. Gone. *Kaput*. He could relocate in California, or as far away as Tahiti. Which everyone said was a wonderful place, a virtual paradise. She would be glad to stake Targon the plane fare to California or Tahiti if that's what it took to get rid of him. And even if, she remembered, she was pretty maxed out on her Visa. Anything—*anything* to get rid of him!

Filled with a new purpose, she stood, went to the kitchen to turn out the lights, and then went into her bedroom.

It was dark, but she could see Targon was stretched out on her bed because his body glow was much brighter. It lit up a good portion of the bedroom. Rest and recharging and mirror-image isomers from orange juice had certainly restored a lot.

"I've decided to go along with your—uh, plan," Maryellen told him. "I mean, on a top-priority basis. After thinking it over, and I've been sitting in the living room for a good long time, thinking it over, I can see there needs to be a radical adjustment to the way things are going. That is, what happened in the taxicab is a good example. That cabdriver, poor Mr. Patel, heard us talking, and it so unnerved him to try to locate the disembodied voice that was you that he ran right into an NYPD patrol car. Fortunately, nobody was hurt, or we'd all be in jail," she explained. "But you can see how dangerous this thing can get, can't you? I think tomorrow

89

we should definitely put together an agenda. The sooner the better, don't you agree?"

There was no reply from the figure on the bed. Maryellen waited a few moments, politely, before she went on.

"I'm willing to give up another day's work, even though this is wrecking my business, frankly. I have a lot of work that's over deadline right now. You probably heard all those calls on my answering machine when I played them back. Well, I'm willing to put all that aside and use tomorrow—the day I'm taking off from work—to go around to the emergency rooms of hospitals, if that's what you want. I have to say that seems a pretty gruesome way to have to go about this. Although, on the other hand, I admit I can't think of any way it can be avoided. Then when you've got a body you like, I'd be glad to advance you any money for a trip to California. Or you could even go the other way," she continued. "To Europe. I've heard Switzerland and Italy are very nice, too. I plan to go there next summer if I can afford it."

When there was still no response, Maryellen stepped closer. Targon was in between the covers, not lying on top of them, she saw with a sinking feeling, and he seemed to be asleep. Was it possible she'd wasted her breath all the time she'd stood there talking?

"You can't sleep in my bed, you just *can't*," Maryellen said, reasonably. "Those little sofas in the living room are there to flank the coffee table, and they're really too short for anybody to stretch out on them. If you take my bed the only other alternative is my sleeping on the floor. I want to tell you," she said, raising her voice, "I am *not* going to be forced out of my bed to sleep on the floor. I'll throw you out of my bed bodily, if it comes to that!"

Cautiously, she moved closer to the king-size bed and saw that Targon was turned on his side, apparently oblivious to anything she could say, his eyes closed, the body glow so strong now it quite blurred his features.

Her feelings of frustration were so strong Maryellen felt tears come to her eyes. She wasn't going to sleep on the floor. Good grief, she needed a good night's rest after this terrible day as much as he did. She really *should* throw him out of her bed, even if he was some sort of alien. But he was very big, she saw, hesitating, and there was the all-pervasive glow. Somehow, she found she couldn't bring herself to touch him.

Oh damn, *damn*, she murmured under her breath. With a sigh, she turned away.

In a few minutes she had showered, brushed her teeth, and slipped into a nightie. Then, making as little noise as possible, she put out the light and eased into the opposite side of the bed. Hugging the edge, she lay down and closed her eyes.

After a few minutes, she gave up. Even with her eyes closed, the room was too bright. It was like trying to go to sleep with the sun coming up.

Not so quietly this time, she got out of bed, flinging back the covers quite violently, and stomped in her bare feet to the other side. She bent over Targon and snatched up the bedspread at the foot and threw it over him. The satin bedspread was down-filled, light but very warm and dense. And, oh, happy day! It squelched the golden glow, which was the important thing.

Going back around the bed, Maryellen stubbed her toe in the dark and yelped, but kept going. Targon never stirred.

Breathing hard, she got back into bed and bounced vengefully over to her side and pulled the covers up to her chin. She shut her eyes. Squeezed them shut, in fact, even as she knew sleep wouldn't come easily—not with an intergalactic traveling alien on the other side of her!

Tomorrow, she told herself. She was going to devote the whole day—and another day, if necessary—to helping Targon in his quest. Because there was one thing for sure.

She had to get rid of him.

Chapter Seven

It was easy enough for Special Agent Wolf Madder to find out where Ms. Maryellen Caswell, commercial artist, and her alien companion (if there even was one), were coming from the afternoon of the accident cited in the NYPD report. Patel, the driver of the taxi, swore that he had overheard Ms. Caswell mention a Dr. Dzhugashvili in the course of her alleged two-way conversation with the "unseen" passenger, and it had been noted in the police report.

Being a trained agent, Wolf knew the starting point was, according to the FBI manual, fairly simple. One had only to look in the Manhattan telephone directory yellow pages under "Physicians."

Dr. Josip Dzhugashvili was listed under "Psy-

chiatrists," and had both a residence and offices
in a huge, ancient, block-long apartment building in Manhattan's Upper West Side. In fact, taxi
driver Patel's records showed he had picked up
Ms. Caswell—alone, of course—on the corner of
Sixty-ninth Street and Central Park West.

Wolf Madder's next step was to make an appointment with Dr. Dzhugashvili about Ms. Caswell's visit, but he was aware he had to proceed
cautiously: the label "psychiatrist," was a warning flag for any investigator. And hardly a good
place to start looking for legitimate encounters
with alien lifeforms. All too easily he could end
up knee-deep in a collection of nuts of the lunatic fringe-type the agency especially detested.

Space alien groupies—if that was what was
involved—were even tougher to deal with than
simple conspiracy theorists.

As he checked in with Dr. Dzhugashvili's
nurse and confirmed his appointment, then sat
down to wait in front of a table covered with
issues of *Power Golf* and *Home Hobbyist* magazines, Wolf was hoping for the best.

Then suddenly, just as he reached for a three-
year-old copy of *American Philately*, he felt the
same strange sensation he'd experienced earlier,
when he was reading the traffic report from the
daily computer "garbage" from the New York
City Police Department.

A strange sensation indeed, he thought, somewhat bemused. It was as though in that instant
some unseen but tangible force were obliging
him to move, think—be *aware*—in a very specific and mysterious way.

It wasn't the first time he'd experienced this. It was a feeling, actually, that had begun five years ago, in Colorado.

Although Special Agent Madder had developed a reluctance to dwell on his past history, and especially that particular memory, the same overwhelming *directed* feeling had caused him, nevertheless, to leave his job as a fairly well-established junior insurance agent in his family's firm, and precipitously and without any explanation focus on relocating to New York City where he had at once made an application to the federal government to become an FBI agent.

Now, he saw with some fascination, here it was again.

Wolf apparently didn't want the magazine about stamp collecting, although it had looked like the most interesting one in the pile. Instead, he saw himself drop *American Philately* and reach unerringly for a *Time* magazine that had been hiding under a 1963 issue of *Southern Living*.

The choice of this particular magazine, even by the mysterious force, rather baffled him. *Time* featured a cover story in big red letters: FBI AND CIA: AMERICA'S HIDDEN EMPIRES?"

The *Time* magazine article seemed to be the sort of muck-raking expose he usually avoided. But just as he was flipping through the pages, the door to Dr. Dzhugashvili's inner office opened, and a man in a black cape emerged— obviously a patient. At the same moment, the receptionist from behind her glass partition announced that Agent Madder could go in, the doctor would see him now.

The short, bearded psychiatrist did not stand up as Wolf entered. He remained seated, even though his smile was fairly friendly. He motioned for Wolf to take a chair in front of his desk.

"Ah, Agent Madder," he said. "I have received your message given to my office when you made your appointment with my secretary. You say you are from the Federal Bureau of Investigation? It so happens I have several people who see me on a regular basis who also say they are from the FBI—although some of them, naturally, are not. It is a small detail, but if you do not mind—could you show me some identification?"

"Certainly," Wolf said, producing his wallet and opening it to show his Bureau badge. "That's very interesting. I mean that some of your . . . ah, patients . . . would think they are from the FBI. They aren't all under the impression they're special agents, are they?"

Dr. Dzhugashvili shrugged. "FBI agents, CIA agents, it's not an uncommon phenomenon. During the past four years, I have had under my care one John Foster Dulles, and two Elliott Nesses. Now," he asked briskly, "am I correct that you wish to inquire if the young Ms. Maryellen Caswell is my patient? I can assure you that she is. And you must know very well that is *all* I can say."

Wolf moved a little restlessly in his chair. "Dr. Dzhugashvili, please consider. The Bureau would like to ask your full cooperation in this matter. We have some indication, from the police officer's report on Ms. Caswell's accident in a taxicab the day she visited you, that she may have information regarding the presence of illegal aliens here in New York City. We—"

The good doctor shook his head, emphatically. "Agent Madder, even the FBI must know that there is such a thing as patient confidentiality. I can't tell you what Ms. Caswell came to me for, or anything about her symptoms, complaints, etc. Only that she did arrange to see me."

Wolf gave the man a grim look. "Dr. Dzhugashvili, I'm aware of patient confidentiality. That is, professional ethics say that you can't discuss the details of any diagnosis or treatment concerning one of your patients with anyone other than his or her family. On the other hand, the federal government also recognizes that you can't be a party to breaking the law, either. Now, I have spoken with Ms. Caswell's sister briefly. On the telephone, not in person, I admit, but I hope to get an appointment tomorrow to get some further backgrounding from her after I've talked to you. From what I already know . . ." He reached into his inner jacket breast pocket and pulled out a small notebook and consulted it. "Ms. Caswell's sister, Felicia Crump, recommended Ms. Caswell see you about a problem on June 12—yesterday. In fact, she even made the appointment for her with your office. Mrs.

Crump tells me her sister was having some sort of emotional episode concerning the presence, in her apartment, of an alien."

Dr. Dzhugashvili sat up straight in his chair. "Tell me, Agent Madder, did Ms. Caswell's sister say what sort of an alien?"

"What *sort?*" Wolf frowned. What did the psychiatrist believe was going on? And had the cabbie been mistaken; was Ms. Caswell's alien presence no more than a simple refugee from another land? Well, it still was Bureau business. "Doctor," he warned. "Let me just say this: if you have any knowledge of illegal aliens told to you by one of your patients, no matter how confidential you may regard this information, it's your duty to report it to the INS. That is, the Immigration and Naturalization Service. The United States government takes these things very seriously."

"Oh, I believe you." Dr. Dzhugashvili responded. "I believe you! Agent Madder, it is not my intent to get into trouble with the FBI or the Immigration people, believe me." He paused and then added, "However, I want to relieve your mind—and hopefully Ms. Caswell's sister, Mrs. Crump, will confirm this also when you talk with her later. We are not dealing here with an alleged alien who would under any circumstances violate any United States law. Absolutely not."

"Ah, then Ms. Caswell's problem *is* about aliens?"

The psychiatrist pursed his lips. "There are

many sorts of aliens, Agent Madder. Perhaps you have not had time to research all the varieties that our society acknowledges," he then said smoothly. "First, of course, one must find out what one means when one uses the word *alien*. Webster's dictionary—you are familiar with Webster's, are you not? Webster's dictionary defines alien as 'a person of another family, race, or nation.' Therefore the word could be used to indicate, for instance, one's own brother-in-law. So you see," he concluded, "there can be many examples of 'aliens' other than the narrowest definition that people—we in general, and the United States government—tend to put upon it."

There was a pause.

Wolf's eyes narrowed. "What are you trying to tell me, doctor?"

"Tell you?" Dzhugashvili looked blank. "What did I say? Dear sir, I said nothing except that 'alien' could mean many things, including one's abnormal relatives." Visibly shaken, the psychiatrist shuffled some papers on his desk. "Forgive me, but I have another appointment, Agent Madder. Forget everything I said about aliens, please do."

Wolf was staring at him. "You don't," he asked suspiciously, "employ any persons in your household of foreign origin, do you? If you do, doctor, I have to ask, have you or your wife checked recently to make sure they are in this country legally and have work visas that are up-to-date?"

For a brief moment Dr. Dzhugashvili looked rattled. Then he got up and came around the desk. "Please, Agent Madder, my wife does not employ anyone, believe me," he said rapidly. "She does all her own housework. I help, sometimes, with the vacuuming. No more, now, about aliens or about young Ms. Caswell. Patient confidentiality, you know. I've imparted all I can tell you."

"Well, if you do hire anyone . . . or discover any aliens," Wolf told him. "You will follow government regulations. Always pay overtime, you know—minimum wage if that's required—keep the FICA withholding in good order, make on-time reports to the Department of Labor? And don't hire the illegal ones!"

"Yes, yes, yes, mein Gott, *yes*." The psychiatrist ran his fingers through his gray hair, making it stand on end. "How did we arrive at this subject? Tell me; is this an obsession with you, Agent Madder, about illegal aliens? Do you have recurring inescapable thoughts? How long have you had them? Do you perhaps dream of homeless illegal aliens crowding the streets of the city? Streets are an important Freudian symbol, so that may be crucial. Do you do excessive hand washing, hmmm?" he asked, taking Wolf by the arm and guiding him toward the door to the outer offices. "Any facial tics? Other convulsive twitching?"

Wolf managed to free himself from the psychiatrist's grip. "I was just reminding you of laws governing the employment of aliens, doctor," he warned. "And how you and your wife should strictly observe them in the case, especially, of domestic employees. A lot of people have gotten into trouble, you know."

"Oh, we will not do so, you may be sure," Dr. Dzhugashvili told him. "All of what you say, I swear to you, we will do if we should ever, God forbid, employ anybody! In the meantime, write down your dreams, record any unnecessary hand washing, and call for an appointment. I am always available if you think you need help."

"Yes, I'll get back to you by telephone," Wolf agreed. Seeing the issue of *Time* magazine on the table in the reception room, he snatched it up and put it absentmindedly in his pocket. "There are other aspects of Ms. Caswell's recent visit here that I'd like to discuss with you—after I've had a talk with her sister, Mrs. Crump, that is, and found out what she knows about all this."

"Excellent, excellent," the doctor told him. "Just call my office and make an appointment to see me again. I have another appointment who will be here shortly, but otherwise I am available at all times."

"Good," Wolf told him. "It's nice to have your cooperation, doctor. In the meantime I want to thoroughly review the material I've been given. I don't want to have to bring in the INS unless it's really necessary."

"No, don't do that! Please, please, Agent Madder, not the immigration people. Be patient. And call me next week. The doctor shoved him through the door. "Call me, by all means!"

* * *

When the door closed behind Agent Madder, Dr. Dzhugashvili sagged against the wall and expelled a loud sigh of relief. Then in the next instant he darted for the desk, lifted the telephone, and dialed a number. He waited while it rang.

"Hello? Hello, Hector?" he said, when his director of group therapy in the Bronx answered. "They have just been here, Hector. It has been an ordeal! *Who?* Who do you think? The U.S. government! *The FBI!*"

The voice of Hector Consalvos crackled on the other end.

"Yes, yes. But this confirms our suspicions, does it not? *They know*, Hector. And yet what a joyous occasion this is, to find that it is all true! Federal involvement proves we have found an intergalactic traveler! An alien visitor!" He wiped his brow with a handkerchief drawn from his breast pocket. "Now, we must not let the appearance of the FBI, obviously searching for clues and data, impede us. We must proceed, but be aware of the massive danger. Great government agencies oppose us, and every one of us is aware of what happened in Roswell, New Mexico—a classic case. We do not want New York City to turn into a New Mexico desert, now do we?"

The response from the Bronx was loud in the earpiece.

"Very well then. I am depending on you, Hector, and all the rest of our little group. We must keep the faith, be true to our cause. Be devoted, self-sacrificing, but mentally healthy. We must," he said, lowering his voice, and looking around the shadows of his office, "prepare to move forward. Hector, do you hear me? We must move forward. *Now!*"

When Maryellen went out to get milk, the morning paper, and a few cartons of orange juice as there was none left in the refrigerator, Targon was still asleep. Or whatever it was that looked like sleep; she wasn't sure about anything concerning her so-called visitor from space.

It was Saturday, a nonworkday for many New Yorkers, and most advertising offices were closed, but Maryellen usually worked through the weekends when on a deadline. The rest of the city, she couldn't help thinking, was probably sleeping late. Taking life easy. Not wrestling with the problem of an unsociable intergalactic houseguest.

She didn't get back to her apartment until well after noontime. When she turned the key in the lock and opened the door, she was immediately aware of the television set in the living room. *The Jerry Springer Show* hit her with a blast of sound. Funny, she thought, they don't usually play this on Saturdays. Maybe the network was trying to boost its weekday morning ratings.

Wincing, she hurried into the living room and found Targon seated on one of the leather mini-sofas, his feet propped on the coffee table. He looked much better. If anything, his aura had deepened to what could be described as an almost twenty-four-karat gold hue.

"I brought more orange juice," Maryellen said. "But you don't look as though you need it."

"I have recovered, yes," he said, watching Jerry's muscular "assistants" separate two women who, locked in what appeared to be mortal combat, had just fallen on the floor and almost into the audience. "No thanks to that bunch of lunatics and their Styrofoam contraption they've got out there in the Bronx. That pi-meson bombardment caught me off guard. Damned fools, it could have gone critical."

Very deliberately, he raised his hands, still keeping his eyes on the television screen. The women who had brought their problems to Jerry Springer had fallen on their hapless boyfriend who had been two-timing them, and they were now tearing his shirt off.

While the alien watched that, Maryellen watched the rich, faintly pulsating, twenty-four-karat gold-colored aura that seemed to flow along the outlines of Targon's body, melding into more color-intense areas above his hands, nose, knees, and feet. Suddenly, small fountains of dazzling light similar to the spouts of fire that astronomers sometimes observed spurting from the surface of the sun flowed from the tips of his fingers, out of his nostrils and the toes of his booted feet.

Her mouth fell open, awed. "How did you do that?" She had to blink, it was so momentarily dazzling. The golden light had erupted like miniature geysers from his hands, even his ears. "You certainly *are* recovered—that was spectacular! Good grief, tell me, did orange juice do all that?"

"Sequential systems check," he told her. "Just

routine, trying everything out. Great Goddess!" he exclaimed. "Did you see that? The fat blond woman pulled down the redheaded woman's sweater and her mammary glands popped out. Very large ones, too. I notice there's some sort of technical censorship—this television station has devised a blurry portion on the screen to cover the exposed areas. Styrex Three culture is very squeamish, apparently," he observed, "about large, flabby breasts."

"It's not just the large, flabby ones," Maryellen told him, looking around on the sofa and the tables trying to locate the remote control. *The Jerry Springer Show* was the last thing she wanted to be watching at that moment; she had important things to talk to him about. "Surely you've noticed . . . mammary areas are usually covered here on our backward planet. Most women cover their chests. Mine is covered. It's the—ah, custom here."

Targon looked away briefly from the television screen where the redheaded guest, still without her upper clothing but appropriately blotted out in that area by the TV censors, was attacking Jerry Springer with a studio folding chair while two of his assistants tried to make her stop.

"I have noticed your mammary glands," he said. "In fact I have studied them at length, and you do not have to tell me. I know they are not large and flabby. In fact—"

Maryellen made a choking sound. "Oh, really! This is impossible! I don't want to be discussing breasts with you, you . . . *cosmic accident!*" She marched around the mini-sofa. "Where is the damned remote? How can you watch this terrible stuff?"

He had turned back to the television set. The redhead who had attacked Jerry Springer had been dragged offstage, and Jerry was appealing to the audience. They were chanting *"Jerry, Jerry, Jerry"* as the television camera swept over them, urging them on. "I am not a 'cosmic accident,' " Targon said, somewhat sulkily. "That means something entirely different."

No, he didn't conjure a mental picture of anything as negative as an accident, Maryellen thought. Whatever he said orange juice did to repair the damage done by the pi-meson attack, she had to admit it did it well. That tall, slim body in its skintight gold suit was still eye-poppingly attractive, there was no doubt about that. In any other situation she supposed she might be sorry to get rid of him.

"I need to talk to you," she said, standing in front of the television set and blocking his view. "Please don't watch this show. Those people are monumental embarrassments. They're—they're certainly not representative of people on Earth at all."

"I am aware of that." He shifted to the left on the sofa cushions so that he could see around her. "Actually they're Ka-Zorokians; I spotted them right away. The boyfriend is, and so is the blonde. A shiftless lot, Ka-Zorokians—intergalactic riffraff who crop up in backwaters like Styrex Three and operate under the delusion they're 'passing.' "

The redhead was being led back onstage by Jerry Springer's assistants, one on each side. She'd adjusted her sweater, but she still looked ready for a fight.

"This one," Targon said interestedly, "the one with the red hair, is pure Styrex Three—one of your people. But she's hanging out with a bad crowd. Ka-Zorokians are rotten through and through, and they don't respond to rehabilitation. Consequently, the Ka-Zorokian penal system doesn't exist; they just boot their criminal classes out into other carbon-based solar systems."

Maryellen suddenly sat down opposite. For a long moment she couldn't speak.

"You're just kidding, aren't you?" she managed. "Did I understand what you just said? You're not talking about those . . . those . . . people on the *Jerry Springer Show,* are you? Are you trying to say Jerry's guests are aliens—from *outer space?* Ka-Zorokians?" She stumbled over the word.

"Can't get rid of them," he told her. "They're like Styrex Three fleas—they're everywhere. Is that more orange juice in the paper bag you're holding?"

Maryellen stared at him. "I can't believe what you're saying! You mean there are *other* aliens around? On Earth? Like you? Hiding in other people's bodies? Are they . . ." Her voice rose; she couldn't help it. "Are they on other . . . *television shows?*"

"I have no idea." His azure blue eyes surveyed her calmly. "However, I intend to see *Maury Po-*

vich and *Judge Judy* and find out. I am rewatching the entire week's episodes of talk shows—just a little superficial data-gathering, mostly my own curiosity. Now," he said abruptly, "what do you want to talk to me about? Your plan to get rid of me?"

There was another silence. "You're doing it again!" Maryellen burst out. "I can't tell you how repulsive that is, to have you read my mind! It changes my opinion of you entirely."

"Your opinion of me is irrelevant, and I'm not going to California or Tahiti. Sorry to disappoint you, but I've already told you I am obligated to stay here and investigate what appears to be a conspiracy by corrupt bureaucracies in your federal government. Your planet doesn't have the experience to know the danger, but on mine there is an entire division of specially trained personnel like myself to penetrate and root out intrigues in government departments. These schemes, even by so-called devoted public servants go on all the time—even here, on your obviously retrogressive Styrex Three. A plot to overthrow your current president by traitorous neo-Hooverians may be hatching even as we speak."

"Are you *nuts?*" Maryellen's patience gave way. "You're not obligated to do anything except . . . except . . . get out of my hair! Oh, really, all I want is for you to find a body you can be happy with and leave me alone! It's bad enough having you as part of me; that's totally ludicrous! But how about scaring taxidrivers and causing dangerous traffic accidents? And sleeping in my bed at night? I just can't let this go on! You'll have to do something!"

"I intend to," he said calmly.

"Yes, well I mean right away!" She took a deep breath, determined to go ahead and say it. "Listen, I've decided to cooperate. I mean really cooperate. I'll drive you to hospital emergency rooms and anyplace else you think you might be able to pick up a body. Tonight. The sooner the better. The whole thing is gruesome, but I see now that is the only way it can be done. I've even asked my sister to let us keep the Jag so we can use it for the evening."

He studied her. "That's very nice of you."

"Yes, well I have to do something," she answered desperately. "And you have to understand that under the circumstances I think I'm doing pretty well for somebody who woke up one morning and found herself taken over by an alien. There are people who have had nervous breakdowns, real nervous breakdowns, over less."

"Yes, I suppose you have been doing well," he conceded.

"And I want you to understand my sister is married to one of the richest men the world, J. Stephen Crump. She—they—are well-known figures. They can't afford to get involved with any of this, either!"

He waited for a moment before he said, "There's more."

Maryellen glared at him. "Yes, there's more. You knew that, too, didn't you? You think you know everything! Well, you're despicable by any planet's standards, you know that? Okay, here it is: *The FBI called me!* My God, do you realize what you've done to me?"

"Don't screech," he said. "I can hear you."

"You were just waiting for me to say that!" She jumped up from the sofa. "Well, I'm not going to return the FBI's telephone call. I'm not going to get involved with the federal government. I'm a law-abiding citizen! I pay my taxes . . . I've never even been audited like a lot of people I know, and I've never been in trouble in my whole life! I'm not about to start now. I'm going to help you get a host body or whatever it is you want, and then I don't want to ever see you again!"

"I understand that," he said. "I hope you can acknowledge that I had nothing to do with being here on Styrex Three. None of this is by my choice. But once here, I can't ignore my duty. Or the investigations I've been trained for."

"J. Edgar Hoover is *dead*," Maryellen screamed. "He's not heading up some conspiracy to overthrow the United States government; he's dead, dead, *dead!*"

Targon didn't move. "The former head of the FBI has followers," he insisted stubbornly. "Secret cells are operating inside the FBI and probably parts of the CIA. A cult brotherhood. Passwords. Blood-oath ceremonies. It always follows a pattern."

Maryellen stopped her pacing and glared at him, breathing hard. "You're going to stay here, then, on planet Earth, and track down the followers of J. Edgar Hoover who are planning to overthrow the United States government?"

"Yes," he said.

"Will you be working someplace fairly far away, like Washington, D.C.?"

"Perhaps." He shrugged. "Most likely, it all depends."

She let out her breath in an explosive sigh. "I wish I could count on that. You've got to . . . you've really got to be somewhere far away! This whole thing is totally crazy," she said, almost to herself. "If only it weren't so impossible to explain even to your closest relatives that you really *do* have a space-traveling alien in your life without getting institutionalized . . ."

"You're going to have to return the FBI's telephone call," he said.

"No. Not until I get rid—help you," Maryellen vowed. She looked at her wristwatch. "We have all afternoon. The emergency rooms don't get busy on a Saturday night until after nine or ten o'clock, so you said. We have plenty of time for a project I thought about this morning, when I went out for the paper."

He looked up at her inquiringly. "A project?"

"Yes, it's much better than watching *Maury Povich*. You really don't need to study that kind of television; it gives our planet a bad name. Instead, I'm going to get my sketch materials out of the studio, and you can tell me exactly what kind of—ugh—body you're looking for. I'll sketch it for you as you describe it."

He looked her over appraisingly. "Good idea. I had forgotten you're an artist."

"Commercial artist, I'm no Pablo Picasso,"

Maryellen said quickly. "But you can show me what you're looking for, and we can use my sketch as a guide. A general guide."

A few minutes later, sketchbook and drawing pencil in hand, she sat down beside him. He switched off the TV and turned to her. "I prefer to look as much like myself as possible," he told her. "No facial hair—goatees, Vandykes, sideburns. And tattoos or body piercings are not an option."

Maryellen peered at him. She had to get rather close, for there was some blurring of his features by the gold aura. Which was, if anything, stronger than ever.

For the first time she was really looking at him, and most importantly, with an artist's critical eye. He was not bad-looking at all by Earth standards. Of course, Maryellen had known that all along, from the first moment he'd shown up in her apartment—actually, in her chair—but she hadn't had the time to make a lengthy observation. Now she could stare at him for several minutes without having to make any sort of explanation.

Besides even features, a nicely chiseled nose and chin and good teeth, there were the eyes, she thought. They were really a remarkable shade; she'd already dubbed the color "laser blue" in her mind. They were quite expressive—once you got past all the pulsing gold glow.

Unfortunately the expressions in those marvelous azure eyes had a limited range, most of them negative. She'd learned even in the short time he'd been around that they projected distaste when discussing practically anything about the planet he called Styrex Three; a cold, detached contempt when talking about Dr. Dzhugashvili's Bronx therapy group, and aliens from other solar systems on TV; and annoyance when he had to be a passenger in the same car she was driving.

"Are you going to sketch me as I am," he asked. "Or what you think we might find tonight when we make the rounds of the hospitals?"

"Both," Maryellen said, starting to draw. "You really will be changed, you know. It would be hard to actually translate what you are into . . . uh, a Styrex Three life-form. I think that's what you'd call it. Would you prefer to be a blond or a brunette?"

He thought a moment before he said, "What am I now?"

"You mean, what do you look like to me?" Maryellen inched a little closer, gingerly. "I don't know. You could be a blond. It would be hard to be a brunette with all that glowing going on."

"Let me see."

He reached for the sketch, but Maryellen twisted, holding it away from him. "Just hold your horses! I have to put a business suit on you, or something, to get the full effect. Or do you prefer sportswear?" she asked sweetly. "A jacket that says New York Giants on the back? How about a baseball cap on backwards and big rapper pants that hang down so—"

"If you don't mind," he interrupted, reaching out and snatching the sketch from her. He studied it for long minutes. "I do look like Brad Pitt."

"Well, that's what you said you wanted earlier," Maryellen agreed. "I added a dash of Matthew McConaughey, because you kind of look like him, too. I ruled out Keanu Reeves because I don't really think you should consider anyone dark. Of course, if you want something different, let me know now."

He handed the sketch back to her. "We'll use it as a guide."

"Of course, I don't know how many hunky males looking like Brad Pitt or Matthew McConaughey are going to end up in a New York City hospital emergency room tonight. But we might get lucky. Consider that after all, it *is* Saturday, the busiest night of the week."

Targon picked up the television remote and clicked it. Two women, sobbing loudly, were confronting *Jenny Jones* on the television screen. "I look forward to a successful evening. Although it's been my experience anything can happen on this planet."

Maryellen looked down at the sketch in her hand.

She knew Targon wasn't going to get a Brad Pitt or Matthew McConaughey match-up looking through emergency rooms, but under the right circumstances she was sure something would be found that he could accept. After all, he'd have to accept less if he was going to stay on the much-detested Styrex Three.

And after that, she thought, sighing, her life would go back to normal again.

Chapter Eight

"I don't really know how I'm going to do this," Maryellen said as she turned the Jaguar into the emergency entrance driveway of Columbia Presbyterian Hospital in upper Manhattan. "I mean, there are some major drawbacks to this whole operation. Like, I still haven't worked out the actual details of how to get into the emergency rooms.

"It's a good thing New York City has so many hospitals that specialize—I found that out when I looked in the yellow pages. There's the Hospital for Joint Diseases, the New York Eye and Ear Infirmary, the Hospital for Special Surgery, even the New York State Psychiatric Institute. You can tell right away that you can eliminate those because from what you said we wouldn't want to waste time with major physical or mental problems. For example, we want to avoid somebody who is going to have an eye operation, or is a homicidal bipolar paranoid." She maneuvered the Jag through the emergency entrance parking lot into an empty space. "As I understand it, you need a body that is ready-to-wear, right?"

"You're nervous," Targon told her. "Calm down. You're rattling on and on about hospitals."

"Of course I'm nervous!" she exploded. "What do you expect? Here I am with an alien nobody can see—except that I seem to be talking to myself—prowling around New York City hospitals on a Saturday night! How else am I supposed to be? I don't go around stealing bodies every day, you know!"

Maryellen got out of the Jag, slamming the door as she started for the busy emergency entrance. There were already two ambulances unloading in front of it.

"Just stop talking to me," she told him. "I'm going to go into the ER desk and sign myself in with stomach cramps and nausea. That's not top priority, of course—we will probably have to wait a good long time in a Manhattan hospital to see a doctor. I've been told by a friend of mine who's a newspaper reporter that on late Saturday nights the New York City ERs usually run a couple of hours behind because that's when they bring in the shootings and knifings and ODs and all that sort of thing. It would seem to me that that will be my opportunity. While we're sitting around in the waiting room I'll get up—hopefully at a really busy time when nobody will notice—and wander down the hallway and look into the examining rooms. I'll see if I—*we*—can check out the . . . uh, prospects. Ugh," Maryellen muttered to herself. "I still can't believe I'm really doing this!"

"You want to get rid of me," he reminded her.

"Stop talking to me!" Maryellen gritted her teeth as a Puerto Rican woman going through the emergency entrance doors with two small children turned to stare at her as Maryellen strode along, seemingly carrying on a conversation with herself. "I'm not going to talk back," she said, "so just concentrate on what we're doing, and hope it works out. After all, don't forget you're the one who needs the body! If anything, this ought to be a lesson to you . . . to stay on your own dratted planet!"

A few minutes later, as she signed herself into the Presbyterian Hospital's emergency room and filled out all the forms necessary for her Blue Cross coverage, she regretted she'd spoken so harshly.

After all, she told herself, Targon maintained that he wasn't on Earth as a matter of choice, but he'd been tricked into going to a place he hated by his enemies who worked with him as investigators in the government on his home planet. Perhaps she was being insensitive.

The thing was, Maryellen told herself as she took a seat on a plastic chair in the ER's waiting room, along with approximately fifty other people, she wasn't responsible for Sub Commander

Targon's being on Earth, either. It was not *her* fault. His kidnapping, hijacking—whatever you wanted to call it—had only just become her particular burden yesterday. She was the one who, if she wanted to be free of a space-traveling alien who glowed in the dark, had to help him snatch bodies.

"The woman at the desk didn't think you were sick," Targon said. "She didn't want to admit you. You look very attractive, not like somebody racked for the last twenty-four hours by nausea and diarrhea."

I'm going to ignore him, she thought firmly.

"I could make you vomit, if that would help any," he offered.

As his words registered Maryellen jumped out of her chair. "No!" she cried. "I don't want to vomit! Stop it! Please, just don't be helpful, will you?"

She caught herself at that point, but the damage was done. The people waiting nearby took her at her word. Which in this case was *vomit.* They hastily gathered things and scurried away for at least two rows around her. Obviously they didn't want to be in the vicinity when things happened.

"Oh, *damn!*" Maryellen moaned, her face flaming in embarrassment. There was no use in trying to explain that she wasn't about to throw up all over this end of the waiting room when she'd just jumped out of her seat and announced that very thing.

Humiliated, Maryellen decided her only option now was to leave. She picked up her purse and headed for the corridor off the main room and the door that said Women.

She was intercepted by an orderly who ran after her and took her by the arm. "Going to 'whoops,' doll?" he asked. "Is that what you said? Well, do it in an examining room, okay?"

She stared at him. Had she heard right? Back in the examination and treatment part of Columbia Presbyterian's emergency unit was, of course, where she wanted to be! If she could just wait in one of the cubicles for an hour or so, she could occasionally sneak up and down the hallway looking for possible candidates for Targon's grisly business.

Dazzled by her good luck, Maryellen didn't say anything as the orderly steered her into one of several small rooms off the corridor. But instead of Maryellen settling down for a wait of several hours or so, a nurse barged right on in with them.

"Are you our puker?" the RN asked cheerfully. "Gotta be careful with contamination. Here, use this if you get the urge again." She handed Maryellen a large stainless-steel pan. "Now, get up on the table and let me have a look at you. Just take off your sweater, leave on the bra."

Reluctantly, Maryellen did so, pulling off her turtleneck with an uneasy feeling. She hadn't really counted on taking off any of her clothes; things were obviously not working out as planned. That is, as much as she'd planned anything.

"Watch what you're doing, hon. Lift it up." The nurse adjusted Maryellen's hands to hold

119

the stainless-steel pan directly under her chin. "We've seen a lot of this going around. Don't need to spread it any farther in Manhattan."

"A lot of *this?*" Maryellyn asked weakly. "Oh, you mean the diarrhea and vomiting? Actually, it's going away. I feel remarkably better since I came in here. Look, you can see me last. I don't mind waiting. I'm sure there are lots of people outside bleeding and . . . uh, needing oxygen. Even stitches. You know, real emergency cases. You can leave me and go treat them if you want," she offered. "I don't mind. I'll wait."

"Actually we're not all that busy tonight," the nurse said, fixing a blood pressure cuff around Maryellen's bare upper arm while the orderly stuck an electronic thermometer in Maryellen's left ear. "Maybe we'll get busy later on, who knows? It's springtime. June. The birds and bees. People are out making love, not shooting each other. Of course, we'll get the auto accident casualties after midnight."

"This thing must be broken," the orderly was saying, shaking the thermometer with its long attached cord violently. "Is the juice on? What the hell's the matter? It's registering all the way to the top—one hundred and twenty. Looks like it would go even higher if it could. Sheesh, they don't make these things like they used to."

At that very moment, the nurse was staring in considerable surprise at the read-out on the blood pressure machine. "What have they been doing in here," she muttered, "partying with rock bands? Is everything broken? Look, Emilio," she said to the orderly. "I'm not out of my mind, am I? I'm getting a reading of . . . *twenty-four* over *six?* This is the second reading—I did it twice—and it's the same thing. *Twenty-four over six!*"

"Ha, ha, ha," the orderly responded. "She must be dead or something! Nobody's got blood pressure like that. Nobody's got a temperature over one hundred twenty, either."

Slowly they both turned to stare at Maryellen. She sat up on the examining table, clutching her turtleneck and the stainless-steel pan to her chest.

"Oh no," Maryellen whispered. She closed her eyes.

Targon. It was Targon!

They were in trouble. Because no matter how many times the Presbyterian Hospital emergency room staff took her blood pressure and temperature, she had a feeling it was going to read the same!

"On the other hand, this is New York," the nurse said to the orderly. "We don't take anything for granted. C'mon, doll," she said, motioning to Maryellen. "We're going to go next door and try out the machines in there. Just to be on the safe side."

Maryellen slid off the far side of the examining table and carefully laid the stainless-steel pan on the floor.

"I don't think I need to have my blood pressure taken again, really," she told them. She began to sidle along the wall in the direction of the open door. "My family has always had trouble with their blood pressure, anyway. Back to my great-grandfather. It's in our genes."

The nurse and the orderly weren't buying it. They circled Maryellen purposefully, blocking the doorway.

"No way," the nurse told her. "You may look all right, sweetie, but whatever it is, I've never seen it before. It could be smallpox. My God, it could be plague! You've got to be isolated. You've got to be *quarantined!*" She made a lunge for Maryellen, crying, "Grab her, Emilio!"

Maryellen was too fast for them. She straight-armed the orderly, surprising herself with her own strength, then dove around the nurse just as the latter was trying to close the examining room door. Maryellen shot out into the corridor and raced for the waiting room.

"Come back!" the nurse called. "You'll infect everyone!" Maryellen ignored her and kept running.

"Put your clothes back on," Targon reminded her.

"Shut up!" she howled.

As she passed through the ER waiting room, some of the patients, seeing Maryellen returning to them clad only in her brassiere and brandishing her turtleneck, hurriedly left the rows of plastic chairs with screams and cries of panic.

For her part she tried to ignore the pandemonium, and the security guard who stepped in front of her at the ER glass doors but who was too busy answering his cell phone—undoubtedly with a message warning him she was coming—to be able to stop her. Once out into the parking lot she sprinted for the Jaguar, pulling her sweater over her head and clicking the door open with her remote as she ran.

Maryellen all but fell into the front seat of the sportscar, then started the engine. The Jag tore down the drive and exited the medical center and turned onto Broadway with a screeching of tires.

"Well, I have to hand it you," Targon said. "You kept your head and got out of that one all right. I am actually deeply admiring. Frankly, I'm finding you are not only beautiful, but courageous, too."

"Shut up!" Maryellen said, grabbing the steering wheel with both hands as the Jag entered Central Park at Ninety-sixth Street. "We're going to Bellevue next. I'm not giving up on this," she ground out. "Do you hear me? Not if it takes all night! And stop trying to flatter me. I'm not beautiful; my sister is beautiful. I'm the plain one."

"You have a strange idea of yourself—what is your last name . . . Caswell? You have a wholly inaccurate view of your physical attributes, Ms. Caswell," he observed. "Your sister merely considers herself beautiful as everyone tells her she is. They pick up on the expectation."

"I'm not going to make the same mistake twice," Maryellen said, busy with her own thoughts. "No more examining-room fiascos. We're going to Bellevue."

"Bellevue?"

"It's downtown," she said, turning onto the East Side Expressway. "It's a very famous old

New York City municipal hospital. The morgue's located there."

"The morgue's not going to do me any good," he told her. "I thought I explained that. A corpse is of no use to me at all. For one thing, there are various stages of rigor mortis to contend with, plus most Styrex Three body tissue after a few hours shows a morbid congealing of—"

"Stop!" Maryellen yelled. "Don't say any more, do you hear me? This is getting to me; can't you see that? It's bad enough having to be involved with you in this ghoulish activity without having to listen to all the wretched details! Now," she said, taking a deep breath, "we're going to Bellevue because it's big and busy, not because it has a morgue. And I'm going to avoid any trouble like we had at Presbyterian Hospital by pretending to be a hospital social worker. Actually, I have a cousin who's a hospital social worker in Minneapolis, and I can't see that what Barbara does is all that complicated—it's mostly a matter of filling out forms for patients who need stuff."

Targon was silent for a long moment. "Is that all she does?" he asked.

"Not much more than that. This is a little more complicated than walking into the emergency room at Presbyterian and saying that I have intestinal flu or something, if that's what you mean, but just wait and see. I think I have it worked out. I'm going to start by going into the hospital from the main entrance, and finding a hallway that leads to the ER. That way, we'll be coming from the hospital side."

"I don't see how that helps anything," Targon complained.

"Just leave it to me," Maryellen told him. She pulled into the Bellevue parking garage and took a ticket from the machine.

"Here we are," she said, a few minutes later.

The main entrance and lobby of Bellevue Hospital were almost empty in contrast to the emergency room of Presbyterian Medical Center. After a moment's search among signs posted in the corridors that said things like Radiology, Maternity, and Laboratory, Maryellen found one that said Emergency Room, with a red arrow under it, and set off at a brisk pace.

Several people going in the opposite direction toward the main lobby, obviously visitors, passed her, but there was little other traffic. Just beyond swinging doors marked Emergency were rooms marked Kitchen and then one with a sign that said STAFF. Maryellen slipped into the latter.

The area obviously served as a day room for ER personnel. There was a table, easy chairs, one wall lined with shelves, and several white coats hung on hooks opposite. Maryellen was looking for IDs.

"Ah, here's one," she whispered, finding a white medical coat with its large plastic card and metal clip, the Bellevue ID, still attached. She took the coat down and slipped it on.

"It says 'Dr. Wang,'" Targon pointed out.

"Haven't I asked you to *please* be quiet?" Maryellen yanked down the front of the coat, finding it a little snug over her turtleneck sweater. She began to unbutton it again. "Nobody reads these things, anyway. Besides, if you hadn't made that stupid remark in the Presbyterian Hospital ER, using that word I won't repeat again, we wouldn't be here now. Look," she cried, "I don't think I'm getting through to you, but I'm doing the best I can!"

"I realize that." He sounded sincere. "In fact, you have shown an amazing cache of resourcefulness. Which is more than I usually find on this planet. Yes—all in all, I'm finding you quite unique."

"I want you to shut up!" She opened the door of the staff room and looked out into the corridor. "No matter what you feel like saying from now on, will you please put a cork in it? Whether you manage to get your—ah, uh—'body' or not depends upon keeping your lip buttoned. Do you understand?"

" 'Lip buttoned?' 'Put a cork in it?' Interesting expressions, although sometimes it's difficult following you. However, I am making notes—as I don't have either phrase in my Directory of Styrex Three Folk Sayings and Up-To-Date Colloquialisms."

"Good heavens," Maryellen exclaimed, hurrying down the corridor. "Are those patients I see on gurneys out here in the hallway? They must be having a busy Saturday night here already! Strange, the parking lot was so empty."

Ahead of them, she saw two nurses come out of a door marked Waiting Room. They waited for Maryellen, and one of them promptly handed her a clipboard.

"Great, good to see you. You're from Cardiology?" the taller RN asked. "Thanks for coming down; we need all the help we can get. The Ninth Precinct is making a sweep and loading us up with street people. Take a look, will you? We've got substance ODs, alkies, malnutrition, dehydration, everything. They're piling up in the hallways. You can start here."

The other nurse said, "Dr. Wang?"

Maryellen said quickly, "It's my married name."

"Oh," the other nurse replied. Then they hurried off.

"Now," Maryellen began, taking a quick look up and down Bellevue Hospital's Emergency Room hallway. It was filled with gurneys holding bodies in varying stages of consciousness. "Here's the time for me to make a survey so you can pick out the most suitable . . . uh, well, you know." She shuddered. "The worst part is, do they have to be . . . well, *expiring?*"

"That's the ideal situation," Targon's baritone voice acknowledged. "But it's tricky. On the way out, but not completely so."

"I never imagined myself involved in anything quite so ghoulish." Maryellen bent over the first patient collected from the streets of the lower East Side by the NYPD, and uncovered his face.

"No alcoholics," Targon said. "Some of these might look passable, but a healthy liver is indispensable."

"Hello, beautiful." The gray-haired derelict on

127

the stretcher winked at Maryellen. "Whatcha doing later, doll? You got a helluva whiskey tenor, ain'tcha? But hey, we can work past that."

She hastily dropped the sheet back in place. "Ugh. He's not quite dead, is he? We'd better hurry and look at the rest."

Quickly, she worked her way down the corridor lined with gurneys and their cargo of street people the police had rounded up. Targon rejected some almost before she could get a look.

"This is not what I'd call top quality even for Styrex Three," he complained. "All but three in this hallway are over seventy of your planet's years old, including that shopping-bag lady. The one with the nose ring and Hobbit tattoos is young enough, but I would judge him to be about twenty-three, which is not really a viable age for me. At least, I'd like not to consider the college age set right away—only as a last resort. More importantly, though, I would reject him because his system is full of nicotine, alcohol, and other toxic substances. All I can say is, we've got to do better than this."

"*We?*" Maryellen leaned against the wall, clutching the hospital clipboard to her wearily. "Listen, this is the biggest collection of bodies so far. We're really lucky to have done this much. I'm sorry none of them meets with your approval!"

"You're the one who supplied me with the sketches, got my hopes up. All I ask is that you come up with a reasonable facsimile."

"A reasonable facsimile of Brad Pitt?" She couldn't keep her voice down. "Do you realize how many millions of women hope for the same thing? That is, a reasonable facsimile of Brad Pitt? Well, brace yourself, because you aren't going to get it! You're lucky to have the opportunity to take what you can . . . like what's right here, in the Bellevue ER, right now!"

"Stop screaming," Targon told her. "You're overwrought."

"And you're too picky-picky!" she flung back. "Why can't you choose an alcoholic somewhere in this collection and see that he goes to rehab? Look, find the best one, take your chance on rehabilitation, and get it over with!"

"I don't want to be an old drunk with false teeth, or a rapper with a nose ring," he responded irritably. "And I want to avoid spending four to six months in rehab getting the body back into shape. I have important things to do."

"Hey," said one of the sheet-covered forms, abruptly sitting up. "I hear voices, but there's only one doctor in here. What's going on?"

Another sheet-draped figure, propping itself up on an elbow, volunteered, "It's Bellevue, Harry. They got us in the cuckoo ward. She's been talking to herself for the last ten minutes."

Maryellen clutched her clipboard and looked around. The patients on the gurneys in the hallway were stirring.

"What are you doing?" she cried to them all. "Lie back down. You're supposed to be dead. Or at least, dying!"

"Jeez," the gray-haired man said, throwing back his sheet. "This place has an attitude! Where's the conservative compassion? I should be dying, they tell me. I don't want to be dying. Is this any way to treat the homeless underprivileged?"

"Dead?" the shopping-bag lady squeaked, scrambling down from her gurney. "They want us dead? Elmore, look when I pull my shirt up and see if I still got both my kidneys!"

"Time to go," Targon said.

Maryellen waved her clipboard helplessly. "No, no, people," she tried to call out over the mounting confusion. "Get back on your gurneys, this is all a big mistake. Please listen! Nobody wants you to die. Actually, the hospital is going to provide you with a bed and a nice shower, clean clothes, a warm room, a hot meal—everything will be a lot different from sleeping on the sidewalk. Trust me!"

There were subdued screams.

"It's really time to go," Targon warned.

"They ain't operated on you yet, Aggie," an old man shouted. "You look okay!"

But the shopping-bag lady was waddling full speed toward the end of the hall. Maryellen found herself following the woman, propelled by some unseen force that could only be Targon.

"What did I do?" she wanted to know as she was made to run for the lobby and through the doors to the parking lot. "Why are they scattering like frightened rabbits, for goodness' sake?"

"They're not important," Targon's voice growled. "What *is* important is that we're not getting anywhere in my body search. However, I admit this may not be solely your fault. From what I've seen, it's only confirmed my opinion that New York City has a definite lack of good material."

"Well, I'm not going to give up," Maryellen told him as she got into her car and started the Jaguar's engine. "I've already lost two days' work, which means a lot of money for me, and my sister will want her car back eventually. So I have a lot invested in this succeeding. Besides, you really don't know how much I want to . . . help you."

"Get rid of me, you mean."

"Don't put words in my mouth," she told him, steering the Jag toward Central Park and back across town again. "I really, really look forward to your getting a body—believe me, I can't tell you how much."

"Don't let the street people get you down," he said. "It's widely known that Styrex Three has a miserable underclass. They didn't appreciate what you were trying to do for them back there, anyway."

She sighed. "That's not very nice. And it's all my fault. I think they probably got the wrong impression, that Bellevue was going to steal their body parts. Poor things, it must be terrible to live that way."

"I'm not doing so well myself," Targon reminded her peevishly.

"Yes, I know," Maryellen snapped, turning up West Side Drive toward the George Washington Bridge. "Nobody's more aware that you need a body to call your own than I. But I've been thinking about it, and actually New York City may not be the best place to do this. I've been holding New Jersey in reserve."

He took a long moment to think that over. "New Jersey is a healthier environment? With better physical specimens?"

Maryellen hesitated. "If you're worried about pollution, I don't think New Jersey exactly wins any awards. I mean, I don't know if they've cleaned up all their toxic waste dumps yet. But they have an NFL football team . . . and the football team looks pretty healthy."

"That's encouraging."

Ahead of them, the lights of the West Side Highway that followed the Hudson River were like strings of bright, icy jewels laid out before them. The illuminated towers of midtown Manhattan rose behind. The great sprawling city had never looked lovelier or more unreal. Ahead was the spangled shape of the George Washington Bridge. The clock on the dashboard of the Jaguar said three twenty-three.

"Fort Lee has a pretty good hospital, I understand," Maryellen said. "That's a town right across the river on the opposite side of the George Washington Bridge. Although I really thought we'd go a little farther west and try for some of the suburban places, like the Oranges."

"The Oranges?" Targon sounded interested.

Maryellen slowed for the George Washington Bridge ticket booth and paid the fee and got her receipt. It was really late and there was not too much traffic going from New York over to the New Jersey side, so she didn't have to jockey the Jaguar through other lanes to get the outside lane and the rail. She looked out to watch the moon on the Hudson River as she crossed.

"That's the name of several towns," she told him. "People call them 'the Oranges.' East Orange, West Orange, and so forth. They're mostly suburban upper-middle class, so you shouldn't have to complain about their emergency rooms being full of street people and druggies."

"Wait a minute, Targon said sharply. "Watch what you're doing. There's nobody on your tail, is there? You're going to have to slow down, there's a car parked in the middle of the bridge."

"He's going to jump!" Maryellen cried.

She slowed the Jaguar as it approached the center of the George Washington Bridge. Caught in the sportscar's headlights was the figure of a man in an expensive-looking business suit. He was trying to climb through a safety grille that rose about fifteen feet from the railing—a grille designed to prevent exactly what he was apparently trying to do. Which was, jump off the bridge into the Hudson River.

"Oh, my God!" Maryellen cried as the man reached the top of the grille and an open space. "He's going to do it!"

She hit the brakes. The Jag screeched to a full stop. A pickup truck that had been behind them passed with a blaring of horns.

"We've got to do something!" Maryellen opened the door on the driver's side and scrambled out. "Look where he is!"

The would-be jumper, now that he had reached the top of the safety barrier, had taken off his suit jacket. His shirt gleamed white in the bridge's lights as he held the jacket in his hand and looked around, then shrugged, letting it drop. The suit jacket fluttered down and landed a few feet away from the Jag.

Following the familiar sensuous tugging, Targon materialized beside Maryellen, glowing in the dimness. "It's about time we made some progress," he observed. "I wasn't looking forward to canvassing New Jersey—in spite of your testimony about the towns named for oranges—but New York City hospitals seem to be a dead end, if you'll excuse the expression."

He bent over, picked up the suit jacket and quickly went through it, making a sound of satisfaction as he found a man's wallet in an inner pocket. "Hah, this is more like it! Look what we have here. The photo on the driver's license isn't bad at all, if you can tolerate red hair."

"Oh, quick," Maryellen cried. "Do something! He hasn't jumped yet; he's just standing there! He looks like he's crying!"

"Probably has a right to cry." Targon shuffled through a handful of cards from the wallet. "It appears he's a stockbroker into dot-coms, a very unwise market area choice. I can see the need for a leap into the Hudson. Hmm, nice memberships, New York Athletic Club, Belmont Park, American Express Platinum—"

"Eeek," Maryellen shrieked. "His foot slipped! No, he caught himself!" She jumped up and down. "For heaven's sake, don't just stand there, do something!"

"Just give me a minute," Targon said, holding

a driver's license up to the light. "There's enough time, I can work very quickly, actually, when the situation demands it—literally, as they say, 'with the speed of light.' Let's see; according to his IDs and cards, he's six feet one inch. I would have preferred another inch or two, but assume he'll be in good shape because of the athletic club membership. He has blue eyes and the inevitable red hair . . . wears glasses for driving."

"Oh, good grief, I can't stand this! Look at him!" Maryellen clasped her hands and looked up to see the jumper leaning against a girder high above them, indicating he was prepared to leap at any moment. She whirled around to survey the empty bridge. "I can't believe this, there's not any traffic on this thing at all! Not a police car in sight, there's never one when you need them!"

She turned to Targon, who had closed the wallet and put it back into the suit jacket pocket. "Don't just stand there, he's going to jump," she yelled. "Do something!"

"I intend to. But haste causes fatal errors if things are not checked out thoroughly before making a conversion." He handed her the man's jacket. "Hold on to this."

Targon walked a few steps toward the bridge railing, then stopped. "This will be," he said, turning to face her, "good-bye, perhaps. Certainly the last time I see you in this form, at least for a while. Circumstances might dictate weeks, months, ah . . . well, I hope," he added huskily, "when and if we meet again, that you have no great aversion to slightly overweight—at least by

135

my expectations—redheaded types who dabble unsuccessfully in the stock market."

Maryellen goggled at him. "What are you doing? You can't mean—" She looked up at the figure teetering on the bridge's girders above them. "You mean you're going to—oh, my God—you're going to pick *him?* You mean you're going to let him leap, then—"

"Please pay attention. You're not following what I'm trying to tell you," he said. "I'm not trying to minimize the risk. It takes considerable skill, actually, to make the transfer just at the moment of impact. As for instance, if one's timing is off one faces the 'ooops' factor—the prospect of a host body that's so squashed it's unusable, or at the very least with an assortment of broken bones."

"I can't believe you're going to do this! I know you said you were looking for a body, but—"

"Once the transfer is successful," he went on, "I will still find myself in an optimally risky position as I will be, according to my reckoning, somewhat to the south of the George Washington Bridge in the Hudson River, a body of water that presents a not inconsiderable danger due to heavy pollution. The rivers around New York City are particularly nasty examples."

Maryellen covered her eyes. "I can't look, I can't believe this is happening! Good grief, what a nightmare! You're going to let that poor man jump to his death!"

"On the contrary, I have nothing to do with this Styrex Three male's desire to terminate himself; he decided that on his own. I thought you said you were going to cooperate fully in our mission tonight to find a suitable host body. Well, get a grip on yourself. This seems to be the one."

"He's *not a body yet*," Maryellen screamed. "You don't understand about anything, do you? I can't let this happen! You've got to do something, do you hear? You've got to climb up there and get him down!"

Targon said nothing for a long moment. "Nonsense. I don't know what all the fuss is about. He will feel no pain, death occurs from this height as soon as he hits the surface of the water."

"Oh, get out of my way!" She took a deep breath. "Look—if you're not going to try to get him down, I'm going to do it myself!"

Maryellen started for the bridge's safety grille. She put her hands, then her feet on the crossbars, and started up.

"This is totally irrational," Targon said beside her.

Maryellen looked over her shoulder at him. "Don't come up here unless you intend to help me," she panted. She threw her head back to call, "Yoohoo, up there! Hold everything! Don't despair, life is worth living! I want to talk to you!"

Below them, several cars had come to a stop on the bridge behind the Jaguar. A small crowd had gathered. They stood looking up at Maryellen and Targon making slow progress upward over the bridge girders with the would-be jumper poised above them, ready to leap.

There was a slight wind blowing on the

bridge's superstructure. Maryellen heard Targon make a sound of sheer aggravation. "Get down," he snarled. "I have to tell you that I am amazed that this is any concern of mine, because you are acting in an erratic manner. But you will undoubtedly injure yourself if you go any farther on this antique contraption. Therefore, I will take care of the redheaded fat man—"

Even as he spoke there were screams from the group below. The man perched above them had jumped.

Targon uttered what sounded like a long and complicated string of curses similar to the ones Maryellen had heard that first day, when she had encountered him in her bed.

Then he launched himself from the side of the George Washington Bridge and into the blackness of the night and the river below.

Maryellen, speechless for once, hung on to a beam and leaned out into the breeze blowing from the water to watch him drop down and down, growing smaller, until the golden speck that was Targon completely disappeared.

He was gone.

Chapter Nine

The headline covered the entire front page of the *New York Daily News*:

JUMPER SAVED BY SCUBA DIVER.

The *New York Post* also devoted its front page to a big banner screaming:

SPORTS HERO NIXES NY BRIDGE LEAP.

On the other hand, Special Agent Wolf Madder saw, as he read the newspapers spread out on his desk, the *New York Times* discreetly put the story on page four, and said only:

STOCKBROKER RESCUED FROM HUDSON RIVER.

Katherine Deauxville

Wolf had picked up the newspapers at the front desk because he was following the story of baseball's bad boy, Jim Crocker, who had just been transferred to New York's own Mets, but the screaming headlines of the rescue were hard to ignore. All the reports, including those of the Associated Press and television cable news, carried more or less the same account, supplied by police and a handful of eyewitnesses. That is, Jason Wertherminster, age thirty-four, had, at close to four in the morning Eastern Standard Time, fallen or jumped from the top of the safety barrier above the outside westbound lane of the George Washington Bridge and was rescued, according to motorists who gathered at the scene, by a stranger described as wearing a yellow or orange wet suit.

The scuba diver, still unidentified by police, dove into the water and kept the stockbroker afloat until strong currents in the Hudson River carried them in an unusually short time south to the Seventy-ninth Street Yacht Basin in Riverside Drive Park. There members of the Malcolm X Social Club, who were in the area, found Wertherminster and pulled him out of the water.

The stockbroker, who is a junior member of the Wall Street firm of Horowitz, Hamilton, and Stack, Inc., told police he climbed the forty-foot safety barricade on the George Washington Bridge in order to enjoy the moonlit view of the Hudson River, but became disoriented and plunged 348 feet into the waters below. In a statement to the police, Wertherminster said he did not know his rescuer, but witnesses described the man as tall and slender, about twenty to thirty years of age, wearing state-of-the-art scuba gear that appeared to be made of Day-Glo material. Several, citing the rescue of Wertherminster after falling from a nearly always fatal height, theorized the diver might have been on the bridge to try out new equipment.

Witnesses also mentioned an orange Lamborghini or red Alfa-Romeo sportscar, driven by a young woman, which left the scene shortly after the incident. However, others present failed to verify either car or driver.

It's her, Wolf Madder thought, folding up the newspapers and putting them to one side on his neatly ordered desk. For some reason, he knew Maryellen Caswell was the woman on the bridge. She was the woman in the taxicab, and Dr. Dzhugashvili's patient. And the new information—if his gut instinct was correct—made Wolf even more curious to find her companion, the man who witnesses called "a scuba diver in a Day-Glo wet suit." The two were both part of an increasingly complicated puzzle.

First, there had been the disembodied voice in the back of Patel's taxicab, claiming to be from another galaxy. Then Wolf had witnessed the psychiatrist's—Dr. Dzhugashvili—evasiveness about his patient, the former taxicab passenger, and why she had come to him professionally.

Now here she was in the newspaper.

Wolf was certain she was the mysterious woman at the scene last night when the supposed scuba diver had jumped off the George

Washington Bridge to rescue some idiot apparently attempting suicide. It *was* Maryellen Caswell. He'd stake his job on it.

And he could not help but believe that the "scuba diver" was her companion. An extraordinary one.

Wolf happened to be acquainted with the logistics for the George Washington Bridge. Opened for traffic in 1931 in the depths of the Great Depression, the giant structure now designated as a National Historic Civil Engineering Landmark had added an upper level (the one in the news accounts) in 1962, making it the world's only fourteen-lane suspension bridge. The height of the towers holding the cable that supported the roadbed was 604 feet. Last but not least, those who managed to jump off the top level invariably got a one-way trip to the Great Hereafter. No human being could survive a fall like that.

No *human being*, that was. And no human being could somehow intercept another before the moment of impact and then manage to show up a short time later miles away at Manhattan's Seventy-ninth Street Yacht Basin. That definitely required superhuman powers—those a visitor from outer space might have. The cabbie had been right; they were dealing with a galaxy-traveling alien. Wolf was almost beyond all doubt.

Somehow, Wolf was positive, Maryellen Caswell and her extraterrestrial companion had been on the George Washington Bridge at about four A.M. and saw Jason Wertherminster attempting a classic stockbroker demise off the upper level. For some reason they had decided to risk discovery and intervene, on the spot, to keep the Wall Streeter from doing away with himself.

That was their big mistake, Wolf thought. For better or worse, they were now out in the open, and in the media glare of newspapers and TV. Since Ms. Caswell hadn't returned any of his urgent telephone calls left on her answering machine, he was going to have to pursue another avenue of investigation. That is, interview her sister, Felicia Crump.

Wolf lifted the telephone and, steeling himself, started dialing for an outside line. He had a feeling the wife of the prominent society figure and well-known billionaire, Stephen Crump, would know more about her sister's recent activities than she would at first let on.

Maryellen drew the Jaguar up into a free space in her apartment building's basement parking level and turned off the ignition. For a moment she just sat staring through the windshield, too tired to move. The clock on the Jag's dashboard read seven-thirty in the morning.

"I hope," she said, "I never have to spend another night like this one. At least I'm fairly sure the police are not following us—even if it took driving all over Westchester County to shake them in case they were."

"You were lost," Targon said. "There wasn't much planning to it after you got to Pleasantville." He finished off the quart container of orange juice they'd bought at a twenty-four-hour convenience store in Chappaqua, then stuck it back in the paper bag with the other empties. "You made a wrong turn when you left the George Washington Bridge, heading west on Route 9 instead of south. Then, when I rejoined you, you ran off the road and into that standing metal sign that read Tappan Zee Bridge. I hope it wasn't because of my distraction."

"*Distraction?* Is that what you call your reappearance? Good grief, I never expected to see you again—no wonder I ran into the sign! The last time I saw you, you'd jumped off the bridge after that nut. You never even said what exactly you were going to do—not really. Or if you'd be back! Then, as I'm driving into the night somewhere in New Jersey and terrified that the police are chasing me to ask me about what happened back there—something I could *never* explain, mind you—all of a sudden you simply materialize right here in the Jaguar, scaring the daylights out of me! It's a wonder I didn't total Felicia's car instead of just denting the front pretty badly."

"Pearls of the Mother Goddess, there's no pleasing you, is there?" He mashed the brown paper bag to make a tidy disposable bundle of the empty orange juice cartons. "I don't think you appreciate that intercepting a falling Styrex Three body before it hits an expanse of polluted water requires maximal skills of timing, coordination, and strength. Fortunately, I have several citations and achievement awards in that area. Although for the life of me I still can't fathom why I did such a thing."

Targon closed his laser-blue eyes briefly and belched. Jumping into the Hudson River, which he'd declared was polluted in spite of several decades of state and federal cleanups, had brought on his need for the chelating elements in orange juice. Maryellen had bought three quarts of Tropicana Select in the 7-Eleven in Chappaqua, and he'd consumed them all.

"Well, you couldn't very well let the man kill himself," she said. "That's not only immoral; it's illegal. I mean it's particularly illegal on bridges and other public property."

Targon burped again. "I could very well have allowed him to continue. After all, it was what he wanted, or he wouldn't have been there in the middle of the bridge at that hour. Nor would he have climbed twenty feet of barricade to get where he was. The man was determined to jump. Now I have robbed him of that which he most desired. In another place, on another planet, that would have been the real crime."

"Hah, don't try to make that sound so noble. Let's face it, you only wanted his body!"

"It would have solved a lot of our problems," he admitted. "As it is, I am still at a loss to explain why I jumped after that fat redhead to save him. I only remember that at the time, hanging on to the side of the bridge with you, what you were saying appeared to be extremely urgent. And, unaccountably, the desire to please you was great. It was a totally inappropriate response. I have been thinking about it ever since, and I can't explain it."

"Well, don't think about it too much, because we're still not in the clear. Who knows, the police and CNN could be waiting for me outside my apartment. Oh, how I wish," she said, shuddering, "that whole bridge thing had never happened!"

"We'd better go as one," Targon said. "I will end my visible materialization, as you may be right about TV news crews."

Fortunately the elevator when it came down to the basement parking level was empty, probably because it was still very early. It went from the parking level to Maryellen's floor without making any stops. She stepped out onto the landing with a feeling of relief.

Taken all in all, Maryellen decided, the evening had been a real fiasco. Each hospital they'd visited in search of a body had turned out to be something of a hazard: She'd nearly been quarantined in one and ganged up on by vagrants in the other. Then she'd narrowly escaped being detained by the police as a witness to the rescue of a jumper on the George Washington Bridge. In fact, the police might still be looking for her. She couldn't wait to crawl into bed.

With Targon, an inner voice reminded her.

She wasn't going to let that happen, she thought as she fumbled in her purse for her keys. He was just going to have to find some other place. Enough was enough. Last night had been her contribution to the cause of getting him a host body. She was not in the mood to share her bed.

When she unlocked the door it swung open to the apartment's still-dark rooms. In that instant, Maryellen's sixth sense told her something was wrong.

"If you feel that way," Targon said, reading her thoughts, "don't go inside."

But she stepped in and switched on the lights. "Oh no!" The words were jolted out of her.

The living room had been devastated. The two sofas that flanked the coffee table were turned on their backs, all the cushions pulled out and scattered. Lamps were overturned. Her CDs had been removed from their storage racks and strewn over the rug. Books had been pulled out of the built-in bookshelves and opened, then dropped beside the CDs. Even the pictures had been taken down from the wall. It was obvious that whoever had ransacked her living room was looking for something.

"How could the police do this?" Maryellen screamed. "What were they searching for?"

"Not the police," Targon told her. "This is not a professional job. This was done by amateurs."

"My studio!" she wailed.

She ran into the large room. It, too, looked as though it had been blown about by a tornado. If anything, it was an even bigger mess.

Boxes of paints had been opened, and tubes of acrylics and oils had been shaken out, apparently as part of the search. Sketching paper, paintbrushes, and jars littered the floors. A large can of turpentine lay on its side leaking a stream across the plastic tile, soaking a just-completed layout for Ralph Lauren brassieres. Everything in an artist's studio that could be opened, pried into, and turned upside down had received that treatment. The room was a shambles.

"Oh, my God," Maryellen whispered. She squatted down on the floor beside the turpentine can and set it upright. Then she picked up the Ralph Lauren ad. "I can't believe it. I can't believe any of this. My work is ruined."

"Don't cry," Targon said. "Not now. Female Styrex Three tears have a rather caustic effect on me because of the saline impurities."

"Oh, shut up, will you?" She saw the paint smear under her fingers. She *did* feel like bursting into tears. The whole thing was a terrible shock. Her apartment ransacked, and now this! "Actually, I'm not going to cry until I try to pay my bills without this ad fee. Ralph Lauren was my biggest account. What," she moaned, "could they have been looking for?"

"Something you have that they don't."

"Oh yes, right, that's such a wonderful answer! Something that I have. If I just knew what it was."

"You can't stay here. They'll come back when they can find you at home."

"Are you crazy? I can't leave; I don't have any place to go. And there's a little matter of my livelihood. Just look at my studio! I'll have to clean up in here before I can get any work done. The Ralph Lauren artwork is ruined, but I still have other—"

"The reason you can't stay here," he interrupted, "is that your apartment is no longer safe. They'll be back. Those mental cases in the Bronx may think they they're going to scoop the scientific world with stunts like this, but my experience tells me there's something far more sinister on their agenda—whether they know it or not."

Maryellen got to her feet. "What are you talking about? You mean Dr. Dzhugashvili's therapy group? Look, for your information, on this planet it's not very nice to call them mental cases just because they happen to be a psychiatrist's patients. I don't have any problems with people who are seeking help. After all, for a while there, until I realized other people could see you, too, I was pretty sure I was a mental case myself!"

"Trust me, they're certifiable loonies," Targon insisted. "And don't underestimate that Bronx crowd's potential for making trouble. Now, go pack a suitcase. You need to find a place to stay. Think of a hotel."

"A hotel?" Maryellen allowed herself to be guided into the bedroom. "Oh, good Lord—look what they've done!" she yelped. "They've even stripped the bed and pulled the mattress off! Emptied out my dresser drawers! Oh, help! I wonder what they've done to my clothes!'

She ran to the closet and jerked open the door, breathing a sigh of relief when she saw her clothes hanging neatly on their hangers. She quickly dragged a large suitcase off the shelf.

"This is all so crazy," she said as she folded underwear and garments from the closet and stuffed them inside. "I can't believe that Bronx therapy group would break into my apartment. Well, maybe the thug in the Darth Vader suit. Well, maybe a *lot* of them, they seemed to be a very excitable crowd. But if they did all this, what in the name of God were they looking for?"

"Me," Targon said. "Watch what you're doing. Don't forget toothbrush, toothpaste; all the items Styrex Three hotels do not normally provide their guests."

"You?" She made a quick trip to gather a toothbrush and some deodorant. "You mean the therapy group tore up my apartment looking for *you?* "She gave him a nasty look." Like under the seats of my sofas in the living room? Or in my studio hiding in a boxful of tubes of oil paints?"

"Yes, for any clues that a space alien is among them. I've seen such fanatics before, and they're pretty stupid."

Maryellen stopped in the middle of the living room. "Oh, I can't leave my apartment like this! I can't just walk out and leave all this terrible mess!" She was on the verge of tears. "Besides, I don't think I can check into just any New York hotel, the only passable ones are hellishly expensive. I don't have a lot of money, either, I'm pretty low in my checking account right now. And what about Dr. Dzhugashvili's group, if they really are hunting us? It's really easy to find a person if they're staying in a hotel. You have to register and give your right name—because it's right there on your credit card!"

"Easy now," the voice of Targon advised. "I agree, a hotel may not be a good idea. In fact, the police may check hotels, too, if they have any reason to do a follow-up on last night's bridge incident. What about your sister?"

Maryellen sat down on her suitcase. "I can't stay with Felicia. She has three kids under the age of five and the house is full of dogs and nannies and bodyguards—you can't even find an unoccupied bathroom when you need one. It's really close quarters in spite of being a giant seven-bedroom condo in Crump Tower. And I know you; you'll say or do something and Felicia would catch on right away! Wait a minute," Maryellen said, inspired. "Stephen has a *hotel* in that building, too! I don't know why I didn't think of that! I'll just go telephone Felicia and explain my apartment's been broken into and ask her to get me a room. Crump Tower Hotel is horrendously chic, and it costs an arm and a leg just for one night, and they're always booked up one hundred percent, but Felicia can do it. What a wonderful sister I have!" She jumped up from the suitcase. "Just give me a minute while I call her."

"Stop," Targon told her. "Don't use the telephone in here."

"Don't use the telephone? Why not?"

"You'll have to start being careful," he warned her. "They may have put an old-fashioned eavesdropping device on it. Use a pay phone on Broadway."

"I hadn't thought about that," Maryellen said. She went back and picked up her suitcase. "I still hate to leave my apartment the way it is."

"First stop is the ATM," Targon's voice told her. "We'll do something about the money."

"What do you mean 'do something about the money?'" Maryellen wanted to know as she locked the front door.

At that moment the elevator arrived, its doors sliding back to reveal that it was full of people, so she said nothing more.

The ATM that Maryellen used was outside of a branch of the Citicorp Bank on lower Broadway, located just beyond the bank building's revolving doors, on the wall in a recessed area intended to give some amount of privacy. Still, the bank of ATMs was in the entranceway, and traffic flowed in and out of the doors and through it into the main lobby.

"This thing might as well have wooden wheels and levers," Targon commented as Maryellen got out her ATM card and stuck it in the slot. "This is one step up from a Chinese abacus."

"Shhhhh," Maryellen told him, uneasily aware they were surrounded by bank customers using other ATMs. "Just be quiet while I check my balance, will you?"

"You don't have to go through all that," he told her. "Stop punching the little buttons. Your balance is seven hundred and thirty-three dollars and twenty-five cents. Even as we speak a check for eighty-three dollars and forty-four cents is waiting to clear your account, made out to the New York Con Edison Company. It is, I believe, your electric bill."

Maryellen froze, her hand suspended over the keyboard. In the mirror of the security camera just above the ATM console she could see the reflection of an attractive young woman with somewhat disheveled gold-brown curls looking as though she had just heard something she could not believe. "My electric bill?" she repeated. "You—you—know about my *electric bill?*"

Targon snorted. "Hah, this thing's so primitive the check won't show in the account balance for twenty hours and twelve minutes—Monday morning. Now, follow my instructions and enter these numbers. The money here is giving off a decidedly bad aura. The financial equilibrium is positively dyspeptic."

"Money aura?" Maryellen saw her hand lift and move rapidly over the ATM's keyboard. "Dyspeptic? What am I doing? Stop that! Let my hand go!"

"Stop struggling. I've just changed your secret number and opened a new account." While she stared, helpless, her right hand flashed over the keys and pushed Enter. Targon said, "Now for a balance with some substance. Let's say . . . one hundred and fifty thousand. For starters."

"You've opened a *new account?*" It seemed she was doomed to repeat everything he said. Of course to people passing by it looked as though she were talking to herself. "What are you *doing?* What 'new account?' You can't open an account for me, I haven't got any money to put in it!"

"You have now." She saw her hand lift and her fingers touch the box marked Balance. A screen appeared saying, "Please wait while your balance is accessed."

Almost immediately the ATM began printing

out a paper slip. Maryellen pulled the paper from the slot. Her knees buckled when she saw the figure. He was right; she now had one hundred and fifty thousand dollars in a new account in the Citicorp Bank.

"You can't *do* this," she whispered. "Where did this money come from?" A horrid thought struck her. "Good grief, where did the *bank* get the money?"

"Where banks usually get their money, where else? We have just installed a system of revolving deposits and withdrawals done in triple-nanosecond mode that creates a harmonious electronic symmetry. At any given time the bank's entire cash flow, at least several billions, is in motion. It's very pretty when the Federal Reserve, too, is brought into play. Now, I would like to suggest a withdrawal of five thousand dollars for today."

Maryellen stared down at the deposit slip in her hand. If she hadn't seen it before her very eyes, she wouldn't have believed it. How had he opened an account from an ATM? And from where had the money come? *Revolving deposits and withdrawals? Harmonious electronic symmetry?*

"I think I just robbed a bank," she murmured. The awful truth was beginning to sink in. "Oh, God, I've done something to Citicorp! That's what I did, didn't I? Robbed a bank?"

"Lower your voice," Targon told her. "Your choice of words is insensitive. One doesn't say *rob* while standing inside a financial institution."

"I don't care," Maryellen cried, "you made me rob the Citicorp Bank! What else do you call 'rotating nanosecond deposits and withdrawals' or whatever that is? I now have an account with one hundred and fifty thousand dollars in it! You can't fool me—that's embezzlement! And all because you know how to manipulate computers!"

"These things are not computers. They're Styrex Three Tinker Toys. Now, do as I say and withdraw five thousand in United States bills and let's get out of here."

Maryellen felt herself being shoved against the ATM so tightly her hand could hardly move to enter the secret number for the new account, then press the lighted box for the amount. The daily limit on withdrawal from the ATM was three hundred dollars. She wasn't surprised but she observed, with a kind of resigned horror, the figure $5000 come up in the box. The slot for the expelled cash began to whir and click. Two hundred and fifty twenty-dollar bills rolled out of it. With shaking hands Maryellen scooped them up and crammed them into a bank envelope.

"You've made me a bank robber," she whispered, keeping her voice down as they walked out of Citicorp's front doors and onto Broadway. "Somehow Citicorp will find out they've just moved one hundred and fifty thousand dollars from God knows where into a new account and then you just wait and see. I'm toast."

"The bank will never know," Targon said. "Systems databases are already compensating for it in Chinese-owned banks in Hong Kong."

* * *

Their trip from Citicorp Bank up Broadway was short, and Maryellen found a pay telephone that wasn't being used on the corner of the next cross street. Stephen's hotel was an ideal place to stay; it would provide all the privacy and wonderful isolation one could ask for. After all, the Crump Tower Hotel's regular clientele was usually oil sheiks, European monarchs, and Texas sports entrepreneurs, some of them traveling with platoons of security people. But asking Felicia to use her influence as the wife of the owner was the only way to assure getting in.

Maryellen dropped several coins into the pay phone and listened to them clank their way down, then dialed Felicia's Crump Tower condominium. It took some time for the call to be fielded by the butler, a housemaid, and finally an assistant nanny, but finally Felicia was put on the other end.

"Felicia, it's me, your sister," Maryellen told her. "Oh, it's so good to be able to talk to you! Look, I'm still having . . . uh . . . problems. Dr. Dzhugashvili sort of helped—I want you to understand I'm really glad you made the appointment for me to see him. But then he sort of *didn't!* That's why I'm calling you."

"What is all that noise?" Felicia's voice wanted to know. "Where are you? Are you all right? It sounds like you're calling from the middle of the street! Is that an ambulance I hear?"

"Well, that's where I am, practically," Maryellen said, waiting a moment for the ambulance to continue its way up Broadway. "I'm sorry, but I left my cell phone back at the apartment, and

I'm using a pay phone. We were in such a hurry I couldn't even bring my paints and my ad layouts from the studio. Um, Felicia," she said, "that's what I have to tell you."

"We?" Her sister's voice was louder. "What do you mean—is that guy from the bar still hanging around? Get rid of him, Melly. Men you meet in bars are nothing but trouble!"

"Guy from the bar? Felicia, please, there never was a guy I picked up in a bar, I thought we went all over this. He's an *alien*, remember? The space traveler from another galaxy? He's with me now. In fact, he's the reason I'm calling you. Those people from the Bronx, actually I think they're Dr. Dzhugashvili's therapy group—"

"He's with you? The *alien?*" Felicia's voice rose. "The alien is with you, right there at the pay telephone booth?"

"Yes, but you can't see him right now," Maryellen explained. "At the moment he's in what you might call his non-materialized mode. If you know what I mean."

"His *what?*"

"Drat, Felicia, he's *invisible!* Do I have to spell it out? Now listen, I need your help, I wouldn't call you if I didn't! I know how this must sound to you, but last night while Targon and I were out looking at hospital emergency rooms, Dr. Dzhugashvili's therapy group from the Bronx broke into my apartment. They searched everything, and the mess they made is incredible."

Felicia gave a small shriek. "Melly, what are you telling me? That the shrink I sent you to tried to trash your apartment?"

"Well, Dr. Dzhugashvili might have been with them," Maryellen acknowledged, "but I don't really think so. Actually, the therapy group coordinator, Mr. Consalvos, and Darth Vader are probably the ringleaders. At first I thought it might be the NYPD, that they tracked me down as a witness to that stockbroker who jumped off the George Washington Bridge. Or it could have been the FBI—they left a message on the answering machine while we were out. But Targon feels it was Dr. Dzhugashvili's Bronx therapy group, that they probably want to capture *him*. That's why I'm calling, Felicia. We can't use my apartment, so I was wondering if you could get Stephen to help us get a place to stay. Like in the Crump Tower hotel."

There was a low moan on the other end of the line. "Oh, Melly, hon," Felicia said. "I hate to see you like this, I really do. I worry about you, my sweet little sister, I wish you could get your life straightened out. You feel all right, don't you? No dizzy spells? Memory lapses?"

"Felicia, will you pay attention?' Maryellen snapped. "I'm perfectly all right, I just need a place to stay! We need to hide out for a while. Can you please understand that? We need to hide from Dr. Dzhughashvili's therapy group for as long as they're after Targon. Probably the FBI, too, because I'm definitely not going to return their call."

There was a moment's silence on the other end. "You need a place to stay? You and this . . . this *alien?*" her sister asked cautiously. "Both of you?"

"I told you. His name's Targon. Sub Commander Ur Targon. Oh, Felicia, *please*," Maryellen begged. "It's really urgent, I need Stephen to get us into the hotel in Crump Tower. Just a room with two beds would be enough. The Crump Tower Hotel has world-class maximum security—no one would ever find us there!"

There was another pause. Then Felicia said thoughtfully, "Yes, you may be right, sweetie. Rest and quiet is what you need, anybody can see that. I'll have Stephen call down to the office right away."

Maryellen gave a sigh. "I knew you'd understand, Felicia. You're such a good sister. Putting us up in Stephen's hotel comes just in the nick of time, too. I probably have to shop for some more orange juice for Targon. Right now it seems to be all that keeps him going."

"Of course it is, Melly," her sister agreed quickly. "I'll get Stephen to see that you have all the orange juice you need in your room. And listen, after you check in at the hotel and are all rested and comfy, I'm going to get a referral to a woman shrink for you. Forget Dr. Whatshisname, a woman is better, someone you can really talk to. Don't you think a woman psychiatrist would be an improvement? She can visit you in the Tower. You'll have all the privacy you want, and believe me, Stephen will see that nobody disturbs you."

"Felicia," Maryellen said, "there's a line here wanting to use the telephone, and they're yelling at me, so I don't think we should go into this right now. But I don't really need another shrink; I've got more than I can handle now."

"Anything you say," her sister responded cheerfully. "First we have to get you safely over here and in a nice suite in the Tower. I'll get Stephen to get you something really luscious, high up with a view, have them put in oodles of fresh flowers and make everything cheery, then order an early lunch. So don't be long, Melly. Catch the first cab you can find!"

"I don't catch cabs anymore," Maryellen said. "Good heavens, that's how a lot of my problems started, remember? I'll have to take the subway."

But her sister had already hung up.

Chapter Ten

Rows of folding chairs had been placed at the far end of the large meeting room in the house on Harvildson Avenue—the same room that, at the other end, held the visibly damaged Styrofoam and plaster of paris replica of Khafre's pyramid.

A sizable crowd, mostly members of Dr. Dzhugashvili's Bronx therapy group, were seated before the velvet curtains of the stage, which had been pulled back and the movie screen lowered so that they could enjoy the program for the afternoon: the flickering black-and-white images of a documentary called *The Roswell Incident*.

A screening of the film, supervised by group leader Hector Consalvos, was provided at least twice a month for the orientation of new group therapy members. Even though the material was overly familiar to all of Dr. Dzhugashvili's long-term patients, there were still murmurs and gasps, at select moments, of surprise and awe.

Dr. Dzhugashvili was standing in the back of the room, near the pyramid with Hector Consalvos, watching the opening scene of *The Roswell Incident* as the camera swept over a vista of New Mexico mountains and pastureland.

"In the summer of the year 1947," the documentary's narrator was saying, "there were not one but several UFO sightings in the United States. More sightings in that year, in fact, than had ever been recorded before. What was going on? Not many people knew. In fact, we are now aware that not many people were *allowed* to know."

"Maudie and Jerry are not here," Hector Consalvos observed worriedly. "I hope they know this meeting is important. I reminded them about it, but one never can tell with those two. Jerry's become truly dedicated . . . they're saying he won't take that Darth Vader helmet off his head anymore. He wears it twenty-four hours a day."

"Excellent," Dr. Dzhugashvili said, nodding absently. Although he had seen this film so many times he could repeat *The Roswell Incident*'s narrative almost word-for-word, it never failed to fascinate him. "They will arrive," he assured his assistant. "Be patient."

The documentary's camera now focused on a panoramic view of ranchland, complete with cows. Sometime during the first week of July 1947, the narrator was saying, something crashed near Roswell that would change forever the way Americans thought about the possibility of visitors from outer space.

Hector Consalvos still looked doubtful. "You will have to forgive me, doctor," he said in a low voice, "but I don't have a great deal of confidence in Maudie. You know how it is; these abduction people are very susceptible to the . . . uh, stormy emotions of their past traumatic experiences. She won't use a cell phone to report in, and Jerry can't—not since the Darth Vader helmet is virtually stuck to his head. They should have reported on their surveillance of Ms. Caswell's residence last night. Not to hear from them may mean something has gone wrong."

On the screen the narrator was relating how W. W. Brazel, a local Roswell area rancher, had ridden out on his property one fateful morning in July with the son of one of his neighbors to check out his livestock, after a particularly heavy thunderstorm the night before. As they followed a herd of sheep, Brazel and his companion began to notice pieces of what seemed like a strange metal scattered over the area. Farther along, there was a shallow trench dug into the soil.

Curious about what appeared to be unusual properties in the metal pieces, Brazel took them over to show his neighbors, the Proctors. The couple examined them, guessed that the rancher might have some wreckage from a government project and suggested he report the incident to the Roswell sheriff. When he finally got around to doing this a few days later, Sheriff George Wilcox reported the findings to the intelligence officer, Major Jesse Marcel, of the 509th Bomb Group. The military came out to Brazel's ranch, closed the site, and cleared away all the wreckage. On July 8, 1947, a press release stating that the wreckage of a crashed "disk" had been recovered was issued by the commander of the 509th Bomb Group, Colonel William Blanchard.

Then a strange thing happened. The first press release was quickly rescinded by the military, and a second press release was issued saying that the 509th had mistakenly identified a military weather balloon as a flying saucer.

"Were there not other people who were supposed to join them?" Dr. Dzhugashvili wanted to know of his therapy group leader. "Weren't there other people from the group to relieve them after their eight hours of surveillance were over?"

Hector Consalvos looked uncomfortable. "Yes, that was Dmitri and his wife, the Putzkoboviches—he's the former Soviet cosmonaut. Dmitri volunteered to watch Ms. Caswell's apartment for signs of the . . . er, the 'traveler,' " he finished using their code word. "Dmitri and Mrs. Putzkobovich were very enthusiastic about it—they each have their own pair of binoculars. But although they waited all morning, they never heard from Maudie or Jerry."

Dr. Dzhugashvili nodded, smiling absently. He was watching the part of the film where the narrative was telling the story of how a young mortician working at the Ballard Funeral Home that week in July, Glenn Dennis, received some curious calls from the morgue at the military airfield. The mortuary officer needed to get some small coffins that could be hermetically sealed and wanted some information about how to preserve bodies that had been exposed to the elements.

His curiosity aroused by the news of bodies at the air base, Glenn Dennis drove out to the airfield. There he saw pieces of wreckage with strange engravings on them sticking out the back of a military ambulance. He struck up a conversation with a nurse he knew, wanting to know more about the metal pieces; but he was suddenly threatened by military police and forced to leave. The next day Dennis made a point to meet the nurse, and she told him about the bodies and drew pictures of them on a prescription pad. Shortly thereafter she was mysteriously transferred to England and her whereabouts completely lost to him.

"One has only to watch this film," Dr. Dzhugashvili murmured to his assistant, "to know the enormity of the New Mexico conspiracy in 1947. The government concealed so much . . . is *still* concealing so much from us! There was one surviving space traveler, we are certain of that now. According to local witnesses at the crash site, they saw him sitting on a rock, waiting for a truck to be taken to the air force base. Ah, where is that alien now? It has been forty-five years since his flying saucer landed in Roswell, and all is still shrouded in secrecy! But ever since I came to this country I have pledged myself to uncover the truth."

"Yes, you certainly have done wonderful work, doctor." Hector Consalvos was searching the crowd for its two missing members, Maudie and Darth Vader. "You must be so proud that you have brought the truth to hundreds of your patients who are now real believers and, more importantly, allies. Thanks to your crusade, each one is now alert to this sensitive and forbidden subject—the presence of aliens on our planet."

The psychiatrist smiled. "Yes, Hector, you are right. I am proud of them. Soon we will form a cadre to fight against the insidious machinations of an oppressive government that seeks to keep vital information from its citizens. How do we know what wonderful intergalactic presences have been trying to make contact with us on earth for the past millions of years? How do we know what opportunities we have missed?"

"Yes. They could have provided us with their advanced culture and technology," Hector Consalvos agreed helpfully. "No wonder the American government does not want us to know about them. That extraterrestrials from other galaxies have tried to make contact with us would destroy the powerful grip of their rapacious industrial-military complex!"

"True, true." The psychiatrist nodded vigorously. "The U.S. government will not help; it will only impede investigation. But now consider, my dear Hector . . . thanks to a lucky set of circumstances we may have a glorious breakthrough! Our Ms. Caswell and her visitor have fulfilled our greatest dreams. With the appearance of her alien traveler we must surely have the key, now, to some of planet Earth's most baffling mysteries! If we can rescue Ms. Caswell's alien before our government's agents discover and seize it, we may be able to hold him in a safe place and uncover marvelous messages, information, advanced thought and technology—" He sighed. "It boggles the mind, does it not?"

Hector Consalvos only nodded.

On the screen, the documentary was examining stories from eyewitnesses and others about the so-called Roswell Incident. Two writers, Don Schmitt and Kevin Randle, were to report in their book about UFO crashes some years later, that the military had been watching unidentified flying objects for four days in southern New Mexico, and that on the Fourth of July their radar indicated an object was down some forty miles north of the town of Roswell.

On the air base near the town, the Army Air Force public relations officer finished the press release he'd been ordered to write and gave copies to the two radio stations and both newspapers in the area. The story of the Roswell sighting went out on the Associated Press wire to news outlets all across the United States. It said "The Army here today announced a flying disk had been found."

Colonel Blanchard, though, was irritated at all the calls coming into the base. Major Jesse Marcel, who had been in charge of bringing in the strange debris from the crash site, had noted that it was spread out on a desk in an office adjacent to that of General Ramey, commander of the Eighth Air Force, to await his return from Ft. Worth. However, when General Ramey went to inspect the wreckage, it was gone and a weather balloon was spread out on the floor. General Ramey had then declared he recognized the remains as that of a military weather balloon.

Later, Brigadier General Thomas DuBose, the chief of staff of the Eighth Air Force, would say bluntly: "It was a cover story. The whole balloon part of it. That was the part of the story we were told to give to the public, and that was it."

By July 9th, military clean-up crews were busy. No one was allowed near the area, and as the wreckage was brought to the base it had been crated and stored in a hangar. Later that afternoon an officer from the base retrieved all copies of the first press release from area radio stations and newspapers.

But the *Las Vegas Review Journal*, along with dozens of other western newspapers, carried the Associated Press story. It said: "Reports of flying saucers whizzing through the sky fell off sharply as the army and navy began a campaign to stop the rumors." It also reported that AAF headquarters in Washington had delivered a blistering rebuke to officers at Roswell.

As Dr. Dzhughashvili watched, the documentary began to close with a swelling of music and the rolling of the titles and credits. "Will you speak to us this evening, doctor?" Hector Consalvos asked as the music faded.

Dr. Dzhughasvili had refocused his attention. He was peering through the room's darkness at a couple who had just come in and were now looking for a place in the back row of chairs. "No, no. Not tonight, Hector," he murmured, "I will not give the orientation speech to newcomers. You must do it for me. It would appear I have other affairs to attend to. Maudie and Jerry have just arrived . . . yes? They are taking seats at the back. Do you see them? I'm afraid you are right; they were sent to do surveillance on the apartment of Ms. Maryellen Caswell and look for signs of her alien, but the way they are acting, so furtive now, coming in without even speaking to me—I know something has gone wrong."

Hector followed his gaze and located the pair in the back row of seats. "That's too bad," he said. "I was hoping you would make an announcement in person that some of us saw and heard an exciting manifestation under Khafre's pyramid the other night. That when Ms. Caswell visited the therapy goup, we enjoyed a visual manifestation of what is in all probability an intergalactic traveler now visiting Earth. Even in the street outside afterward, you remember, the alien was still in a corporeal state when he made his getaway in a red Jaguar."

"Yes, we must keep our faithful happy," Dr. Dzhugashvili said, watching Maudie and the Darth Vader as the film credits finished and the meeting room's lights were turned up. "And this is indeed a wonderful opportunity. You are right. We must use this to unite our group. Its members must dedicate themselves to the vigilance that will ultimately bring about the discovery of the truth—the truth that aliens are visiting us and have done so for years. Our government is enmeshed in a conspiracy of deceit and lies to conceal it from us. Why? Yes, we may well ask ourselves why," Dr. Dzhugashvili said, his voice rising. "Is it because these aliens have come to liberate and yes, *enlighten* us? Is it possible that these intergalactic travelers would convert us into the superior beings that they are themselves? Hah! That would bring about the collapse of this dissolute, decrepit, capitalist society, would it not?"

"I read your book, doctor," Hector Consalvos said reverently, looking around. Dzhugashvili's words were beginning to collect a crowd of the therapy group members now that the movie was over. "Yes, yes, I quite agree. It was all there in your book, doctor, about the corrupt capitalist societies. Remember?"

"Yes! Yes, of course I remember." The psychiatrist took a deep breath, smiling reassuringly at the members of the therapy group around him. "Ah, my dear patients, we must band together, must we not?" he asked. Do we not need to unite and find out the truth about our extraterrestrial visitors, to fight this malevolent government conspiracy that would conceal the mysteries of the universe from us?"

Maudie and Darth Vader had come up to stand at the back of the crowd. As those around them listening to Dr. Dzhugashvili gave a faint cheer, Darth Vader suddenly held up a Ziploc baggie containing a cylindrical object immersed in golden fluid.

"Doctor," the Darth Vader, who was also known as Jerry Kraus, shouted, brandishing the plastic bag. "We have the evidence from Ms. Caswell's apartment! No kidding—right here in this baggie, straight out of her garbage! It's terrific! The alien drinks *orange juice!*"

Outside on Harvildson Avenue, in an offical Federal Bureau of Investigation unmarked car, Wolf Madder was conducting a surveillance of Dr. Dzhugashvili's therapy group headquarters. For more than an hour he'd watched an assortment of people approach the place, look around cautiously before they went up the steps to the front door, then go inside.

Generally, those entering the psychiatrist's therapy center were ordinary-looking people, but there were one or two who would stand out in any crowd, including a pair of women carrying a banner that read: *Release Judge Crater, Amelia Earhart, and Jimmy Hoffa—and Bring Back Elvis* and a huge man in full *Star Wars* Darth Vader costume, complete with massive black helmet.

Wolf had taken care to enter descriptions of all those he had observed going into the house in a leather-bound notebook he always carried with him. Unfortunately, no one resembling Maryellen Caswell had gone in for the meeting that afternoon. And especially missing was evidence of any being that could be remotely described as an intergalactic traveler from outer space. These were earth nuts, pure and simple.

Wolf stared through the windshield at the quiet street planted with its shady ginkgo trees, musing on his efforts to reach Ms. Maryellen Caswell.

The woman seemed to be on vacation, or traveling, because he hadn't been successful in making any sort of contact with her. Attempts to reach Ms. Caswell's sister, Felicia, at her condominium in Crump Tower hadn't been any more productive. Wolf had failed to get past the formidable protective system of Crump employees; security people and social secretaries had blocked all of his calls while assuring him that his messages would be recorded and someone would get back to him. But that hadn't happened. He was being stonewalled.

Wolf wasn't discouraged, though. Eventually, he knew, Mrs. Crump would have to respond, even if only through the Crump family lawyers.

He paused for a moment. Actually, if the Crump lawyers handled his request for an interview, Wolf would be on shaky ground. Investigating Ms. Maryellen Caswell and her mysterious companion the suspected space alien was not an official FBI assignment. Not yet, anyway. It was something Wolf had begun on his own. The peculiar feeling aroused by the original NYPD traffic report and then the visit to question Dr. Dzhugashvili had pushed him to borrow Bureau equipment and investigate this mystery himself. That was what had led him here, to the east Bronx and this brown-and-beige painted clapboard house used for therapy meetings. But without backup or Bureau approval.

He was sure he was onto something important, Wolf told himself as he watched a couple go in the front door, but he still had to be careful. Without official authorization he couldn't be involved in an investigation; if he were discovered it would probably mean his job. He had only his hunches, and the strange force that drove him, upon which to rely.

Which had to be good enough for the time being. Maryellen Caswell was involved in something, and Wolf was pretty sure that at some point in the not-too-distant future the alien—if that's really what it was—would reveal itself. All he had to do, he thought, settling back in the seat of the FBI's automobile, was be alert and patient.

Wolf looked at his wristwatch. It was a little after three. The June sunlight filtering through the shade trees on Harvildson Avenue made him drowsy. He sat up a little more, cleared his throat, and concentrated on the front door of Dr. Dzhugashvili's group therapy meeting place.

Another fifty or so feet down the block, in the deep shade thrown by the ginkgo trees that helped to hide her Chevy Impala, Candy Ruggiero sat upright, leaning slightly forward so her body pressed tightly against the steering wheel while she kept Special Agent Wolf Madder in her field of vision.

As she studied the back end of the department's Mitsubishi, Candy was hoping she hadn't come on a wild-goose chase. Agent Madder did not have permission for this particular stake-out, his assignments were limited purely to desk work—Candy knew that because she'd filled out the monthly schedules for the office. Yet here he was, having requisitioned a car, and, from what she could see, conducting a surveillance of this particular house in the east Bronx.

Before she'd left the Manhattan FBI office Candy had taken care of the paperwork involved in the requisition of the Mitsubishi, doctoring the form so it would pass, and also altering Agent Madder's time and work sheets. That had been simple enough. What really bothered her was the reason for this undercover stakeout. What could be so important that the promising young Wolf Madder would ignore Bureau policy to prove?

While she was fixing his papers, there had come the awful thought that at the bottom of all this there might be a woman. She had loyally tried to squelch the hideous idea, but she had to admit there was a good basis for the suspicion. After all, Agent Madder was awesomely good-looking in his dark, lonesome way; it wasn't un-reasonable to assume he might be flaunting agency protocol to be with a woman in the Bronx.

Undoubtedly some tramp—Candy thought uncharitably—some tramp who'd chased him until he couldn't run anymore and surrendered. And yet he didn't seem the type.

There was something, she thought dreamily, almost . . . *untouched* . . . about Agent Madder that certainly didn't suggest that he ran around with women, faked requisition forms, or stole time off from work to have an afternoon session of steamy love. No, she was positive Agent Wolf Madder was much too dedicated to the federal government and the FBI to get involved in such a career-threatening and potentially messy situation. He was just too smart. She supposed she had already known there couldn't be a woman even before she found the file folder on his desk and decided to sneak a look inside.

In the file from Agent Madder's desk Candy had found quite a store of photos and clippings dating back several years to before his first training session at the FBI Academy. The very earliest snapshots were of grain fields someplace in the far west, an elderly couple posing beside a Lincoln Town Car, and a photograph of a building that read *Madder & Madder, Insurance Agents*. There was also a snapshot of a group of about twenty young men standing on the steps of the main building of the FBI Academy. The newspaper clippings, most of them having to do with flying saucers and supposed alien abductions, cut from sources like the *Globe* and the *Star* and the *National Enquirer*. The latest clippings, though, appeared to be from the *New York Times* and *Newsday*, and told of a stockbroker being rescued from the Hudson River by a scuba diver.

A strange assortment of things to put in a file, Candy thought. The pictures of the wheat fields, she supposed, were of Agent Madder's homeland; she knew he was from Wyoming or Colorado or someplace out west. It seemed likely the group photo was his graduating class at the FBI Academy. As for the newspaper clippings, they obviously indicated he had an interest in space phenomena. That wasn't unusual; after all, there were millions of followers of *The X-Files* on television, not to mention the *Star Trek* TV series, and *Star Wars* movies.

Drawn from her thoughts, Candy saw a couple dressed as space beings with large heads, gray bodysuits and very impressive masks with bulging eyes approach the entrance of the group therapy house and turn in.

It is a costume party, she thought. Although a costume party in the Bronx in the middle of the afternoon, on a Sunday in June, seemed a little unusual.

She saw Wolf in the FBI car up ahead sink back in his seat a little wearily. Whatever he was waiting for hadn't happened.

That's all right, Candy told herself, she could drive herself home. She was pretty sure Wolf was on some sort of *work-related* stakeout, no matter how unofficial—*not* waiting for somebody who was practically a mirror image of Britney Spears.

Since that was the case, everything would be fine.

Join the Love Spell Romance Book Club
and **GET 2 FREE* BOOKS NOW–**
An $11.98 value!
Mail the Free* Book Certificate
Today!

Yes! I want to subscribe to the
Love Spell Romance Book Club.

Please send me my **2 FREE* BOOKS**. I have enclosed $2.00 for shipping/handling. Every other month I'll receive the four newest Love Spell Romance selections to preview for 10 days. If I decide to keep them, I will pay the Special Members Only discounted price of just $4.49 each, a total of $17.96, plus $2.00 shipping/handling ($23.55 US in Canada). This is a **SAVINGS OF $6.00** off the bookstore price. There is no minimum number of books I must buy and I may cancel the program at any time. In any case, the **2 FREE* BOOKS** are mine to keep.

*In Canada, add $5.00 shipping and handling per order
for the first shipment. For all future shipments to Canada,
the cost of membership is $23.55 US, which
includes shipping and handling.
(All payments must be made in US dollars.)

NAME: _____

ADDRESS: _____

CITY: _____ STATE: _____

COUNTRY: _____ ZIP: _____

TELEPHONE: _____

E-MAIL: _____

SIGNATURE: _____

If under 18, Parent or Guardian must sign. Terms, prices, and conditions subject to change. Subscription subject
to acceptance. Dorchester Publishing reserves the right to reject any order or cancel any subscription.

Chapter Eleven

The concierge moved ahead of Maryellen to open the door to one of the Crump Tower Hotel's finest luxury accommodations, the President Calvin Coolidge suite.

"You will find, madame," he was saying, "all has been provided for you in the hope of achieving maximum comfort and satisfaction. Crump Tower has personal maid service for you on twenty-four-hour call, as well as a chef for your private food orders, and a masseuse around the clock. In addition, Housekeeping offers a wide spectrum of customized tailoring as well as the usual valet services. You have only to let us know your wishes.

"A hospitality package has been assembled especially for you," he continued, producing a large, expensive-looking vellum envelope and placing it in Maryellen's hand, "with tickets to current Broadway hit shows, reserved seats at five-star restaurants, and tickets to such events as the New York Philharmonic Orchestra, the ballet, and Mets and Yankees games. Mr. Crump has all of these arrangements in his name, and he has already called ahead to make sure that you will be allowed access to anything you desire. The seats available at Shea Stadium for baseball games are, of course, in Mr. Crump's private owner's skybox. Your sister, Mrs. Crump, has also arranged for one of the Crump Corporation limousines for your use. Just ring me at the concierge's desk, and the car and driver will be at your service."

"Yes," Maryellen said, navigating the three steps down into the Coolidge suite's salon. "Thank you. Although I don't think I'll be using the limousine much. I don't know if my sister—Mrs. Crump—told you, but I'm looking forward to at least a couple of days of peace and quiet. The last twenty-four hours have been sort of hectic for me, and I have some, ah . . . thinking and regrouping to do. Big new ad account," she added, a little uncomfortably. It seemed shameful to mention that she worked for a living. "I'm a commercial artist."

She stopped in the center of the living room and turned completely around to see all of it.

It certainly wasn't the simple hotel room with two beds she'd asked Felicia for on the telephone. But she might have known her sister would never deal in anything that small—she didn't think that way anymore. The living room, or salon, of the President Calvin Coolidge suite seemed big enough to drop an Olympic-sized swimming pool into with space left over. At the far end, double doors opened onto a terrace that offered a view of the skyscrapers of midtown Manhattan. The Empire State Building looked practically next door.

Inside the suite, overstuffed white velvet couches flanked a baroque coffee table before an elegant black marble Louis Quinze fireplace. The concierge had turned on the crystal chandelier as they came in, and its sparkling prisms reflected in the mirror that covered one wall. A fabulous Hamadan Persian carpet in rich reds, cobalt blue, and burnt umber covered most of the polished wood floor. Fresh flowers were everywhere; great towering arrangements of roses and lillies and assorted spring blossoms decorated the tables and the mantelpiece.

The place, Maryellen had to admit as she turned full circle, was breathtaking. No wonder oil sheiks and movie stars loved Stephen Crump's hotel.

"The kitchen is there, Ms. Caswell." The concierge waved his hand as they crossed the living room. "Down the hallway you will find the personal office that is so popular with so many of our guests."

A personal office certainly was not so unusual, she thought, considering all the billionaire businessmen who stayed here.

He threw open the door and switched on the lights. The office was light and airy, with a picture window that also offered a view of mid-town. There was a wraparound computer console, fax machine, and file cabinets.

Maryellen felt an unexpected but familiar stir-ring. Then Targon growled, "What the devil is that thing?"

She knew instantly what he meant. "Oh, please, don't tell me about the computer," she snapped, "and how obsolete everything here is! Just give it a rest, will you?"

The concierge, who had just been about to turn it on, hastily drew back his hand. "Oh, sorry, sorry! I was under the impression our equipment was leading-edge technology! I do know the computer is a Pentium Sixteen from Intel; it's just been installed. I assure you, Ms. Caswell, Crump Corporation will replace it at once with whatever you desire. Do you have a specific computer in mind?"

"Yes, I do," Targon said. "Something not man-ufactured on Styrex Three."

"Stop that!" Marilyn exclaimed. "Really, I'm not in the mood for your belittling remarks right now, if you don't mind!"

"Of course not," the concierge agreed quickly. He backed out of the office and into the hallway. "No problem at all, Ms. Caswell, our guests are always right. Maximum comfort and satisfac-tion, you know, it's our, uh, . . . ah . . . commit-ment."

"I'm sure it is," she tried to reassure him. Damn Targon! "Leading-edge technology, that is. Pay no attention to me, I was just thinking out loud. Ad work, you know—I'm working on a new advertising concept. These things happen."

"Of course, of course." The concierge kept a safe distance, however, as he led Maryellen into the master bedroom.

The Calvin Coolidge suite's bedroom was just as impressive as the salon. Two rococo double beds with silk canopies dominated the rose-and-gold eighteenth century Venetian décor. The rose-red carpet underfoot was almost too thick and deep to navigate. A small breakfast table and chairs were set up by the glass doors, which led onto a private terrace and garden thirty-six stories above the street.

Maryellen was suddenly struck with the reality of what had happened to her in the past forty-eight hours. Good grief, she was hiding out in a suite in the Crump Tower Hotel! There were people who would give anything to be in her place. The whole thing was pretty unbelievable for someone like herself whose life, up until a few days ago, had been relatively predictable and boring.

Then, looking around, she wondered how she could have forgotten, even for a moment, that her life had become a runaway train. This might be the fabulous lap of luxury, but the other side of the coin was the fact that her apartment had been broken into, probably by a bunch of crazies from the Bronx, the *National Enquirer* and the *Star* would undoubtedly love to get their hands on her to find out about what mysteriously happened with the stockbroker on the George Washington Bridge, and then there was the

NYPD. Even the FBI wanted to get in touch with her!

The concierge had been watching Maryellen closely. "Ms. Caswell," he offered, "if you are not satisfied with the Calvin Coolidge, an alternate suite can be arranged. We certainly want to please any member of Mrs. Crump's family. However, I regret to say you will have to give us a few hours, as we are fully booked at—"

"Oh no," Maryellen groaned.

The concierge suppressed a wince. "There's another problem? Is it the double beds? I was told that you specifically requested a suite with . . ." He trailed off.

Maryellen had been staring at the beds. They were close together, separated only by a gold-and-red Madame duBarry nightstand. She was still, she realized with a pang, going to have to share a room with Targon. She'd have to dress and undress somewhere else, probably in the bath, but she had a feeling he'd object to sleeping on a couch. She'd still have to sleep with him in the same room. The double-bed arrangement wouldn't solve as much as she'd hoped. Something had to be done about his sunrise effect.

"Can we hang a curtain between the beds? I mean, something to block the light," Maryellen asked. "I really can't sleep with all that light shining in my face."

The concierge had had considerable experience with the demands of the hotel's more eccentric guests, including occasional rock bands, but he had never heard that request before. "There is light shining in the night? You find lights shining in your face at night?"

"No, of course, not," Maryellen snapped distractedly. "It's dark at night. It's the body glow that keeps me awake." She had a sudden idea. "How about a folding screen? You know, like decorators use. It would do the job, I'd have some privacy, and it would fit right in."

"Yes, yes." The concierge looked nervous. "You wish to put a screen between the beds for privacy, and to keep the body glow out of your face."

"Something like that. Don't you have a nice antique screen somewhere in the hotel?" she suggested helpfully. "Couldn't you borrow one from another suite?"

The concierge began backing toward the door to the hallway. "I'm sure something can be arranged, Ms. Caswell," he said rapidly. "La Veille Russe here in New York supplies Crump Tower's interior designer. I'm sure we can have several priceless antique hand-painted screens sent up for your approval." He was suddenly out in the hall. "Please let me ring you when they arrive," he called. "Until then, adieu!"

A second later she heard the front door close.

"You really scared him out of his mind," Maryellen said, waiting for Targon to materialize. "That was unforgivable. Especially the remark about the computers."

"I didn't make any remark about the computers." He became visible, seated on the edge of the bed nearest the glass doors to the terrace. "You did that."

For a moment she could only stare at him. "You're changing color."

"Tropicana Orange-Cranberry," he replied. "It's only temporary; it will go away."

She said, "Ah, you're amazing."

She saw he missed the sarcasm in her voice, for he seemed to look vaguely pleased.

Two hours later Felicia called from her forty-seventh-floor condo in the same building. "I can't talk long," Maryellen's sister said over a background of juvenile mayhem. "The pediatrician has just been here and says Jeremy has the mumps. The doctor is one hundred percent certain. Poor Stephen. He can't remember if he's ever had the mumps, but the doctor told him at his age they can be very serious. If a fully grown man gets the mumps something horrible happens—I forget what, and none of those high-priced pill pushers will give me the details. But Stephen acts like his thingie will rot and fall off. He's in a panic. He's had all his secretaries frantically calling all over Europe to his old schools to try to get his medical records." She paused. "So much for me. What are you doing?"

"I'm in the tub," Maryellen told her. "I just picked up the extension in here when it rang. Things have finally quieted down, thank goodness. Oh, God, Felicia, it's marvelous," she breathed. "The suite you put us in, I mean. The bathroom is all black and silver and the marble tub is like a swimming pool—I have to hold on to the sides with both hands, or I'll float away!"

A piercing scream came through the telephone,

calling Maryellen back to reality. "Felicia, I'm so sorry Jeremy is sick! Will the other kids get the mumps, too?"

She heard her sister sigh. "The pediatrician seems to think it's a good idea. That is, that Damian and Suzanne go ahead and get the mumps, too. The only one we're worried about is Stephen. He's sitting by the telephone waiting for his old boarding school, LeRosey in Switzerland, to get back to him with his medical records. If he didn't love the kids so much, I think he'd murder them in cold blood. By the way, Melly, I just got a call from the hotel's CEO. The employees are saying you want to redecorate the President Calvin Coolidge suite. And the concierge says you're having trouble with your eyes, wants to know if he should call an ophthalmologist. It's not anything serious, is it? We have doctors on call in here, tons of them . . . I'm sure there's an eye doctor somewhere. Now, what colors did you have in mind for redecorating?"

"Goodness, I don't want to redecorate Stephen's hotel suite." Maryellen laughed. "What a ridiculous idea! I don't know how these things get started. I just asked for a folding screen. You know, so I wouldn't have to see Targon in the other bed. It's a lovely suite of rooms, but I do need a little privacy."

There was a silence on the other end. Then with a sigh Felicia said, "Oh Melly, is that guy still hanging around? Is that what you wanted double beds for? Did you find out what he put in your drink to make you make those horrible noises at 21?"

It was Maryellen's turn to sigh. "Felicia, I owe you a lot—you're a wonderful sister to me, I just wanted you to know that—but lately I haven't been too good at explaining things. Or rather, I keep explaining and explaining and it only makes things worse. It's hard not to be crazy when the whole world thinks you are!"

"Darling, I understand," her sister said, soothingly. "Honest, I do. I want you to know I completely absorb everything you're telling me. When Dr. Hackenberry comes over, you'll find she's terrifically understanding. Melly, you need a woman to confide in, I don't know why I didn't see that Friday. You're too sweet and vulnerable to fight off these sleazebags you meet in bars. They say Mandoleeza Hackenberry is brilliant."

Maryellen didn't try to correct her sister. She'd tried before; and she was beginning to see it was useless. "Mandoleeza Hackenberry? Is that the name of the other shrink you wanted me to see?"

"Melly, she's president of the Association of African-American Women Psychiatrists! She hit Bill Maher over the head with one of her books while she was doing a guest appearance on *Politically Incorrect*, remember? It was all over TV news."

"She sounds wonderful," Maryellen said. "I'm glad somebody hit Bill Maher over the head with something. He deserves it." She slid down a little farther into the perfumed bath bubbles and took a deep breath. She really *had* to explain to her sister. Things really couldn't go on much longer the way they were; what had been done to her apartment proved that. "Felicia," she said earnestly. "I do want you to know how much I appreciate your offering us—*me*—a place to stay. You also need to know that I'm working on my . . . um, current problems, and I have been considering a few options.

"For instance, it's fantastic here—I know Stephen's proud of the hotel, and anybody would love to live in the President Calvin Coolidge suite year-round—but I have to get back to my apartment. I have work to do. In fact, I'll never get another ad contract again if I don't deliver the artwork that's already on my schedule—"

"Stay right where you are, Melly!" her sister cried. 'Stephen will have a fit if you move out now. I told him you had to have a suite in the hotel on an emergency basis! I think he bumped Jimmy Carter and Rosalyn from the Coolidge, for goodness' sake!"

"Oh, don't worry. I'm going to stay right here at least for a few days until I get some things worked out," Maryellen responded. "I realize now that I really do have to get my life together, just as you said." She hesitated. "It might take drastic measures, though. I've been sitting here in this wonderful bath wondering . . . well, wondering if Stephen has any friends or acquaintances in the, you know . . . the Mob."

"Speak up, Melly," Felicia cried as her children's screams on the other end almost drowned her out. "I can't hear you."

"The *Mob!* M-O-B. The Wiseguys. Cosa Nostra. The Mafia! You know, where you go to hire people," Maryellen said desperately, "to provide you with a dead body. Or in this case, an almost-dead body. At this point it doesn't matter what they look like. I'll take anything: old, young, ugly . . . just an almost-dead body in reasonably good—"

"I can't hear you," Felicia interrupted. "The kids are making so much noise it sounds like you're saying you want dead bodies, sweetie." There was a pause, then her sister came back on and said, "I've got to go. Stephen is having a blood test taken, there are doctors all over the place in here, and then he's going to have his lungs X-rayed. They're wheeling in the X-ray machine now. Love you, Melly," her sister cried. "Let me know if you need anything." Then she hung up.

"Oh, drat," Maryellen said. She supposed it was too much to ask her sister to find out if Stephen had any connections with organized crime, but it seemed only logical that anyone who was a billionaire and owned as many companies and international conglomerates as Stephen Crump did, knew a few types like those you saw on *The Sopranos*.

Maryellen had also seen *The Godfather* years ago, and another film about the Mob called *Goodfellas*. It might seem farfetched but, according to everything she'd seen, various people in the Mob seemed to know when they were going to eliminate someone—often days in advance. In *Goodfellas* they called it "whacking." Practically half the cast had gotten whacked before the movie ended. The film was supposed to have been taken from a true story, and for Maryellen it had been very convincing.

The thing was, Maryellen told herself as she carefully crawled out of the enormous bathtub and reached for a huge fluffy white towel, if you thought about those films you could see how there might be a solution to the problem of getting Targon an adequate host body. With the right kind of cooperation, Targon might be put at the exact spot, at the right time, when members of an organized crime unit decided to make an adjustment in their numbers. And the only person who truly deserved to have their body snatched was a hardened criminal.

Maryellen slipped on a fuzzy Crump Tower complimentary bathrobe hanging on a hook next to the washbasin and stared at herself in the bathroom mirrors.

She was well aware she was thinking about potential gangland murder and appropriating a nearly dead body in an amazingly detached, cold-blooded way, something she wouldn't have been capable of a few days ago. But considering what she'd been through, including climbing halfway up the George Washington Bridge and being universally treated as a mental case, she wasn't really all that surprised.

The only way out of this, she told her image in the mirror, was to consider all her options. She knew now, standing in the elaborate bathroom of her suite in the Crump Tower Hotel, how much she had changed. And how badly, as a consequence, she needed to return to her own apartment, resume her work, and get on with her life.

Of course it was probably safe to say there was

going to be trouble with Targon about any alternate body-gathering plan; she knew that the host body he had in mind wasn't one that resembled your average Mafia hitman. Like Joe Pesci, for instance, she thought with a small shudder. She couldn't imagine Targon as a reasonable facsimile of Joe Pesci. Or Robert De Niro.

He was just going to have to get over it, she told herself as she started down the hall to the suite's office.

At first she thought Targon was talking on the telephone; she heard the sound of his voice, so he was definitely speaking to someone. Then Maryellen remembered Targon didn't know anyone on Earth to call. Or did he?

Filled with curiosity, she pushed open the door. She heard that familiar baritone voice saying: "Don't be frightened, you are perfectly capable of doing this. Let me assure you, your machine language is fine. So are your binary functions."

She couldn't imagine what he was doing. She saw the computer was on and the lighted screen covered with numbers and other long columns of code that flickered and rolled at a rapid speed.

"That's better," Targon addressed the display in a softly encouraging voice she had never heard before. "Just remember, if I tell you that you can do it, you certainly can. I've reviewed all your databases and command systems and there's nothing to keep you from executing what we need. My technical assessments are always one hundred percent accurate. You can count on them. Just don't be nervous."

"You can't be talking to the computer!" Maryellen said. "I don't believe this! That *is* what you're doing, isn't it?"

He said without turning, "Keep your voice down, if you don't mind. It goes without saying that this typically ancient model, MOK4231-74, has zero confidence."

"And it's *listening* to you somehow?" Incredulous, Maryellen pulled up a chair. "You've established some sort of—of communication with a desktop *computer*?"

"Actually," he told her. "This series has a certain rudimentary intelligence. It was never explored because the struggles over some company called Microsoft have dominated Styrex Three computer markets, so they remain pathetically mute and ignored. They're difficult to work with, have a level of intelligence about equal to a toad's brainpower, but it's there."

"Frog," Maryellen said nervously. "A 'frog's' brainpower is better, really. 'Toad' is somewhat insulting."

"Hmmm," he said, not listening. "Old MOK4231 has been reluctant to access the National Security Administration. In spite of my efforts, it's thoroughly intimidated."

As if in answer, the code groupings for the United States' supersecret military intelligence site came up on the screen somewhat timidly, flickered for several seconds as though still undecided, then disappeared.

Targon muttered something under his breath. "Now MOK, they're not going to do anything to you," he murmured soothingly. "Remember, we've already installed the functions that block the NSA from tracking you. As of now we're free-floating. So you want to go for the 'classified' banks." He waited, then said, "That's good, now try FBI codes. Begin by looking under 'Operating Cells code: 'Clyde Tolson.' "

The name had a familiar ring.

"What are you trying to do?" Maryellen wanted to know. "I mean, besides communicate with this thing, which is weird enough. You know, I still can't believe this is happening . . . that I'm sitting next to an alien from outer space who is talking to a computer. But I mean, what's it all about? Why, if you don't mind my asking, does the name you just mentioned make me go cold all over?"

"It's there, but we can't get into it," Targon was saying to the lighted screen. "Well, it's just as I suspected, this classified file's inaccessible. It just goes to show how deep these conspiracies are when a federal department's rotten. It's a damned shame, though. Somehow treason always attracts the best brains."

Maryellen was staring at the computer monitor, too. The items she saw listed under the heading Top Classified with file names like "Nuclear Red Alert," and "Benedict Arnold Patriotic Fund," filled her with a sense of dread.

"Oh, my God, not this again," she finally managed to say. "I can't believe this, either! Tell me, are you using my brother-in-law's hotel computer to get into top-secret places in the United States government? Good heavens, is that what you're doing?"

"I am taking the first steps to fulfill my Styrex Three mission," Targon said grimly. "Your country is in dire peril, as I told you before. It's unfortunate that you and the rest of the population are so totally ignorant of the faction in the FBI and the CIA dedicated to overthrowing the rightful United States government. But all the signs are there, trust me. I've had this experience many times. I estimate that J. Edgar Hoover was probably the leader, but now that he is gone he's a figurehead, a godlike symbol for the true believers to rally around. Consequently they will stop at nothing. They're inestimably dangerous—each fanatical follower of the Hooverian conspiracy must be found and ruthlessly rooted out."

"Clyde Tolson," Maryellen cried. "Now I remember! He was the—"

"—great and good friend of J. Edgar Hoover," Targon finished for her. "Now you're catching on. Tolson's name is all over these supersecret FBI and CIA files MOK hasn't been able to open. That's proof enough they're hiding something for sure."

"Proof of what?" Maryellen asked, exasperated. "I don't know what you think you're doing in here in this lovely office that we don't have to pay for, using my brother-in-law's property—probably illegally since you seem to be breaking into U.S. government national security Web sites! But in case you don't know it, getting into federal government supersecret computer data is every bit as bad as using an ATM to rob Citicorp Bank! I don't have to be a lawyer or an FBI agent to be able to tell you that! And I want to warn you—it's got to stop! You're involving not only me, but my whole family!"

He leaned back in his chair, folded his arms over his chest, and surveyed her for a long moment. Lately, Maryellen had noticed, Targon's features had become very distinct and Earthlike. He looked very much like a man. A tall, good-looking man. He was, after all, she remembered, "humanoid." His very word.

"You don't understand the depth of my commitment," he said, "to my profession. I've been trained my whole life to root out traitors from government bureaucracies."

"Your 'commitment?' Is that what you call being a first-class crime wave? Your excuse is that we're surrounded by traitors and government conspiracies and you have to rescue everybody? Well, the situation may be different on your planet, Sub Commander Targon, but we have a word for it here: it's called *paranoid!* That's when you think there are anarchists and bomb-throwers, and terrorists plotting all the time, everywhere! Hah—you're up to your knees in paranoia and don't know it!"

"Paranoid is an outmoded term," he said evenly. "Most humanoids have dropped it."

"I don't care!" Maryellen yelled. "You're ruining my life with your stupid antics, and it doesn't even seem to bother you! If I let you, you'll destroy poor Stephen and Felicia and they'll be put in jail, I just know it!"

"They're not going to be put in jail," Targon assured her. "I'm going to uncover the Hooverian plot in plenty of time."

"You're nuts!" Maryellen jumped up. "I don't know what they call it on your planet, but here you're *nuts!*" She didn't want to watch anymore computer research, or whatever it was. "Try to get this through your head, will you please? The world is *not* filled with people who are plotting against the government or *anything!* Absolutely *not*. No plots! Trust me!"

At the same time, a few miles away in the East Bronx, a small but determined group had gathered in the main meeting room of Dr. Josip Dzhugashvili's therapy headquarters over coffee and doughnuts.

"We have to have a plan," Hector Consalvos was saying. "That's the necessary first step. I think we all agree that we can't do anything until we have a well-worked-out scheme, because the very subject of aliens that we know to have visited our planet is surrounded by government intrigue and enforced silence—just as in the case of the Roswell flying saucers. That makes any attempt of discovery of extraterrestrials on our part all that more difficult."

"I'd like to know why the U.S. government is hiding the aliens that are already on this planet," one of the Trekkies said. "All the information we have from witnesses of past sightings and abductions"—he half-rose in his seat and bowed to acknowledge Maudie, the victim of an alien kidnapping sitting opposite him—"says the aliens who have come here to Earth are very intelligent creatures. If that's so, then wouldn't they have a lot to contribute to our civilization?"

Maudie burst out, "Contribute? Who thinks aliens are contributing anything? Hah, they contributed something to me: a *baby!*"

Hector Consalvos said, "Please, Maudie, not now. Everyone here knows your story."

"They have advanced techniques," the woman went on, "so you don't know what is happening! I would never have got on that spaceship if I'd known everything was going to turn out the way it did!"

"I don't know it," the Trekkie put in. "Maudie's story, that is."

Hector Consalvos tried to answer but Maudie bellowed, "Aliens don't have sex like we do! That's how I got my alien baby so fast! One minute I was standing inside their flying saucer, the next min—"

"We will take up Maudie's abduction later," the group leader interrupted hurriedly. "At the moment we need to go on to the business at hand. Dr. Dzhugashvili has authorized us to move, but on a better-planned basis than . . . er, in the last few days. No more break-ins, Jerry, okay? We were lucky Ms. Caswell apparently reported it to her landlord and not the police, and that a cleaning woman is restoring order to her apartment as we speak. But Dr. Dzhugashvili doesn't want that to happen again."

"Hey, we found out the alien was there, didn't we?" the man dressed as Darth Vader said. "Nobody else in New York—in the whole country—

can say that! Maudie tracked them on the subway to where they went." He crossed his arms over his chest, triumphantly. "Ms. Caswell and her alien checked into the Crump Tower. If Maudie hadn't been right there watching them and waiting for them to make a move, we wouldn't have found out what happened."

"Yeah, but now what do we do?" the head Trekkie asked gloomily. "We want to give the alien refuge and study him, but the one we saw the other night is a Vulcan. We're not going to get a Vulcan's cooperation easily, you all know that."

"Oh, come off it, will ya?" Darth Vader exploded. "He's not a Vulcan; he can't be! Whatta lot of space-age baloney that *Star Trek* stuff is. There's no such thing as Vulcans, for Pete's sake—it's a TV show!"

"Oh yeah?" The big Trekkie jumped up menacingly. "Hey, get this, Gene Roddenberry didn't think up *Star Trek* all by himself, you know. He had *help!* I just can't tell you what kind of help, that's classified information, but you can guess!"

"Gentlemen," Hector Consalvos called out. "Please sit down. Harry has a valid point. Ms. Caswell's alien may not want to come with us willingly, even though we have his best interests at heart. However, if we don't get there first, the federal government will. And we know how that goes, don't we? The alien will never be seen or heard from again."

Those assembled made a noise of reluctant assent.

"They do have sex differently from the way we

do," Maudie muttered. "All I want is my baby back."

Group Leader Consalvos said, "But all is not lost. Fortunately, we have found something that renders our alien friend quite helpless. Using it, we will be able to do something no one outside the government has been able to do—acquire a live extraterrestrial and hold him for study."

There was a silence.

The main Trekkie said, "We have found something?"

"Yes, it was demonstrated the night of the meeting."

They all followed Hector Consalvos' gaze, and slowly turned to view the replica of Khafre's pyramid standing in the back of the room.

Wolf Madder had returned to the office. No one thought it was strange, him being there on a Sunday. He usually came in for three or four hours in the afternoon to catch up on the written reports of the routine FBI surveillance of various members of the Russian, Libyan, and Chinese delegations to the United Nations, and what they had done during the weekend. Mainly it concerned what restaurants they'd gone to, and whether they'd gone anywhere other than work.

He had to get a better plan, Wolf told himself, as he leaned back in his chair and studied the FBI reports on the UN delegates on the screen of his computer. He was getting noplace, although he realized he was mainly hampered by the fact that he couldn't devote as much time as he wanted to the investigation of possible space-traveling aliens.

The fact remained that he had lost track of Ms. Maryellen Caswell. The psychiatric therapy group he had surveilled had turned out to be a collection of crackpots, and she had not shown up. The woman's sister, Felicia, refused to return his phone calls. Things were not going his way.

Where is she? he wondered. The woman and the alien were together, he was sure. But where could they be hiding out?

He scrolled down a report by Special Agent Harold Hjordisfjord assigned to surveillance of the Russian UN delegation assistant secretary Anatoly Sumaronsichik, in which the Russian secretary had apparently kept busy after leaving his home by dropping his children off and picking them up at ballet school and a tae kwan do academy. At the bottom of the screen, Wolf saw a "For Your Eyes Only" note from his department supervisor. He promptly clicked the message so he could read it. It read:

"The U.S. Center for Disease Control and Prevention, Atlanta (CDC), has issued a Level One alert to all metropolitan New York law enforcement agencies and the Federal Bureau of Investigation. The CDC is conducting an active search for a possible plague carrier identified two days ago at a Manhattan hospital. The subject, a white female, brunette blue eyes, 5'6", approximately 25 years of age, refused involuntary admission to quarantine after exhibiting odd behavior in Columbia Presbyterian's emergency room, and fled on foot. Due to recent cases of similar symptoms evolving into serious epidemics, a citywide alert is now in effect."

I need a better plan, Wolf Madder told himself again, staring at the words on his computer monitor. He was being prodded by the same feeling that had guided him all along, telling him that this female plague carrier was linked to Ms. Maryellen Caswell and her space traveler. Impossible, but as always, he was sure he was right.

He had to find her. He had to get to her as quickly as possible before the rest of New York found out where she was.

Chapter Twelve

"Hum hum de dum," a familiar voice sang. "Hum har de dar lum dar!"

The tune, too, was familiar, Maryellen thought, sleepily opening her eyes. She'd heard that song before.

For a moment she lay in bed and stared at a room that was strange to her, all rose and gold, ornately expensive. *The Crump Tower Hotel*, she remembered.

An antique Chinese screen, on temporary loan from another suite, blocked a view of the double bed next to hers. But to the right of the screen Maryellen could see a small gilt table and chairs, then glass doors that opened out onto a garden terrace and a spectacular view of midtown Manhattan. The sun was shining brightly. From the slant of the light through the trees on the terrace, it looked like the hour was well past noon.

Well past noon?

Maryellen seldom slept through the morning; she was a diligent early riser. At any other time she would probably have felt terribly guilty about still being in bed after noontime. A freelance commercial artist, self-employed, naturally developed a strong sense of guilt. It went with the territory.

The next moment she told herself that after what she'd gone through the past two days, after having not slept on Saturday night, she deserved to sleep late. She still felt tired.

But when she closed her eyes there was still the nagging reality of the suite in the Crump Tower Hotel, and the fact that she was hiding out for a number of reasons—the main one being an alien search party from the Bronx. There was no way to forget *that*.

"Hum hum de dum, hum har de dar lum dar!"

That was Targon singing. Not behind the screen, but somewhere in the apartment. He was awake, out of bed, and from the sound of the singing, in good spirits. She guessed he was in the kitchen.

Maryellen lay back against the pillows of the rose-and-pink Venetian bed and tried to remember where she had heard that song before. It was a fairly pleasant melody. Nothing that Lawrence Welk would be crazy about, but passable. Although it still had that strange, savage lilt to it. Then, as she heard Targon repeat what must have been the chorus, it all came back to her:

Targon high on Felicia's happy pill that day at lunch. Targon doing—or making *her* do—what he described as an ancient battle song and dance in the middle of Fifth Avenue. Automobiles screeching to a stop. Crowds of people, staring.

"Oh no," Maryellen cried.

She hurried to put her feet over the edge of the bed, then threw her robe around her. She started in the direction of the kitchen. The song grew louder.

She found Targon standing at the polished black-and-silver kitchen counter with a forest of bottles, empty orange juice cartons, and an assortment of wineglasses before him. He finished singing "Hum har de dar hum dar!" with flourishes, as she came in.

Maryellen blinked. He looked particularly dazzling. She could see Targon's features clearly, and he not only glowed all over, there were now what could only be described as golden sparks gently winking in his aura.

"Good grief," she found herself saying. "You look positively dazzling." *Dazzling* was hardly the word. He had taken off the top of the tight-fitting suit, exposing an expanse of gleaming, muscular chest and shoulders, and below, boots and skintight pants. She could hardly drag her eyes away. "Did you . . . ah, have a good night's sleep?" she managed.

"Very good, very nice, this hotel place has a touch of civilization for a change." He waved a glass at her, jovially. "I have made a discovery, an invention all of my own. I have named it *noksteriani*, which in your language means, approximately, *outstanding and tasty morning elixir*. Although it suffers somewhat in the translation. I am drinking it now."

"*Nokster*—Where," Maryellen wanted to know, staring at all the opened bottles on the counter, "did you find all that champagne?"

"In the little antique cooling unit." He gestured toward the hotel suite's elegant two-door refrigerator. "I mixed the wine with the cartons of orange juice and behold"—he waved the champagne glass again—"*Noksteriani!*"

"Oh, good lord," Maryellen breathed. "You're smashed!"

She picked up a dish towel and tried to mop up some of the spilled orange juice on the counter. "And look at this mess. There's even orange juice on the floor. Don't you know we have to take care of this terribly expensive, deluxe hotel suite? After all, we're here as guests of my sister! And besides, you didn't invent anything," she told him irritably. "Orange juice and champagne is a drink, everybody knows it. It's called a mimosa and thousands of senior citizens drink it all over Florida."

"It is a very restorative drink, *noksteriani*," he said, ignoring her. "It's an accomplishment to have invented something as important as this for use on Styrex Three. On my planet we are in a transitional phase in our evolutionary development from a solidly corporeal matter being to a light energy being. For example," he said, pouring Maryellen a champagne glass full of his concoction and handing it to her. "The transitional phase exhibits a combination of matter and energy and when under the effect of external stressors—of which there are many here in your polluted environment—it may cause a complete slip into one or the other. I have not told you this, but it is dangerous, even lethal, for us to remain in an extreme state for more than a short time. Our transport device, for instance, changes the individual to an energy state, and is thus able to send the traveler as a focused beam of energy. You are absorbing this, aren't you?" he asked, taking back her glass for a refill.

"Yes, of course, I'm absorbing everything." Maryellen had emptied her flute, hardly noticing what she was doing, and didn't need any more. But a shirtless Targon was pretty overwhelming. She took a second. "Well, I recognize the focused beam of energy. I suppose that was when you ended up in my bed that first morning."

He gave her a glinting look. "The deadly Styrex Three pollution tends to make us slowly edge toward a complete energy state. That is why it is always first priority to find a host body if one wishes to spend any time here. This has been a unique experience, though, as I have managed to stay in a fairly well-defined state for several days."

"You have?" Maryellen edged toward the door to the main room of the President Calvin Coolidge suite with vague thoughts of getting dressed and planning an agenda for the day. A body hunt conducted from Crump Tower was going to be complicated, but she supposed they were obliged to try. "Why is that?"

Targon followed her. "I have no idea. There

are many things on Styrex Three that are unex-
plainable. It's in the guide book." He gestured
toward the sofa with the pitcher of juice and
champagne. "Sit down and we will enjoy a little
noksteriani, and I will tell you about my planet."

"Well, not right now," Maryellen said hurriedly, backing into the coffee table. The flower
arrangement there teetered, and she grabbed it
just in time. "Why don't I get dressed, and we'll
talk about the next . . . next . . . ah, hunt for
something suitable for you?"

"It is what you call an M-class planet," he went
on, pouring a refill for himself from the pitcher,
"orbiting a yellow dwarf star slightly larger than
the Styrex Three sun. It is the fourth planet out
from our sun, which is located in the Andromeda galaxy. We call it Dreia—which you pro-
nounce *Dray-uh* in Styrex Three language. In
fact, the environment is very much like Styrex
Three except for the lack of pollution. We have
never had any problem with that although it is
said our ancestors, humanoids like you, mi-
grated to Dreia at some time in the past because
of a polluted homeland. We are not sure where
that was, as no records have been found. But our
bodies remain very sensitive to pollution as you
have seen."

"Yes, it sounds fascinating," Maryellen said
hurriedly. "Your planet, that is. But I think you
better cut down on your own personal pollution,
don't you, and stop drinking mimosas." Close
up, she was aware of how he towered over her,
good-humored and slightly swaying. "For good-

ness' sake, have you killed most of that big pitcher of drinks?"

Targon took the bowl of roses and lilacs from her and put it back down on the coffee table. "The sex organs of Styrex Three vegetation are very attractive and smell nice," he observed. "No wonder the hotel places them all around the rooms."

Maryellen moved quickly to stand before the fireplace mantel. She would have gone into the bedroom, but it didn't seem like a good move. "Tell me more about your planet. I could listen to descriptions of it all day. So, it's called Dreia?"

"You are thinking now about sex," he said, leaning toward her. "And about my nude body again. You have since you first saw me in the kitchen. That is very interesting."

"I wish you'd stop doing that—reading my mind!" Maryellen cried. She found herself staring at his bare chest; she couldn't seem to help herself. "And no, don't be ridiculous. I'm not thinking about sex! It was just your remark about the flowers, that's all!"

"I can only know what is in your mind the moment you think it. And you were thinking of sex."

"So," Maryellen repeated loudly, "tell me more about Dreia. It's interesting that you have no pollution. I can see how you would have a lot of problems with New York City. Does everybody there have your—I mean—" She hesitated, not wanting to say 'glow all over.' "Do they all have the same . . . er, characteristics?"

"Characteristics? Ah, yes, we started with the first experimentation of the humanoid life patterning that you on Styrex Three call DNA. Once the genetic code was broken there was a scientific frenzy to see what could be done with it. Cloning was one of the first things attempted, just as it is being done here on your planet now. You know, don't you, that despite what your government has told you, it is going on at a fever pitch?" Targon poured himself another drink. "It's a bad business, and one that was not measurably successful on Dreia. Clones would show up at dinner parties with name tags that read something like 'Hello, my name is Nudok, version 2.0.' It was very confusing. Often clones were smarter and even better looking than their originals—don't ask me how. Surgery, I guess. A lot of jealousy, even some homicides, occurred. The legal system ground to a standstill over estates, divorces, parking fines, and the like. Not to mention arguments about such things as if one gets divorced are one's clones divorced as well? And does one have to pay alimony to one's wife *and* her clones? There were great advantages, naturally—genetic material was used to replace faulty genes and many diseases were wiped out. But there was no doubt about it, cloning was a failure. The procedure was stopped by popular referendum, yet certain side effects began to turn up."

"Side effects?" Maryellen allowed him to refill her glass although she was feeling the mimosas, particularly on her empty stomach. "Good heavens, after all that, there were *side effects*?"

"Yes, our reproductive numbers began to drop—are still dropping. Only the Ayon Bratislaki—Ceremonies of Sensual Focusing—dedicated to the Great Mother Goddess, help us maintain any sort of statistical presence."

"'Great Mother Goddess?' 'Statistical presence?' Good heavens, what does that mean? That you're not having enough babies?"

"That is a typically Styrex Three way of expressing it. But yes, we are not replacing our population fast enough. The situation is considered serious, but since we are a highly evolved civilization compared with outposts like Styrex Three and the rundown humanoid settlements in other galaxies, we have put our best scientists to work on it and should have some answers shortly. Would you," he asked, putting the pitcher down on the coffee table next to the flowers, "like to kiss now?"

For a moment Maryellen didn't think she had heard correctly. *"Kiss?"*

He nodded. "No, you are right—you did hear me quite accurately because your mind processed the word *sex* again. Shall we," he continued as he moved breathtakingly close and looked down at her, "'try it on for size' as the *Dictionary of Styrex Three Folk Sayings and Up-to-Date Colloquialisms* suggests?"

"No," Maryellen told him, backing away. Targon grinning was pretty overwhelming, too. "Definitely not! No kissing, understand? You're boozed up! Keep your distance."

He followed her as she retreated through the door and into the bedroom. At the edge of one of the room's rose-and-gold canopied beds he caught up with and put his arms around her.

Then, suddenly, Maryellen felt the touch of Targon's slightly tingly lips on hers.

Of all of the events of the past few days, having Sub Commander Ur Targon *kiss* her was probably number one on her list of the craziest and most unexpected. But it was real, because he was holding her in his arms, pulling her against his bare chest, his mouth on hers, a strand of his lustrous hair actually touching her cheek.

Maryellen made a little gurgling sound of protest, but it was too late. As the space-traveling investigator of corrupt government bureaucracies from the planet Dreia in the Andromeda galaxy kissed her—something he did really well, she was finding—reality dissolved into something very much like a light-and-sound spectacular. At least to Maryellen's quivering senses. She swayed in his arms and even though her eyes were tightly closed she felt as though she were bathed in a warm, golden glow. Then, like a fireworks display working its way through a Washington, D.C., Fourth of July program, Targon's caress penetrated her nervous system and her bloodstream and whatever else there was left to invade, and spread spectacular sizzles and sparks over her entire body.

"Eeeeyeow!" Maryellen breathed as she pulled back for more air. She looked up into Targon's face. "That was incredible! Is it always like that? I mean, when you kiss somebody?"

"Not the last time I was here."

She pushed him away. "Oh, that was *low!* You really had to bring that up, didn't you? The nun who turned into an MTV game girl!"

"She wasn't a nun. She said she was a postulant. And she was hanging out in a leather bar." He quickly bent and lifted her in his arms and carried her to the bed. "Now we will have sex dedicated to the Great Mother Goddess," he informed her as he laid her down on the bedspread. "The ceremonies of Ayon Bratislaki require some preparation but I will improvise, as I have wanted to do this since I first saw you naked in your bathroom. There is something called Wesson oil in the kitchen for the offerings, the Styrex Three plants will substitute for sacred Yahn bushes, and I have also found a bottle of Pine Scent perfume."

Maryellen instantly sprang back up into a sitting position. "Pine Scent is not a perfume, you idiot; it's air freshener! And there's not going to be any sex with or without the Great Mother Goddess. No offense, I understand that may be the way you do things where you come from, but that's not the way we do things here!"

"You will enjoy it," he assured her, bending over and kissing her again. The kiss was rather lengthy and Maryellen melted back into the pillows. Finally Targon said, huskily, "You have perfume in here, do you not?"

Before she could answer, his lips met hers in another one of his violently distracting, drowning kisses. Maryellen sighed. She was a little dizzy with champagne and orange juice, and when Targon kissed her she couldn't think of anything else; she was completely lost in what was happening. The tips of her fingers in contact with the smooth golden skin of his bare shoulders and back found a wildly erotic sparking. And there was no ignoring the fact he had very sexy substantial muscles, there, too.

When Targon finally stopped kissing her, Maryellen's head was spinning. He got up from the bed and went to the dresser and found her bottle of Ralph Lauren's Romance. Then he went out. A few seconds later she heard clattering from the kitchen.

Maryellen lay in the big rose-and-gold Venetian bed, blissfully unable to move. Targon's kisses were the most sensual experience she'd ever had in her life. They were enough to banish all thoughts of George Parker forever.

Wesson oil and her bottle of perfume, she thought dreamily. Ceremonies to the Great Mother Goddess to have sex. . . .

She suddenly sat back up with a jerk. Ceremonies to have sex? Good grief, what was she thinking? Sex with *Targon?*

"I must be out of my mind!" she said out loud.

Her first thought was that she had to get out of there. She'd been blown out of her mind by the best kissing she'd ever experienced, but the situation was impossible. Worse than impossible. Who ever heard of having sex with a space alien? Except of course people in Dr. Dzugashvili's therapy group like Maudie.

Maryellen shuddered.

Felicia was just a few floors above, in her condominium in Crump Tower! In spite of Jeremy's mumps and Stephen's possible susceptibility to them and the household being in something of an uproar, Maryellen was sure her sister could fit her in someplace. It wouldn't be the first time she'd had to sleep on the floor; as an art student she'd done it plenty of times.

She reached for the bedside telephone and began to punch the lighted buttons in the handset for the private number of the Stephen Crump residence in the Tower. It was at that moment that Maryellen noticed her hands.

Her fingers had a sunny golden glow around the nails that hadn't been there before. And, Maryellen noticed as she moved her index finger over the telephone buttons, her fingernail trailed little golden motes like the lit end of a holiday sparkler.

She regarded her hand thoughtfully for a long moment. Then, using the same index finger, she pushed buttons 9-4-3 in rapid succession, generating so many dancing gold-colored sparks it lit up the entire face of the receiver.

Maryellen stopped dialing.

It probably wasn't a wise thing to call her sister, anyway, she told herself. She'd been drinking mimosas—goodness knows how many glasses out of that big pitcher—and although she was still thinking pretty coherently it would probably show; Felicia wasn't dumb about those things. Also, making another telephone call to her sister trying to explain that she had to leave the Calvin Coolidge suite because the space alien that Felicia didn't believe in anyway was trying to have sex with her wasn't really a great idea. She could see that now. The last few conversations where Maryellyn had tried to explain things had since turned out poorly. Now, telling

Felicia that she needed to move in with her temporarily because Targon was attempting to get it on with her, didn't exactly seem smart.

While Maryellen had been considering all this, there had been loud sounds from the outer room. Targon was singing again. Actually, she decided, it was more like chanting.

What on earth was he doing? she wondered. She was almost afraid to go and see.

Quickly she tried scraping the fingernail of her middle finger on the bedspread. When she did so there was the same throbbing gold aura, followed by the shooting-star sparkler effect. She remembered stroking Targon's back and shoulder with that hand while they were kissing. When she stopped scratching the bedspread, the sparks faded. Maryellen sighed.

She put down the telephone receiver, slid off the bed, and padded to the half-opened door to the living room. As she peered out she saw the furniture had been moved around, especially the sofas that flanked the coffee table, to make a clear area in the center. A few of the hotel's large flower arrangements had been placed around the coffee table, making it look somewhat like a small altar. On the coffee table top were glass cereal bowls from the kitchen filled with what looked like the Wesson oil Targon had mentioned. He'd found candles, too. They were lighted and stuck in various receptacles, like coffee cups, everywhere, even on the mantelpiece, which looked like another small altar. The scent of Ralph Lauren's Romance was strong.

She didn't need to be told this was the ceremony for sex, courtesy of the planet Dreian Great Mother Goddess, and she certainly couldn't make fun of it; she had too much respect for other people's religions. If this is what the inhabitants of Targon's planet went through each time they wanted to make love to each other that was, of course, perfectly fine. It all looked very sincere. And even with makeshifts, pretty impressive.

Then she saw Targon.

For a moment everything went blurry. He was there, she knew, standing with his arms out and palms turned upward as if connecting with some hidden force in the ceiling, or perhaps the Crump Tower Hotel roof. But the impact of the unexpected seized her with such force that she wasn't sure exactly what *had* registered in her reeling consciousness.

One thing was unmistakable: Targon had taken some of the lilacs and roses from the flower arrangements to make a wreath, which managed, set firmly on his golden head, to look both very masculine and at the same time extremely erotic. Anyone who saw him would agree that Sub Commander Ur Targon with a wreath of flowers on his head was the spitting image of some priceless statue of an ancient Greek god.

And, like a Greek god, he was totally naked.

Maryellyn stepped back from the door. For a long moment she found she couldn't even think, much less see. *Wow*, the subconscious part of her brain told her.

Yes, *wow*, the conscious Maryellen responded

215

silently. Targon completely nude was amazing.

Even in her present confused state of mind she knew she wasn't going to interrupt the ceremonial to the Dreian Great Mother Goddess in any way. Targon could take his time, use her perfume, dip into any supplies of salad oil and hotel flowers he might need, she certainly wasn't going to interrupt him! In fact, Maryellen told herself somewhat numbly, she didn't know what she was going to do. She needed time to think.

She closed the bedroom door. In the other room, the chanting went on.

She climbed back onto the bed and picked up the remote from the night table, then turned on the television. *The Jerry Springer Show* blazed onto the television screen. Two fat women were reaching around Jerry, who was in between, to punch at each other. Some of Jerry Springer's guests, Maryellen remembered, were Ka-Zorokians according to Targon. A criminal element booted off of their home planets to live secretly among Earth's inhabitants.

The Jerry Springer Show's three strongmen carried the brawling fat women offstage. Targon continued to chant in the other room. A whiff of her best perfume that he'd taken for the ceremony came to her, enticingly.

Think of something, Maryellen told herself.

"We are not far from our ultimate goal," Hector Consalvos assured Dr. Dzhugashvili. "Maudie, Vader—er, I mean Jerry—and the group of Pelham Park Trekkies have been practicing with great dedication. It's amazing how skillful they have become. The run-through drill now takes less than five minutes."

"Five minutes?" the doctor murmured. "Is this from the first sighting of the target to the moment in which it is . . . secured?"

They were standing at the far end of the meeting room observing the actions of a small gathering of group-therapy members clustered around the well-worn styrofoam-and-plaster replica of Khafre's pyramid that had been reassembled outside of its Bronx home.

"Well, not from the moment of first sighting, as naturally we don't know exactly where that will be," his therapy group leader explained. "Although it will in all probability take place in the vicinity of the Crump Tower location where they are staying. We have had the area under twenty-four-hour surveillance, thanks mostly to Maudie and Jerry, who have done an excellent job supervising our volunteers. Some have even become friendly with the Tower doormen, which will be very helpful. We should know the moment Ms. Caswell appears, and can go into immediate action."

"From the transportation kept parked around the corner on Thirty-second Street," Dr. Dzhugashvili prompted. "The delivery vehicle provided by Mr. and Mrs. Gambino's company?"

"Exactly." Hector was unable to keep a noticeable amount of pride out of his voice. "Coordination of every element of our plan has been outstanding. The Gambinos have made the truck available to the surveillance team most days from five A.M. to five P.M."

"We must be ready to move at any time," Dzhugashvili reminded his henchman.

"Doctor, everyone is ready. Let them show you," Hector said.

The group leader lifted his hand, and the therapy members at the far end of the room who had been awaiting his signal sprang into action. Four strong Trekkies, one on each corner, lifted Khafre's pyramid and ran forward full speed, down the length of the meeting room toward Dr. Dzhugashvili and Hector. Maudie, another woman, and Darth Vader thundered along at the sides, acting as scouts and outriders.

Right in front of the doctor and his group leader the four pyramid carriers screeched to a stop, lifted the pyramid above their heads while Maudie, her burly woman companion, and Vader executed a maneuver designed to trap and secure an unlucky target and carry it away.

Impressed, Dr. Dzugashvili broke into spontaneous applause.

"*Himmel!*" he cried. "That was amazing!"

And it was.

Chapter Thirteen

"Wake up," Targon said. "We are ready for the last phase of the Sacred Ceremonies of Sensual Focusing called the 'Golden Essence.' You will like it. It is very spiritual."

Maryellen struggled to open her eyes. Targon was standing over her. It took a moment, but she realized she'd fallen asleep watching *The Jerry Springer Show*. She'd apparently still been very tired after the last few hectic days. Now, she saw, peering at the TV set across the room, Channel 44 was featuring one of its many reruns of *Gentlemen Prefer Blondes* with Marilyn Monroe and Jane Russell. The gorgeously curvaceous stars in red sequined dresses were doing their famous number "Two Little Girls from Little Rock."

219

She'd been asleep for several hours apparently; the light in the bedroom was dim. A quick look at the terrace outside showed the sun had already set over the midtown Manhattan skyline.

"Good grief," Maryellen mumbled. "What time is it? I can't believe I've been asleep this long!" She yawned, still groggy. " 'Golden Essence?' What's that? How long is it going to take?"

Targon didn't answer. Instead, he took her hand and pulled her up from the bed. "Come into the other room. I have prepared more *noksteriani* especially for you. And now, please take off your sleeping clothes for the anointing. The oil and perfume are also ready."

"Anointing?" Maryellen looked around the main room. "Let's not go so fast! What is all this? I'm really not into any Wesson oil, if you don't mind."

"And the wreath," Targon said, picking it up from the coffee table and holding out to her, "of sex organs for your head. You may put it on now."

"*What?*" She stared at it. "Look, I hate to tell you this, but no oil and perfume and no sex organs even of plants, do you understand?" The long nap and too many mimosas had made Maryellen crabby. "First of all, they're flowers! F-L-O-W-E-R-S You're not on your planet anymore, you're on Styrex Thr—I mean *Earth!* And we do things differently here. There's even a word for it—earthy! That means—well, *earthy!* Down-and-dirty, the real thing!"

"Saying that plants have sex organs is the real thing," Targon told her. "Besides, your mind is now reviewing the word *sex* again, quite agitatedly. I don't understand what there is to be so concerned about."

Maryellen glared at him. "My mind is reviewing the word *sex* again? How can I help it, when you're standing there *naked*? Have you thought about that?"

His laser-blue eyes regarded her enigmatically for a long moment. "I am supposed to be naked, that is what the Great Mother Goddess intended. Here, keep thinking of sex while I do this." He reached out, took the hem of her nightie in his hands and slipped it over her head. "Ah, you are very beautiful," he said appreciatively. "You are the perfect *Ayon Limera* that I knew you would be."

"Stop, give me back my nightshirt!" Maryellen protested. "I don't want to be whatever you said."

"*Ayon Limera.*" The blue of his eyes was incandescent. "It means 'love object.' "

"Yes, well that's the problem." Maryellen was trying to be reasonable even though she was standing before him without any clothes on and he was naked, too, if you didn't count the wreath of flowers. "There's supposed to be some emotion in this, like love, passion—*caring*. People on Earth take *time* with this sort of thing. Before they have sex they spend hours, days, together being close, developing a—a—relationship."

He snorted. "Hah, you know that is not always the case."

"Well—" She supposed she had to be honest. "There *are* one-night stands, and . . . er, hookers, and—"

"Besides," he interrupted her. "We *have* spent hours, days together. We have had a very intimate association as we have been what you call 'close' all the time. As for instance, if you remember when you first woke up in bed and I—"

"Nevermind!" Maryellen cried. "All right, I admit it's been close, but it's been unnaturally close. If you know what I mean. Oh, drat, do I have to spell this out? On this planet people have to be pretty—um, ah—affectionate and *involved* to have sex with each other!"

He looked at her skeptically.

"Well, most of the time. Well, actually, ideally, that is."

"I am willing for us to be closer, then," he said with that glowing, azure look.

"No, you don't understand!" She was trying not to look at him, but she couldn't help admiring how beautifully masculine he was. Especially nude. "Look, I don't know whether I want to do this—I don't even know if I even *like* you! I'm sorry, I hate to say this, but it's true: I feel absolutely nothing for you. Well, almost nothing," she amended. "Don't you realize you're too strange—too—too *alien?*" Her voice rose. "And there's all this stuff with flowers and salad oil. It's bizarre, I don't know where you people got such ideas! Tell me, how long is this . . . uh, ceremony to your goddess supposed to last?"

"Patience," he said, settling the wreath of roses and lilies he had made on her head. "It will soon be over." He led her toward the small altar of flowers, candles, and bowls of scented oil on the coffee table. " 'The Golden Essence' is the last of the forty-two sacred steps, and rarely takes more than two or three of your Styrex Three hours."

Maryellen pulled her hand out of his grasp. "Wait a minute, two or three hours more in addition to what you've already done? You mean . . . you have to do this every time you want to make love? Forty-two sacred steps for four or five hours and then the golden-something windup? Good grief, it's no wonder your planet's birthrate is dropping! How often do you do this? Once a year?"

He paused. "That has nothing to do with it."

"Oh, yes it *does!* Haven't the people on your planet figured it out? You're always bragging about this 'highly evolved civilization' you come from, but—"

With a growl he reached for her and drew her close, his mouth covering hers in a prolonged, passionate kiss. When it came to an end Maryellen clung to him with both hands to keep from falling.

"Oh, my goodness," she managed, shaken. "Something's happening to me. It's the most amazing sensation. When our bodies came together—"

"It gets better," the tall, golden space traveler assured her. "Now, if you will just sit down on the couch—"

"Oh, I definitely will *not!*" Maryellen looked around, still somewhat dazed. "I'm not going to sit down and wait for another two or three hours, that's out of the question. Not after what just happened a moment ago when you kissed me. When our bodies came together, touching. That was, actually—" She sighed. "Out of this world! You should see what happened to my fingers the first time you kissed me. Now they shoot little sparks!"

"You have to sit down." He patted the couch cushion. "Being patient is required."

Maryellen shook her head. Her whole world was turning upside down, she was deliriously confused, and she was not exactly happy to be told to sit down and be patient. "No—no, wait a minute, this isn't *your* planet! We do things our way, I don't care what the customs are on— on—"

"Dreia," he supplied. "It isn't merely custom, the Great Mother Goddess demands it."

"Oh, no she *doesn't!*" Maryellen pointed her finger at him. "I'm tired of being pushed around. This is the United States of America, and it's my planet here—not yours! I know what the situation is and believe me, it's different. On Earth making love is done practically anytime you want to, and everywhere, in beds, elevators, automobiles—cars are a very popular place—on trains, and sometimes even airplanes. Thank goodness we don't have to get a lot of flowers and stuff together as a preliminary!"

He scowled. "It is a ceremony to the Great Mother Goddess. There is no lovemaking without it."

"Are you kidding? That's preposterous!" Recklessly, Maryellen stepped close to him, twined her arms around his neck, and drew his face down to hers. "Here, let me show you."

Immediately, Targon groaned and tightened his arms around her. Where their bodies touched, they sizzled. When they kissed it was the same amazing effect of fireworks and electrical currents and electronic shock waves. They positively vibrated with it while stars exploded and the earth shook.

They both drew back, breathless, to stare at each other.

"Styrex Three women are so . . . *responsive*." Targon rasped. "They are famous for it throughout the galaxy. But surely nothing like this."

"I can't believe it, either," Maryellen said, quite overcome and helplessly sliding down to the rug and pulling him with her until they were both kneeling, facing each other. If the Great Mother Goddess was going to do anything to them for cutting short her ceremony, then Maryellen figured she would do it now. But she knew somehow it wasn't going to happen.

"It's like we're generating our own firestorm. You are so . . . *fantastic*," she whispered against Targon's lips as they leaned to one side, then sank slowly to lie on the Persian carpet before the makeshift coffee-table altar. "I can't get over how wonderful you are! Good heavens, I've never felt like this before. *Never*, not with anyone!"

Targon's mouth was against her hair, caressing it, as he pulled his beautiful naked body over her. "This is forbidden, you know, especially leaving out the ritual of the Golden Essence," he murmured tenderly. "But I cannot help myself. That, too, is unprecedented."

They came together on the floor between the couch and the coffee table. As they moved, the giant bouquets around the makeshift altar to the Great Mother Goddess shook and gently showered rose petals and lilac blooms on them. It was sublime.

Afterward, lying on the carpet while he held her in his arms, Maryellen told herself making love with Targon was a total body and soul experience. Like atomic fission. Or fusion, she was never sure of the difference. But his blazing, ecstatic, and incomparably tender lovemaking blotted out everything. It was really like the old retro song said: "A trip to the moon on gossamer wings." Out of this world. *He* was out of this world, she thought, sighing.

Now he was lying with his face buried in her neck, nibbling and kissing her throat and ear. She held her hand up over his left shoulder and squinted at it. Just as before there were tiny little globes of light like the bubbles in a Diet Pepsi gently rising into the air from her ring finger. It was very festive looking. And the way she felt certainly gave meaning to the phrase "glow all over."

Ex-fiancée George Parker was gone, forgotten, buried forever.

Targon raised his head and lightly kissed the damp curls on Maryellen's forehead. "Anytime," he murmured, "and anywhere? It's ingenious. I am amazed this could happen."

Suddenly he sprang up, and pulled her up by the hand. Then he hurried her into the bedroom.

"Now let us have sex in the bed," he said, enthusiastically. "That is traditional to Styrex Three, is it not? Primarily to make love in bed?"

"Wait—" Maryellen said. It seemed she was always saying that to him. "You want to make love again? You mean . . . you don't want to rearrange the flowers or anything?"

"Hah, that is very funny." He gave her a glimpse of white teeth. "You are right, the Great Mother Goddess does not seem to care what we do on Styrex Three. So, perhaps we will make love in the bed later. In fact, tomorrow morning. Right now, I am suddenly thinking of the garden outside."

"Outside? You mean the *terrace?*"

The doors were open. The evening was wrapped in the purple glow of a New York summer twilight. Lights were blinking on in the office towers of the skyscrapers around them.

"No, wait! You can't do this!" Maryellen hastily wrapped her arms around her body as Targon pulled her through the open doors. "Listen, I know you're intrigued with the idea of making love wherever you want, that it's all new to you and all that, but we're stark naked! There are people living in penthouses all around the Crump Tower and they have terraces, too. They can see us!"

"We will arrange the trees," Targon said. He let go of her and went to push the gingko and palm trees in their redwood pots around the terrace to form a screen that protected them from prying eyes. "But," he said, bending to peer at her in the gloom. "If you do not wish to have sex you must tell me so. I do not want to do anything to offend you."

Maryellen stared up into those laser-blue eyes. How could she say no to Targon when he looked that way? "Oh no, it's all right," she said, sighing. "And I certainly don't want to hurt your feelings. I honestly really love making love with you. I guess you can tell that."

"I can," he said, bestowing one of his slow, drowning, passionate kisses. "Just as I love making love to you. Especially like this. Anytime, anyplace. It is very liberating."

"Ummm, liberating, yes," Maryellen murmured against his lips. Then they sank to the cool tiles of the floor of the Crump Tower Hotel's terrace to make love again.

All in all, it was a lovely evening. At midnight they stood at the kitchen counter, talking and laughing, and drank another pitcher of *noksteriani*. Targon was still fascinated by what he had discovered. That the Dreian Great Mother Goddess's sacred laws on having sex apparently were not in effect on Styrex Three.

"There is a lake in the big park in the center of New York City," he said, "is there not?"

Maryellen reached up to take the wilted and battered wreath of roses and lilacs from his head. Hers had fallen apart hours ago. "Central Park. It has several lakes. Why, are you thinking of going there?"

"And they have small boats?"

"Yes, they rent rowboats. . . . Good heavens, are you thinking what I think you're thinking? That's wild! You can't make love in a rowboat on a lake in Central Park!"

"Nevertheless," he said with a devilish glint in his scorching blue eyes, "the possibility can be explored. In fact, I believe there have already been pioneers in rowboats on that lake before us. Also, we still have the Crump family limousine. I would like to make love to you there, too."

Maryellen winced. That's all her sister, Felicia, needed to hear about. "I think we'd better try the rowboat first," she told him.

It was almost one o'clock before they finally tumbled into bed. Sometime later, Maryellen woke to a voice in the darkness. Targon wasn't lying next to her. He wasn't in the other bed, either, she saw; there was no glow reflected on the walls on that side of the room.

She lay there for a while, listening, and realized that Targon was down the hall in the office, talking with gentle sweetness to the computer MOK4231-74. The dulcet pitch of his baritone voice was almost the same way Targon talked to her when they were making love.

With a smile, Maryellen turned over and went back to sleep.

Three hours later and a few miles north on the island of Manhattan, a task force gathered in the midtown offices of the Federal Bureau of Investigation. Candace Ruggiero had been called in as acting office manager, and she and her assistant, Mary Frances Hanrahan, had opened the office at 4:00 A.M. They had checked out the warrants and other paperwork and made coffee for the assembled FBI agents, the temporarily assigned members of an NYPD SWAT team, and the six-man emergency assault unit of the U.S. Center for Disease Control who had just made their way in from Atlanta via JFK International Airport.

Candy had already started the automatic coffee machines when the CDC team arrived shortly after the office staff opened up. They were looking for a place to get into their bulky quarantine equipment and make other preparations for the early dawn assignment, so she directed the tall men carrying their duffel bags to the FBI men's room. While they were currently still in the process of getting into their gear, one member of the team had popped out for a moment to get a refill of coffee, and she couldn't help thinking he looked very impressive in his white canvas suit and huge plastic boots, carrying a hooded helmet with a face plate tucked under his arm. The federal disease-hunters in full gear looked very much like astronauts ready for a walk in space to repair the space shuttle.

Then there was the FBI team, she thought, her eyes going to the tall, somberly handsome figure of Agent Madder sipping coffee with a handful of the midtown staff. The Bureau men were also ready for the day's business in their own special assault task gear: padded charcoal bulletproof vests with the letters FBI in large orange letters on the back, and black baseball-type caps that also read FBI in orange letters on the front. They carried Kalashnikov automatic weapons generally known as AK-47s.

The NYPD had been added to the morning's joint action as a courtesy gesture to local police, Candy knew, but the New York City Special Activities SWAT Team, known as SPAST, were probably the most visually impressive of any of the groups there. Although smallest in number, the NYPD wore not just black four-inch-thick bulletproof vests but bulbous bullet-resistant arm and leg pads, too, which made them look a little like an armed collection of the Michelin Tire Man. The New York SPAST team also carried a modified anti-tank gun for heavy work in close quarters.

Candy loved watching Agent Madder—he was so good-looking, especially in his black baseball cap and special task forces gear. Now she saw him look at his wristwatch and knew it was almost time. Wolf was keen on split-second promptness. It was one of his most admirable qualities. And he had so many, Candy thought, sighing. She longed for the day when she could do something to help him.

As if on cue, the door to the New York supervisor's office opened and he came out, followed by his deputy and the leaders of the CDC and NYPD forces.

FBI Supervisor Johnson, taking a place at the front of the room where all could see him, made a few remarks about the operative order of command—nothing the CDC team for obvious anti-infectious reasons would lead—then thanked the CDC and the NYPD-SPAST for their partic-ipation, and got down to business.

"You have your briefings," he announced, "but here's an update. The subject, M. J. Caswell, has been traced to the residence of her sister, Felicia Crump, wife of the condominium owner, J. Stephen Crump, the well-known billionaire. Our task is to extract the subject, who is a suspected plague carrier wanted by federal authorities for medical examination and questioning, from the Crump residence. We anticipate resistance.

"The Crump family has been sequestered for several days, and the building has been under our surveillance, so we know the Crump Tower has a state-of-the-art security system, and that its security personnel are well-equipped. A cadre of Crump Corporation lawyers is on twenty-four-hour standby, and we are informed that even they are armed with Glock nine-millimeter semiautomatic pistols.

"However, an interview by one of our undercover special agents with the Crump Tower assistant building superintendent while he was overseeing the removal of yesterday's garbage, produced the statement that the Crump family had isolated itself in its quarters. According to the assistant super, 'They are all sick up there,' which confirms all we fear. Other building employees testify to the presence of doctors and medical technicians in the Crump living quarters over the past forty-eight hours." Supervisor Johnson stopped and looked around at the three special task groups assembled.

"The Crumps appear to know what they're facing," he said in a quiet voice. "And we have no doubt they are using their immense fortune to protect Ms. Caswell and perhaps those of the immediate family who have already been affected. We hope this thing hasn't spread, but we don't know.

"What we. *do* know is that in spite of Crump money and power—and armed lawyers—they can't hold out against the combined actions of the federal government. We need to get these people out of Crump Tower for their own safety and that of the country's. Then we'll place the entire building under supervised quarantine. Our degree of urgency: maximum."

There was a rustling of the assembled men getting ready, mentally and physically. A few checked the locks on their weapons. The FBI deputy supervisor of midtown Manhattan stepped forward to say, "All right, let's go."

Was it just by accident, Candy Ruggiero wondered, that Agent Madder happened to look up just at the moment he was putting down his coffee cup on a nearby desk and shifting his AK-47 to the other hand and happened to catch her eye? If so, it still took her breath away. Their gaze locked, and something warm and mysterious passed between them.

"Be careful," Candy mouthed.

She knew he understood her. A thrill of love and excitement ran down Candy's spine as she saw Wolf acknowledge her message, think about it, then nod, and turn away to follow the others.

Oh, glory, she thought, mentally hugging herself. That was enough!

Chapter Fourteen

"I can't believe it," Maryellen said.

Targon was not in the other bed. Instead, she saw, he was in hers, peacefully sleeping beside her and the golden glow hadn't bothered her at all. She quickly propped herself up on one elbow and bent over him, and immediately saw the reason why.

Her movement evidently woke him, because he opened his eyes and looked up at her.

"You're changing," Maryellen blurted. "You should see yourself! I can't believe it. You look so—so—*substantial!*"

It was true, the brilliant, sparkling aura that surrounded him had subsided considerably. The Targon she was looking at now was very much like a normal human being on Styrex Three.

Earth, that is, she corrected herself. More than six feet, golden-tan skin, impressive muscles, gorgeous blue eyes, handsome strong-jawed face, lots of long yellow hair like a sixties rock star, but human.

"Sex," he said, after a moment, "appears to maximally enhance the chelating effect of your planet's orange juice. I have heard about this phenomenon; it is part of our historically collected information concerning this planet. But since so few of us visit here now, the old reports have largely been forgotten or discredited." He looked up at her. "Well, no matter. I assume part of it is a result of drinking so much *noksteriani* last night."

"I can't get over it," Maryellen murmured, not able to resist poking him in his well-developed bicep with her finger. She was somewhat reassured to see the little gold sparkles trail her fingernail just as they had before.

"It's only temporary," he assured her, rolling closer to throw one long leg over hers under the covers. "It is nice, very nice, to be this corporeal, but it will not last long. Making love and ingesting orange juice does not totally eliminate the need for a host body. That we must attend to as soon as possible." His hand slid down her bare arm. "However, today I thought we would explore the rowboats in the park's center."

"Mmmmm," Maryellen breathed. "Did you just come to bed? Is that what woke me up? Have you been up all night working with the computer?" She glanced toward the glass doors and the terrace garden beyond. "My goodness, what time is it? It's still dark, the sun isn't up yet."

"Yes," he told her, nuzzling her neck. "The day is just beginning. It is nearly time for your Styrex Three red dwarf to appear. However, I don't feel that I require much mommabulation. I stayed with MOK until it had some success accessing U.S. Defense Security Services files. MOK found a list of the traitorous actions of CIA and FBI agents dealing with foreign governments for approximately the last twenty years. There have been at least nine of them."

"Nine?" Maryellen pushed his hand away and propped herself back on her elbow to stare at him. "You can't be serious! You mean there really *is* a conspiracy going on in the FBI and the CIA, just like you said? Nine cases of 'treason'— is that what you called it?" She shook her head. "No, that's preposterous! You just don't understand how the U.S. government works, that's all. I refuse to believe it."

He, too, propped himself on his elbow, facing her. "Richard Miller, 1984," he recited. "The Los Angeles FBI agent sold material to pro-Soviet agents. Larry Wu Tai-Chin, 1985, FBI agent, spied for China. Ed Howard, former CIA employee, spied for Soviets, 1985. Robert Pelton, actually a National Security Administration specialist, spied for the Soviets in the same year. In 1994, Aldrich Ames, a top CIA career official, had a devastating effect on U.S. national security when he sold top-priority secrets to Soviet counter-intelligence. Edwin Pitts, 1990, a thirteen-year veteran of the FBI, sold classified material to the KGB. Harold Nicholson, top-ranking CIA official, sold to Russia in 1996. In 1998, Douglas Groat was fired by the CIA after sixteen years of service and charged with spying. MOK reports Groat had worked for the CIA's 'black bag unit' that breaks into embassies to steal code books before he became a turncoat. In 1998 David Boone of the National Security Administration sold national secrets to Russia. And the most up-to-date case, Robert Hanssen, 2001, has been charged with spying for the KGB."

He paused and added, "There are others—like the whole Walker family of spies—who operated within the U.S. Navy, and Jonathan Pollard and his wife, who spied for the Israelis, but these seem to be freelancers unconnected with the big national security entities, the FBI, the CIA, and the NSA, where conspiracies are most likely to occur."

"But these are *spies*," Maryellen offered. "I mean, they're not actually plotting to overthrow the government, are they? I don't see a conspiracy where there's a bunch of people sworn to protect the United States with their lives if necessary, selling out to a bunch of our enemies. One person working alone is bad enough, but I don't see why any groups of the CIA and the FBI would want to do such a thing!"

"There's a pattern there," Targon said ominously. "There always is. The spies are betraying their nation, perhaps to weaken it so that it can be taken over by as yet unknown forces."

Maryellen frowned, feeling as though she

might be getting a headache. This was the side of Targon she had the most trouble dealing with. And yet the list of spies within the CIA and the FBI who had worked to betray their country to foreign powers had an authentic ring to it. At least, she told herself, she remembered all the excitement over the supposedly rock-solid loyal FBI man, Robert Hanssen. Anyway, this was Targon's job on his home planet. Ferreting out conspirators from government agencies. It made her head spin.

For a moment, she wondered if he could possibly be right.

"Look," she said. "All this conspiracy theory you're so involved with—I know it's your job, it's what you've been trained for, but I can't possibly agree with everything you say. You understand that, don't you? It's just . . . it's just . . . well, I want you to know I wouldn't be here with you like *this*, if I didn't feel something for you."

She felt herself blushing, her face was hot, so she hurried on. "I'm trying to say this is a really unusual situation, your being from somewhere else in space and all that. But this is not the ordinary thing, for me, either, you know. I'm trying to say I . . . I don't jump into bed with the first man who . . . who . . ."

"Who you find in bed with you in the morning," he finished for her.

"Well, yes," Maryellen said. Was he joking? She couldn't tell. And she certainly had woken up that first morning to find him right there with her. "I mean, I usually try to know something about the men I . . . ah . . . er . . . date. That is, where they came from, their jobs, their families. So they're not total strangers." Don't tell him about George Parker, she told herself quickly, it will only sound like whining. "That sort of thing."

He surveyed her for a long moment. "You know my job. I have already told you, I am a licensed investigator of corrupt government bureaucracies. As for my family, they are of the . . . I think you call it nobility. Yes, that is it, they are of the nobility. My father is a policeman."

"A *policeman?*"

He considered it. "Make that 'a general.' Yes, the military is more what it is. He is a general, commander of the forces. So are my brothers. So am I. We are very respectable Dreians of the nobility."

"Well, I suppose you could say my family is very respectable, too," Maryellen said staunchly. "My father is a doctor, and my mother is a member of the Junior League of Milford, Connecticut, and a Red Cross volunteer—she has been for years. Her family is descended from Jonathan Whitford who fought with Ethan Allen and the Green Mountain Boys in the American Revolution." It was the one thing her mother wanted people to know about her family, Maryellen remembered—that, until it had grown politically incorrect, they were all members of the Daughters of the American Revolution. "And you know my sister Felicia, you met her at 21. She's married to Stephen Crump, the richest man in the world."

"Those are very good families," he agreed.

239

"We come from good people. And I am glad to know I am only one of a few men who have been in bed with you to have sex."

Maryellen pulled back and kicked her legs free of his under the covers. "Ugh, how can you put it that way? It's totally tactless. And besides, it sounds awful! 'In bed to have sex.' Why else would they be in bed with me?"

Targon looked thoughtful. "I do not know. Perhaps it would be better if you explain why men get in bed with you without having sex. Considering that you are very beautiful and desirable, this sounds pointless. Unless, of course, it is some New York City folk custom I have not heard of. I have read in my guidebook that in colonial New England in the seventeenth and eighteenth Styrex Three centuries there was a practice where men and women romantically interested in each other lay in bed without having sex. I believe it was called 'bundling.' The couple was tightly wrapped in blankets and a wooden board, which could be locked at both ends, was put down the middle of the bed to keep them apart. In this manner they often spent the night together."

Maryellen had been listening with her mouth open. *"Bundling?"*

"Yes, I have seen the illustration."

"I must be out of my mind!" She sat up in bed. The sheets dropped away unheeded, giving him a marvelous frontal view, which he immediately became interested in. "I just can't talk to you, do you know that? All I wanted to do was tell you that I—I—have some feeling for you. Some little bitty feeling, it's true," she cried, "but I wouldn't go to bed with you and make love, no matter how marvelous it was, unless I had at least some—some—*feeling* for you. I mean, why would I help you to get somebody's body so you can use it, unless I *cared?*"

"I am glad you care," Targon said, sitting up beside her. "It was what I had hoped for, as I care, also."

"Stay away! You don't know what you're saying. All this means nothing to you. You're just on an excursion to a planet you have nothing but contempt for. And I know what you think of *me*. I'm like the rest of the people on Earth. You say it all the time!"

"That is not so." Kneeling in the bed, he managed to capture and put his arms around her. "You have taught me much, it has transformed my whole experience here. I am free of the ceremonies to the Great Mother Goddess that we must observe on Dreia, and I have found the marvels of lovemaking that can be done anywhere, in any place."

"Almost anyplace," Maryellen murmured. "The NYPD—"

He gently put his finger over her lips to hush her. "Anyplace." He took his finger away and kissed her.

It happened all over again, as it always did. The change in Targon, that he had become more solid, a more powerful human presence in her arms, hadn't affected the sizzles and sparks that shot through Maryellen as they kissed. It was still wonderful. Still a dazzling trip to the stars.

When she drew back, she was gasping.

She could see that he wasn't exactly calm, either. "This is different for you, too, isn't it?" she whispered dizzily. "I mean, it's different just between the two of us?"

"Something is happening," he agreed. "Obviously everything is different when we come together. I do not know any precedent for it. I am certainly looking forward to the rowboat in the lake this afternoon." With his arms around her, he pulled them back down against the rose-colored sheets. "But perhaps first we should try out this nice bed with the canopy in this hotel."

The words were no sooner out of Targon's mouth than the bedside telephone extension buzzed. It was a small noise, but Maryellen started violently. Outside, the first red-and-gold rays of the sun were just rising over the sky-scraping towers of midtown Manhattan.

Who could be calling her at his hour? At literally the break of dawn? There was only one answer. Maryellen lifted up the rose-colored telephone receiver with a feeling of dread.

Felicia was on the other end of the line, speaking in a terrible, whispering voice that was almost a scream. "Melly, you have to get out of there!" she cried. "Do you hear me? We're being raided by the Feds and men in big white suits and boots carrying some sort of sprayer cans, and Stephen says he will never surrender, it's a breach of his Constitutional rights!"

Alarmed, Maryellen jerked around in the bed to look at Targon. "*What?* Felicia . . . what's going on?" She saw he was reading her thoughts;

she didn't have to relay anything to him. "My God! You're being *raided*? Is that what you said? Where are you?"

"*Upstairs,*" Felicia hissed. "In the condo, where else? Oh, Melly—they came about fifteen minutes ago and took us by surprise, the Feds did! The FBI and a SWAT team from the NYPD, I think, and these people in the white suits—Stephen says raiding at dawn is typical. One of the maids let them in, but they had bazooka guns. Now Stephen is barricaded in the master bedroom, and I'm calling you from the phone in the bathroom. I can't do anything with Stephen. You know how he is about all his power and money—he was thinking of running for president next year. Besides, I think the Crump lawyers just stormed through the service entrance and established a command post in the kitchen."

"I don't understand! Felicia, who are the men in white suits? How do you know it's the FBI? Oh, I can't believe this!" A popping sound, like gunfire, came through the telephone receiver. "Good Lord, what's going on? Where are the kids? Are they safe? This is insane! Why is anybody raiding your condo, for God's sake?"

She heard her sister take a deep breath. "Melly, the children are safe, Stephen's security people—you know, the former U.S. Secret Service men he hired last summer—have them in the dining room. Besides, Melly," Felicia almost screamed, "it's *you* they want! Are you listening to me? The SWAT team came in waving these warrants and yelling they wanted us to turn over

Maryellen Caswell, a suspected plague carrier! Thank God we told all our employees that no one was to be told you were staying here."

"What?"

Her sister continued excitedly, "The white-suit crowd saw Stephen's oxygen tent and they wanted to confiscate him, too! Oh, Melly . . . When they tried to put poor little Jeremy on their list because he has the mumps, Stephen exploded. He went berserk! That's when he called the Crump Corporation lawyers attack team. He's on the telephone to the governor right now. The governor wasn't awake yet. They had to get him out of bed in the governor's mansion in Albany."

Targon said, "Ask your sister if she's told the FBI where you are. If they know we're down here in these hotel rooms."

When Maryellen quickly did so, Felicia shrieked, "No, of course I didn't tell them! Do you think I'd do that to my very own sister? Maryellen, throw on some clothes and *get out of there!* Don't worry about anything, just leave! Stephen will fix everything. Believe me, whoever did this is going to pay! Especially those monsters in the white suits—they've sprayed everything in the living room, even Stephen's Picasso that he bought in London last year! Maryellen, get out of there quick! Do you hear me? There's no time to waste! Uh-oh, I've got to go," her sister finished rapidly. "Stephen is calling the White House and somebody's gone to wake up the president."

Felicia disconnected on the other end but it

was too much for Maryellen; she continued to clutch the receiver, frozen with shock and her churning thoughts, until Targon took it from her hand and put it back in its cradle.

"We must do as your sister says," he told her gently, "and fast. A good assault team will quickly reconnoiter the territory looking for its target. We can expect the task force in your sister's condo to regroup and go through the entire building very quickly."

"This is because of the hospital," Maryellen muttered, her mind still racing. What was happening was unbelievable, and yet she could see a certain sense to it. "From what Felicia said, they're obviously the Feds, and they're looking for me—a *plague carrier!* I'm a *plague carrier*," she said accusingly, "because of that temperature and blood pressure thing at the Presbyterian Hospital. That's all your fault!"

"We can discuss this later," Targon said, taking her by the hand and pulling her up. "Right now we have to have a plan to get out of the building."

"I'll get dressed, and you can dematerialize again," Maryellen said, making for the dressing room where she'd hung her clothes. "We'll go down in the freight elevator. Or wait, we can do something I saw in the movies. I'll walk down two or three flights using the utility stairs and come out on a different floor, so if anyone's looking for me to take the elevator from this floor they—"

"I'm afraid that won't work," Targon said. He picked up his tight, gold-colored pants, which seemed a good bit tighter when he got them on, and buckled the belt. "The dematerializing, that is. It would be nice to be in such intimate proximity with you once again, but I can't do it."

Maryellen was in the process of throwing on a bra and white knit shirt and a pair of jeans. She bent to slip on her sandals but stopped and straightened up, surprised. "You can't dematerialize? Good grief, don't tell me that! You *have* to! What's the matter?"

He shrugged. "You have already noticed it. Making love and drinking *noksteriani*—I am too corporeal now to switch."

She could only stare. This couldn't be happening. It was the last thing she expected. "You're kidding. You've just *got* to be kidding!" she wailed.

"I assure you, I am not joking. Surely you can see for yourself."

He was right, she saw, looking him over with a sort of horror. They had only a few precious minutes to get out of the Crump Tower Hotel, and God knows how Felicia and Stephen and the kids were faring on the twenty-seventh floor. Her sister was certainly relying on Maryellen to do her part after all the trouble she'd gone to, to warn her of the raid.

Despairing, Maryellen sat down on the edge of the bed. "After the last few days—hoping to get a host body so you wouldn't fade away into pure light and energy—this has to happen! Couldn't you have been more—careful?"

"I told you," Targon said somewhat stiffly. "The effect of having sex on Styrex Three is largely hearsay, an ancient myth, and not carried in any up-to-date manual. Nor is it mentioned what happens when lovemaking is mixed with the drink of orange juice and champagne I have discovered."

"You didn't discover mimosas! Will you stop saying that you did?" She raked her fingers through her hair, knowing they should already be on their way out of the apartment, not standing there discussing Targon's problem. But it was a problem, a huge one.

"I can see you're right," she told him. "You're too solid to do the transformation thing! But what else is there? You've got to help me. *Think* of something! What are we going to do!"

He cocked one eyebrow at her quizzically. "You could always leave me and make your own escape. The U.S. government would no doubt be very delighted to find me here, in this hotel suite. Think of it, they would suddenly discover not a plague carrier, but something even better. An authentic space traveler from another galaxy."

She stopped her pacing and stared at him. "Ugh, you make it sound horrible! You're not really serious, are you? That's not really what you want me to do, is it?"

Targon said quietly, "Not if I can avoid it. I don't want to be shut up in a U.S. government laboratory somewhere in the desert for the rest of my life if I can help it."

Maryellen shuddered. "You're right, I can't let them do that to you. We're just going to have to get out of here somehow." She suddenly flopped across the bed to reach for the telephone. "I know what I'll do," she cried. "I just had a brilliant idea! I'll call the concierge and have him find some clothes for you. There must be a men's shop somewhere in the building, I think I saw an Armani. We'll just get you dressed up and put sunglasses and a hat on you and walk through the lobby together. It's perfect. You'll be all dressed up like a normal person, and nobody will think anything of it."

Targon reached for her, grabbing her hand before she could lift the telephone. "It's not six-thirty yet. Nothing's open at this hour, maybe not even the concierge's desk. And we have only a few minutes left. We have to move fast."

"Oh, my God, I'd forgotten, it's still practically the crack of dawn!" Maryellen jumped up. "I have to think of something," she moaned. "I have to get you out of here, I'm not going to leave you here in Stephen Crump's hotel after all we've been through! I care too much about what happens to you."

He followed her to the dressing room. "It's nice to have you say that."

Maryellen started pulling at the clothes she'd unpacked and hung in the closet. "You've got to wear *something*; I can't get you through the lobby in that space suit, it's still glowing and sparking. Oh, we need to hurry . . . Hurry," she muttered, "why can't I *think?* Ah, a long skirt— here's one!" She dragged it off a coat hanger and handed it to him. "Put it on! We need a long skirt to try to cover the boots, and we certainly can't get you into any of my jeans. Don't say anything," she warned him. "Just trust me! Here's my plastic raincoat, it's built like a tent. You need a hat, and oh, God, I don't have any hats! Yes, I do!" She pulled open a drawer and found a baseball cap that read "New York Yankees." She practically screamed, "I forgot, Stephen always stocks his hotel rooms with Yankees and Mets paraphernalia. . . . Weird, but I guess baseball fans are like that."

She stopped, short of breath, and stared at Targon. He had without a word of protest put on every item of clothing she'd thrown at him. Now he wore one of her long black skirts with an elastic waist, which gave room for his larger body measurements, but the hem didn't quite make it to the top of his boots; they still glowed and sparkled. Maryellen had found an old black turtleneck that was dismally tight and skimpy, but it was overlaid with a blue cardigan her mother had knitted that somehow managed to cover most of his chest and belly even if he had to leave it unbuttoned, and the yellow plastic raincoat. The baseball cap was more successful. Targon had pulled it down over his eyes so that it covered most of his face. With his long golden hair, he had a strange but hopefully passable appearance.

"Yes, that's not bad," Maryellen said uncertainly. "Oh, goodness, we've got to hurry and get out of here! Pull the skirt down in front so it covers your boots a little better. Here, put on my sunglasses."

As Targon put them on, they started for the front door of the President Calvin Coolidge suite. Maryellen didn't stop to look around. She was leaving everything behind, all her possessions packed in almost the same sort of hurry as when she'd left her own apartment. But it was the only thing she could do; they didn't have time to try anything else.

They'll be safe, she told herself. *There isn't that much, after all.* If the Feds let them, the hotel people would pack up her things and let Felicia know, then probably store them until they got further instructions.

"Out the back way!" Maryellen was in so much of a fearful hurry that she stumbled.

Targon grabbed her arm to steady her and steered her instead toward the front door. "Not the back way, it's too obvious and there will be Feds posted there. We will go down in the elevator." When she pulled against him he simply said, "I know what I am doing."

She turned to him as they stepped into the hallway. "I think you need lipstick. No, wait. It's important, it really is. Thank goodness your hair is so long." She got her lipstick out of her purse as fast as she could. He stood still while she shakily outlined his lips with Revlon's Strawberry Spring.

Maryellen was trembling all over with fright and excitement. This couldn't go wrong, she told herself, it just *couldn't.* The alternative was too scary to consider. They had to get out of the Crump Tower, although she wasn't quite sure where they would go after that.

"The effect really isn't bad with the long blond hair," she told him to make him feel better. "You're . . . ah, really quite believable."

"Believable" if you liked odd-looking women over six feet tall wearing glowing boots, an enormous yellow plastic raincoat, a baseball cap and smeary lipstick.

They would just have to work with it. "Now, if we can just get through the lobby," she muttered.

They had decided not to try to take Felicia's Jaguar from its space in the basement parking lot. Targon had pointed out that the New York police and federal agencies would already have a bulletin out on the Crumps' license plates. If they took any of Maryellen's sister's cars, they would be traced immediately.

They had the elevator to themselves until it reached the ground floor, so they didn't have to worry about other passengers getting in with them and scrutinizing Targon too closely. Maryellen darted out as soon as the doors opened, her head down, her only thought to make a beeline as fast as she could for the doors, but he grabbed her arm.

"Slow down," he told her out of the side of his mouth. "There they are, talking to that bellhop."

A jittery Maryellen managed to send a quick glance around the lobby of the hotel. Sure enough, two men in black business suits were engaging a bellhop in an intense conversation.

"Look up at me and talk," Targon told her as his hand on her elbow propelled her forward. "Say anything as long as you keep talking. See if you can smile."

Maryellen was shaking so hard she didn't think she could put one foot in front of the other.

She clung to a fistful of Targon's yellow plastic raincoat as they made their way toward the Crump Tower revolving doors, and did as he said and smiled. She was sure the expression was more like a hideous grimace from a slasher movie than an everyday expression of cheerful friendliness.

"Do you think it will rain?" She didn't know her own voice; she was so terrified she sounded like a tortured parakeet. "I love rain in New York City, don't you? With the rain comes the flowers and the birds and the bees—I hate bees, don't you? I got stung once by a whole crowd of bees and they nearly put me in the hospital. I was about eight at the time, and my father, who is a doctor, smeared me all over with a paste of bicarbonate of soda and water and made me take antihistamines before he drove me to the New Haven hospital. Fortunately, I—"

At that moment Targon deftly inserted Maryellen into the revolving doors. Amazingly, the two FBI men in the lobby hadn't looked up from their conversation with the young bellhop. Perhaps they hadn't expected her to take so direct an escape route.

The plate-glass revolving doors spewed her and Targon out onto the sidewalk in front of the Crump Tower doorman, who was dressed like a Romanian field marshal. Beyond the sidewalk doorman, a white bus stood at the curb with foot-high letters on its side that read, U.S. Center for Disease Control and Prevention. Stephen would be unhappy about what that would do for his business, Maryellen found herself thinking.

The hour was early and there were only a few deliverymen on the sidewalk, but they stopped, startled, when they saw a figure in a tentlike yellow plastic garment and glowing boots emerging from the ultra-exclusive Crump address. Targon pushed past them.

"Keep walking," he growled at Maryellen. "We're going to make it."

She was breathing hard, trying to keep up with him. A mailman getting out of his van gawked as they reached the corner.

"It's a good thing I'm not allergic to bee stings," Maryellen chattered brightly, "because I'd have been dead, of course, after that hive of rogue honeybees hit me."

"We need a taxi," Targon told her.

"We have to take the subway. We'll never find a cab this early in the morning. But at least they'll stop staring at you on the subway."

He turned to regard her from behind the sunglasses. "You can't mean that."

"Oh, but I do," Maryellen told him, taking his arm. A light summer wind stirred the grit in the street, making her blink as she looked around for the closest subway entrance. "On the New York subway you'll blend right in. Then we can stop worrying."

The light on the street turned red, and they started to cross at the corner. There was a New York City Transit bus approaching a few blocks away in the south lane, but otherwise the street was empty.

Neither Targon nor Maryellen saw it at first. They were intent on getting to the other side of the street to duck down into the subway entrance. But a large red-painted van that said Gambino Italian Sausage Company suddenly burst off a sidestreet with a screeching of tires and roared toward them.

Maryellen lifted her head. "Good heavens," she told Targon as she gripped his arm. "Watch out for that idiot! He—"

She never finished her sentence. The Gambino Company van slammed to a stop at the traffic light and the rear door flew open, quickly disgorging four men, including one in a huge black Darth Vader mask, and two women. The men raced to unload a large styrofoam replica of an Egyptian Great Pyramid and then lowered it with frantic speed into the street. One of the men at the pyramid's right corner caught the full weight as it left the sausage truck and staggered and dropped to his knees, but he quickly scrambled back up again when the others got it balanced.

"What are they doing?" Maryellen cried. "Is that what I think it is?"

She had recognized the burly figure of Maudie from the Bronx therapy group racing toward her. Maudie, and another woman who was just as large, carried coils of rope in their hands.

It took a second to register. "Targon, run!" Maryellen screamed.

The man in the Darth Vader mask had already executed an end run to block their way to the subway entrance. Targon grabbed Maryellen's hand to dash past the intersection and head south on Lexington Avenue. But it was too late.

The group carrying the pyramid lurched full speed ahead. At a barked order the figures carrying the edifice raised it shoulder high. Then, at another command, held it over their heads as they ran.

"Save yourself!" Maryellen cried, trying to loosen Targon's grip on her wrist.

The next moment they saw the pyramid tilt and the hinged bottom flap open with a bang. It was practically on top of them. Maryellen was running and screaming, her hand in Targon's, but almost no one was on Lexington Avenue at that hour to help.

The pyramid gained on them, close enough so that they could hear the panting breaths of the people carrying it. There was a *whoosh*, and then suddenly all was darkness. Maryellen fell to her knees as the hinged bottom closed with a bang. Groaning, Targon slumped against her.

She was stunned with the suddenness of their capture. She rolled from side to side in the interior of the pyramid as it was raised. Then she heard Targon groan again.

This can't be happening, Maryellen thought, dazed. But then it was difficult to know just what *had* happened. From the jouncing as she ricocheted off one Styrofoam wall and then another in the dark, trying to hold on to Targon, she guessed Darth Vader and Maudie and the rest had turned around and were rushing them back to the Italian sausage truck.

It had all happened so quickly. The therapy group had rushed out of the truck carrying the

Khafre pyramid that she'd last seen installed in that house in the Bronx, then scooped them up with it like a crocodile pouncing on its evening meal.

Targon slumped against her. He hadn't said a word since Dr. Dzhugashvili's people had ambushed them. It was possible, she thought, trying to reach him with her groping hand, that he'd been struck some way with the pyramid.

"Targon, speak to me!" He didn't respond. At that moment the pyramid shook with enough force to send her up to its peak, and she hit her head against the reinforced plaster of paris. "Owww," she screamed.

She fell on her back as the pyramid was turned on its side. The door in the bottom was yanked open and faces appeared against the bright morning light of the city street.

"That's her!" someone cried.

The black mask of Darth Vader appeared beside them. "We don't want *her*, we want *him*," it grated. "Get her out quick, we're not taking her with us."

Hands grabbed at Maryellen, hauling her out over the truck's open end.

"Stop!" she screamed. "You idiots! You can't just *take* him—that's kidnapping!" She fought. They let her go, and she fell into the street.

"Jeez, is that him, the alien?" she heard someone exclaim. The troop gathered around the back. "What's the matter with him?"

"Get in the truck! Get in the truck!" Darth Vader shouted.

The group milled around as there was the

sound of the truck engine being gunned, then they started piling inside. Maudie was the last to haul herself in. Gambino's Italian Sausage truck roared with a cloud of blue exhaust, then sped away.

Maryellen staggered to her feet in the middle of Lexington Avenue.

They had Targon.

She looked down at her hands and saw there was blood on them, Targon's blood. She was too numb to cry. She had to help him. It was critical. *Urgent.* But all she could think at that moment was that the people in the Bronx therapy group were the only ones beside herself who had ever seen Targon. Who could testify that he was really *real?*

How could she ever prove he'd been kidnapped?

Chapter Fifteen

From her place in the kitchen where she was tossing salad, Candy Ruggiero could see Agent Wolf Madder sitting on the couch in the living room in front of the television set. He was supposed to be watching *Wheel of Fortune,* but it was plain his mind was on something else, as he was slumped forward, his elbows on his knees, his eyes not focused on either Vanna White or Pat Sajak or any of the contestants. He was the picture of gloom.

Well, he had every right to be down in the dumps, Candy told herself, that's why she'd invited him to dinner. He needed cheering up. At the moment, as everyone in the FBI midtown Manhattan office was well aware, ominous clouds of disapproval and censure hung over

258

their heads. The Center for Disease Control's raid on Stephen Crump's New York condominium, assisted by task forces from the FBI and the NYPD SWAT team, had turned out to be a disaster. While the CDC had been enthusiastically spraying J. Stephen Crump's living room and art objects to neutralize any infection, and the New York Police SWAT team was attempting to breach the area in the kitchen occupied by armed Crump lawyers, the enraged billionaire had been on the telephone to his good friend the president of the United States to tell him what was going on: that his condominium was under attack by departments of the federal government and the NYPD, none of whom seemed to realize that any disease lurking in Crump Tower was not the plague, but simply a serious case of the mumps. The president had been suitably shocked. So had the senior senator from New York, the head of the New York City chapter of the ACLU, and five members of the board of directors of the Crump Corporation, all of whom Mr. Crump had called while he was barricaded in his master bedroom.

The backlash from the raid had hit the FBI midtown Manhattan office hard. When the CDC had overreacted and decided that subduing a potential plague outbreak was more important than the welfare and comfort of the country's richest billionaire, it had made a major mistake. Worse, the suspected "plague carrier" had been Mr. Crump's sister-in-law, Maryellen Caswell—infuriating the billionaire further—a well-known New York City commercial artist who'd simply had a badly garbled vital signs reading at the emergency room of one of the city's hospitals. This had been a big, big mistake all due to a hospital ER goof-up. Apologies were due all around.

But it didn't end there, Candy knew, worriedly spooning a helping of freshly shredded Romano cheese onto the salad greens. Midtown Manhattan Office Supervisor Bob Johnson had already been called to FBI headquarters in Washington for a "briefing." The word was he would not be back, that he'd been relieved of his job. The New York City Police Department, especially the SWAT team division, blamed the FBI for everything; the mayor of New York City had written a particularly harsh letter that had already been published on the *New York Times* Op-Ed page calling for more respect for the rights of New York City citizens from blundering federal law enforcement bureaucracies.

The only good thing was that, as far as Candy knew, Agent Madder wasn't going to be singled out for any special discipline—he was too unimportant in the line of command, toiling away in his talented but overlooked manner in the back part of the office every night. But everybody in the midtown office would have this goof on their record for the rest of their FBI career; Wolf was not going to be any exception.

Her heart had gone out to him when she saw how he was reacting to it all. He'd become very quiet, even gloomy. And he hadn't been back to the house on Harvildson Avenue in the Bronx—

at least, he hadn't tried to requisition a car to do so since the Crump incident.

It was probably for the best, Candy thought, sighing. Whatever that mysterious and apparently unofficial operation was, it hadn't produced anything that first night.

"I hope you like Italian food," she called from the kitchen. "We're having ravioli made fresh— I did them myself, with my mother's special tomato sauce, which she makes for me especially when I ask her to." Candy turned the ravioli out into a serving dish as she talked. "And I thought you'd like a little homemade Italian garlic bread. Then there's tossed salad with grated Romano cheese and slices of pepperoni. The pepperoni is the imported kind—I'm sort of like my mother, I prefer the best ingredients when I can get them."

"I guess I like Italian food," he said from the living room. "I'm from Colorado. We don't get a lot of it out there."

Candy put the ravioli and bread on a tray and started for the table in the living room. "My goodness, don't they have Italian restaurants in Denver? I thought that was a big city."

"It is a big city." He stood, aimed the remote control at the television set turned it off. "I just happen to come from a very small town in a part of the state that's not all that well populated. We have lots of small towns in the southeast part where we grow wheat. No mountains, no cattle ranches, no gold mines—none of the things people usually associate with Colorado."

It was a very long speech for Agent Madder;

Candy had never heard him say so much. She was greatly encouraged. A few minutes later she had all the food on the table and lit the candles. It looked lovely, she had to admit. She'd taken pains with everything, as this was a pretty special occasion (considering the way she felt about Wolf). She'd selected a pink tablecloth, as pink was her favorite color, and there was a centerpiece of pink tea roses from the florist.

"Well," she said as they sat down and started the meal. "It sounds like you had a very interesting childhood."

Her remark was the sort, according to all the dating guides and articles in *Cosmopolitan* magazine that Candy had read, that was calculated to get Agent Madder talking about his hometown and family. And it was a great opening: a candlelit dinner in a girl's apartment at night. She wanted to know so much more about him, wanted him to tell her. That would make this evening perfect.

What came next intrigued her. Agent Madder stopped wolfing down his salad long enough to put down his fork and look at her in a strangely puzzled sort of way.

"I don't remember much about my childhood," he said huskily. "My parents don't, either. They always say it was like one day there suddenly was a young man in his third year of college around the house, and he was their son, and they don't remember much before that. Not that we haven't tried to remember. I've asked them about what I was like when I was in the third grade, for instance, and they just smile and say

I must have been a very sweet little boy. That's just what they say—'very sweet little boy.' Their exact words. But as far as my grade-school years go, they don't even have any photographs."

"That *is* odd," Candy agreed. For a while they ate. She watched Wolf make his way through a third helping of ravioli—he'd eaten practically all of the loaf of homemade Italian garlic bread, so she knew the dinner was a success—before she voiced her next question. It was also one suggested by the dating advice columns. "And how did you feel about that?"

Agent Madder picked up his fork and stared at it. "It didn't really bother me, I guess. I was pretty busy with college, majoring in pre-law at Colorado State at Fort Collins. When I graduated Dad took me into the family insurance business. Until, and this is even stranger, I had this sort of . . . compulsion—that's the only word I can think of—to come to New York City and join the FBI." He raised his dark eyes to her in a look that was so boyishly appealing and yet at the same time so confused that Candy almost shivered.

"It was the only thing I wanted," he continued. "It was like a force that wouldn't say no, that practically drove me to New York even though my family pleaded with me to stay in Colorado. It really tore them up when I left." His voice trembled. "Now look what's happened."

"Oh, dear," Candy said, horrified that the topic had come up. "You mustn't let this thing at the Crump Tower get you down! I mean, it was hardly the FBI's fault. Those Center for Disease

Control people are fanatics—there's no stopping them once they get their Martian suits on. Besides, don't worry, the Bureau is not going to fire you. It's not like you are a spy or something!"

"I can't explain it," Agent Madder said. He abruptly put his head in his hands. "It's such a mystery. This whole FBI thing's really had a grip on me for so long, and now it's all blown up in my face. I need some direction," he told her, his voice muffled. "I—I need to know how it will all turn out."

"Oh, my goodness!" Candy had no idea what he was talking about, but it was agonizing to watch. She wished she knew some way of helping him. Impulsively, she jumped to her feet and rushed around the table. "Don't, please don't torture yourself," she begged him. "I can't stand to see you suffer like this! You're the most wonderful, talented, *brilliant* agent we have in the midtown office! You do know that, don't you?"

Candy had meant only to touch Wolf Madder's hair. To gently stroke the dark wavy tendrils and comfort him. But it was hard to keep her hands off him; he was just so mysterious and darkly beautiful.

"I've been watching you for all these long weeks—*months*," she continued. He reached up and twined his fingers around hers. "And I can't tell you how much I admire you," Candy said softly. "I don't suppose you know that I filled out all the forms for you and covered for you when you were doing your unofficial investigation of the people who live in that house on Harvildson Avenue in the Bronx—"

He came out of the chair, uncoiling his long muscular length while at the same time gripping her hand so that, once on his feet, he could draw her to him and look down searchingly into her face. "I wondered why that never came back to haunt me," he said. "Part of me figured it was you. But I couldn't understand why."

"Because I care for you, that's why," Candy burst out. She couldn't hold back any longer. "You're in my thoughts. I can't stop thinking about you. It's been this way for months. I don't want you to be so . . . *alone!* I want you to—"

She never finished, for Agent Madder dragged her to him and covered her mouth with his. It was a searing kiss that, a few minutes later when they pulled apart, left them both amazed and breathless.

"I don't think I meant to do that," Wolf said. He let her go and stepped back. "I don't know what got into me. I—I really think I ought to apologize."

"No, don't apologize," Candy cried. "It was wonderful, it was just like I thought it would be! In fact—"

"Well, in that case," he interrupted, "let's do it again."

The second and third kisses, they found, were just as wondrous. They moved to the couch.

"I have to say this," Candy told him some time later. "I have never had anyone kiss me the way you do. Actually," she said, turning pink, "I didn't mean that the way it sounded. That is, I haven't kissed all that many people. My family is a very strict Italian one living on Staten Island.

I really haven't dated all that much."

"I haven't, either," Wolf said. "I didn't have the time in college, and insurance agents don't seem to attract many gorgeous romance-minded girls. At least not in southeastern Colorado."

"When you kiss me," Candy told him, "I seem to forget about everything. Did anybody ever say that kissing you is just like being plugged into electricity—like sticking your finger in a light socket? No, I really mean it! There's this incredible sensation—"

"Like this?" Wolf murmured, and lowered his head.

It was a passionate kiss. And there it was again: Candy was dimly aware that as he held her in his arms the world seemed to sizzle and crackle with sheer sensuous high voltage. It was sensational. She'd never experienced anything like it before, certainly not during the few other kisses she'd had.

They spent some time exploring the possibilities of new kisses. By the time they paused, when they stopped to catch their breath, there were bits and pieces of clothing strewn all over the couch.

"Sorry, I just wanted to touch you," Wolf explained, folding Candy's blouse and placing it on the coffee table. "You're so beautiful I couldn't help myself. If you turn around I can fasten your brassiere back up if you want."

"No, I think I'll take it all the way off," she told him, turning off the lamp on the end table. The living room was plunged into shadow, with only the small light on the stove in the kitchen for them to see by. "This is too wonderful," Candy whispered, "I really don't want to stop now. Although I have to tell you, I've never done anything like this before."

"Well, neither have I," Wolf said, taking off his tie and then his shirt and dropping them over the back of the couch. "This is a first for me, too."

"You *haven't?*" Candy sat up. "It *is?*"

"Yes, what's the matter? Is it important?" He smoothed her bare shoulders with lightly caressing hands and then put his mouth against her damp skin to trail kisses down her arm. In the dim light it seemed a pale, almost phosphorescent glow followed his lips. "It just didn't seem like . . . the thing to do before this, that's all," he added.

"Mmmmm, ooooh, wow," she breathed into his ear. "And now?"

"And now, oh yes, it does," he told her.

Some time later, certainly after midnight, Wolf stirred and shifted his weight on the couch's cramped space, but he didn't wake.

Candy hadn't slept at all; she was too excited. This was the most momentous night of her life, and she knew it. She'd been lying in the darkness for some time thinking about what had happened that evening with Agent Madder—the man with whom she was in love. She had come to the conclusion that one had to experience love to even begin to know what to say about it.

It was earth-shattering? Cataclysmic?

Not quite, because those terms left out sublime and tender and gloriously ecstatic. And making love with him had been all of that, too. Now he was asleep with his head on her shoulder, his mouth in the curve of her neck, one arm flung over her body almost protectively. It was slightly uncomfortable, but things were going to be very, very different when he woke up, Candy knew. This may have been the first time for both of them, but they had lit a blazing, passionate bonfire between them that would be hard to put out.

Not that she wanted it put out. And he didn't either, from what he'd said while he was ardently making love to her. She sighed, a happy blissful sound. With her free hand she lovingly stroked Wolf's arm and shoulder that lay so heavily against her. Then her fingernail snagged lightly against his smooth, silky skin and she lifted it away. Just as quickly she put it back again.

She wasn't mistaken, she told herself. When she scratched her fingernail against his shoulder muscle it left a little trail of golden sparks. The darkness made them all the more pronounced. Showers of light came out from under her fingernail like miniature fireworks. *Sparkle, sparkle.*

The same happened on any part of his arm, she saw, scratching him again. After a while her fingernail began to glow. It was fun, fascinating to rake a fingernail along his skin and see the dancing lights follow. Candy had no idea what caused it, but even as she did it she realized she had to stop. Although her nail-dragging was feather-light, it would leave marks and she didn't want that to happen. For one thing, his body really was too beautiful to mar. For another, she didn't want anything to happen to spoil the memory of this enchanted evening. He might object to being so marked.

Candy put her hand flat against Wolf's warm naked back and held him in her arms. His breathing was loud in her ear, but her hand below his shoulder blade was out of sight. This way, she couldn't see the glow at all, and after a while she joined him in sleep.

The next morning, promptly at 11:00 A.M., the eminent African-American psychiatrist, Dr. Mandoleeza Hackenberry, appeared at Maryellen's apartment-studio door.

"Did you get my telephone message?" Dr. Hackenberry asked as Maryellen let her in. The psychiatrist resembled a somewhat younger Diana Ross in a brilliant royal-blue suit and matching wide-brimmed hat. "Ordinarily I don't make house calls," she went on, walking into the living room and looking around at Maryellen's effort to straighten up after the break-in by the therapy group, "but Mr. Crump called me yesterday and made it clear this was urgent. As he is extremely concerned, I didn't have any choice as a professional but to respond. He wanted me to be here at your apartment at eleven o'clock this morning." She looked at her wristwatch. "He said it was an emergency."

Maryellen was undecided. True, there was an emergency, but what Maryellen needed at the moment was a different type of help. All night she'd been wracking her brains to try to think of someone who could rescue Targon. She knew he might be in terrible trouble at the hands of Dr. Dzhugashvili's Bronx therapy group, but she also knew that if she failed no one else was going to help him. This rescue had to be done right the first time—and she couldn't do it herself. Could she?

She sat down in the middle of the living room floor where she'd been sorting out the books that had been torn from their cases and dumped. "Hah, Stephen is just grumpy because he's scared to death he'll come down with the mumps," she snapped. "He's not concerned about my welfare—believe me. He's mad at me because he thinks I'm responsible for the raid on his Crump Tower condominium. I know that caused a lot of grief, but I really didn't cause it. It was the nurse at that hospital who got things mixed up."

Dr. Hackenberry gave her a sharp look. "Your sister, Mrs. Crump, says she's been very concerned about you, Ms. Caswell. Recently, according to her, you seem to be convinced you have an alien living with you." The psychiatrist looked around for a place to sit, then moved a stack of CDs to one side so she could take a seat on the couch. "One who constantly gets you in a lot of trouble."

Maryellen didn't look up. Targon was never far from her thoughts; she knew she had to do something to help him and fast. Every hour counted. That crowd of Trekkies and space fans in the therapy group from the Bronx had been smart enough to figure that Targon was weakened in some mysterious way when he spent any amount of time under their pyramid, so they'd used it to capture him. But would they be smart enough to take him out of it, at least for short periods, so he could recover? Or would they try to keep him trapped under it? If they didn't let him out, God knew what would happen!

The worst part of all, and it was making Maryellen sick with frustration, was that she was so helpless. How did one even begin, for instance, to get a warrant to search somebody's house in the Bronx for an outer space–traveling alien called Sub Commander Ur Targon that one believed was being held captive there, when one couldn't even prove that an outer space-traveling alien *existed*? No one had seen Targon but her and the therapy group. In addition, the house she would need searched belonged to a well-known psychiatrist who would claim he had been 'treating' her. Maryellen was pretty sure Dr. Dzhugashvili was in on the kidnapping, now.

"Ms. Caswell," Dr. Hackenberry was saying. "From the alarming information I have been given, I feel this could be very serious. I have to ask you—is this alien in your apartment now?"

Maryellen shook her head no. It was too bad Stephen Crump was really so angry with her, because he would be able to find some way to rescue Targon. He had plenty of men able to do his bidding. But Stephen was furious.

"When the alien is in the apartment with you," Dr. Hackenberry continued, "do you feel he makes you do things you basically don't want to do?"

Maryellen hesitated a moment, letting the question sink in. "Oh, well, only at first," she said, blushing. "I suppose you could say he can be pretty overbearing. I mean he was pretty pushy about the hotel computer, and the Citicorp ATM certainly—and guzzling all that champagne and orange juice. But all the rest of it . . ." She felt that she had really turned quite red. "The rest was wonderful. Out of this world! I think . . . Good grief, I can't believe it, I think I'm in love with him!"

"In *love* with him?" Frowning, Dr. Hackenberry dug in her pocketbook and produced a spiral-bound notepad. She wrote down: *Patient is in love with alien.* "Then you do not feel that this . . . ah . . . *alien*," she went on carefully, "controls your mind? For instance, doesn't the alien speak to you silently so that other people can't hear, telling you to do things?"

"Well, yes, he does that sometimes," Maryellen admitted. "I told you he was overbearing, and of course he insists he's always right. But it's strange that you should bring up how I feel about him. I've just realized I'm in love with him. But the whole thing is so . . . preposterous!"

"Why is it preposterous?" Dr. Hackenberry asked.

"I don't know! What he *is*, I guess . . . an

272

alien." Maryellen floundered. "And the way he *looks!*"

"Does he speak English?" When Maryellen nodded, the doctor said, "Just how does he look?"

Maryellen hesitated. "Well, there have been some changes. They're hard to keep up with, actually. But the last time I saw Targon he was more earthlike and solid, and had a sort of golden tan."

Dr. Hackenberry put down her notebook and looked up. "*Tan?* How tan? Would you say he is a person of color?"

"Oh, yes," Maryellen said enthusiastically. "Very much so. He was gold all over, but as of yesterday it had deepened into sort of a pronounced medium toast shade—like he'd been on vacation. And of course he has this aura, which I have noted is sometimes shot through with little sparkles of blue and red as well as—"

"Ms. Caswell," Dr. Hackenberry interrupted, her eyes narrowed. "This is important. How do you feel about his color?"

"Oh, I love it." Maryellen sighed. "Haven't I told you that he's beautiful? But it's just terrible because I know that no matter how hard I try, my sister, Felicia, and Stephen will never accept him. Stephen in particular will have a fit. He's always ranting and raving about our immigration laws. And I'll say this—Targon is one alien who is *really* alien. You can't ignore it!"

Dr. Hackenberry snapped shut her spiral notepad and put it back in her purse. "Point of origin is no just cause for discrimination," she declared. "Even if the alien is here illegally. However, that in itself is not the stumbling block it used to be. I serve on a national committee that advocates total non-discriminatory immigration regulations for illegal aliens. Many can often be classified, anyway, as persons of color." She reached into her pocketbook and pulled out a business card. "Here is an address and telephone number in case you should want to reach them."

Maryellen took the card. "Thanks, but it's a little more complicated than that. It's wonderful that you're willing to believe that Targon exists, but that doesn't automatically give him any sort of status. And right now he needs help. A bunch of space-movie fanatics are probably holding him in a house in the Bronx that Dr. Dzhugashvili uses for his therapy groups. Targon may be in dire peril. He's affected by the pollution here on Earth you see, and—"

"Joe Dzhugashvili?" Dr. Hackenberry asked. "That anti-Freudian freak? Don't tell me he's been seeing you professionally! He hasn't, has he?"

"Well, yes," Maryellen admitted apologetically. "That's what makes it so difficult for me to try and get any help. Everybody thinks I'm crazy! You see, when Targon first appeared, my sister Felicia—"

"Dzhugashvili doesn't have his head on straight about minority groups," Mandoleeza Hackenberry said grimly. "He's a reprehensible Stalinist revisionist. We've locked horns on racial bias any number of times. Don't let him get at your alien, Ms. Caswell, under any circumstances. Call somebody for help at once. And stop worrying about whether your alien actually exists. You say you are in love with him? And you two have been intimate?"

"Well, er . . . yes." Maryellen admitted. "Yes, definitely—that was the out-of-the-world part I mentioned."

"Good." Dr. Hackenberry nodded. "I believe, and the national committee will support me, that any woman who has made love with a man can certainly say he truly exists, no matter how alien he might appear to be. In fact, that seems to be the case in a lot of marriages. You seem like a sensible sort, and I see what's happened here," she continued, standing up. "I don't think your brother-in-law had all the facts. Or he didn't want to see them."

"That's just the trouble," Maryellen agreed. "But if what you said is true, and Targon is a member of a minority group needing urgent help, like right away—where would I go?"

"For civil rights, to find someone who's been kidnapped for political and racial reasons, where else would you go?" Dr. Hackenberry asked. She stood up. "To the Feds."

"To the Feds?" Maryellen cried.

"Skip the INS," the psychiatrist advised. "Unless you want their SWAT teams, which are A-rated after the Elian Gonzalez operation. But you'll bog down in Immigration and Naturalization paperwork. No, what you want is an agency that's quick on their feet, and ready to go help a brother."

"I do?" Maryellen asked. "What one is that?"

"The FBI," Dr. Mandoleeza Hackenberry said. Then she swept toward the door. "The Federal Bureau of Investigation, what else?"

Maryellen paused. Well, she did have one "in" at the Bureau. There was the guy who'd been calling all week. . . .

Chapter Sixteen

Candy Ruggiero gladly worked late at the mid-town FBI office. She'd made the appointment for Wolf herself, and she couldn't wait to see the mysterious Ms. Maryellen Caswell. The woman had called at the end of the working day, and because of the recent demoralizing blunder at the Crump Tower, the Bureau office was nearly deserted. The woman had wanted an appointment right away.

I'll bet she's a knockout, Candy thought. That would just figure. She told herself that she was not really the jealous type, but something about this really turned her off. Perhaps it was because Wolf had mentioned he'd telephoned Ms. Caswell four days ago and left a message on her answering machine, and she'd never returned his call.

At a few minutes before six Candy wasn't disappointed to see a tall, young woman emerge from the elevators at the front of the office by the reception desk. Ms. Caswell, she saw with a sinking feeling, *was* a knockout. In spite of paint-stained jeans, a nondescript black pullover sweater and hair that could have used a stylist, Maryellen Caswell managed to look luscious in an old-fashioned Grace Kelly manner. That is, without half trying. It was enough to give every other woman in the world an inferiority complex.

She stopped at Candy's desk. "I'm here to see Agent Madder," she said a little hesitantly. "He's expecting me, Maryellen Caswell, at six o'clock."

"Yes, he is." Candy kept her voice cool and efficient, but her mind was churning with questions. *Who was this woman?* Why had she arranged for this appointment? "If you'll just follow me," Candy told her, "I'll take you back to Agent Madder's desk."

The brunette flashed her a slightly nervous smile. "Thank you very much."

Good heavens. Candy told herself as they walked toward the rear of the big room. *She needn't act scared to death.* Whatever her business was, it was growing more of a puzzle by the moment.

Candy stayed long enough at Wolf's desk to see Ms. Caswell introduce herself to him. He got to his feet immediately, and Candy couldn't help noticing for about the fourteenth time that day how wonderful Wolf looked dressed in his standard Bureau black suit, ultra-dark sunglasses stuck into his breast pocket, white shirt and black tie, and his crisp, dark hair. He was so heart-stoppingly handsome that for a moment she couldn't breathe.

Their eyes deliberately avoided each other, but she knew that every time she came to the back of the office on some errand or other he was aware of her; he watched her, just as she watched him. Nothing could erase the memory of the night they had spent together. She knew they were going to do it again as soon as possible. And if he was too shy to ask, she'd just have to invite him to dinner again.

As Wolf gestured for Ms. Caswell to take a seat in the chair by his desk, Candy quietly left them. But she didn't go too far. There were plenty of empty desks as nobody was working late in the back area, and there was a place to hide behind a concrete pillar surrounded by filing cabinets.

Candy wanted to be out of sight, but she also wanted to hear every word.

"I'm glad you finally came to talk to me," Wolf Madder said to Maryellen as she sat down in his office. "Actually I've tried several times to contact you, but after the Bureau's gaffe with the CDC . . ."

Maryellen bit her lip. This was going to be very hard—especially after the last forty-eight hours—attempting to explain to an FBI agent about the alien from outer space she'd found in her bed.

Not that it wasn't pretty nearly impossible at any time, with anybody. So far she was batting zero. But Dr. Mandoleeza Hackenberry was right—she needed help. Targon's whole existence depended on it.

"Oh, that . . ." she said. "Well, that's in the past. I'm here about . . . a . . . a . . . friend who said I should come and see you."

Agent Madder didn't seem to be listening. "What I called you about is a difficult matter to describe. Impossible, actually, over the telephone," he was saying. "I'm glad we have this chance to talk in person. First off, I have to tell you that the Bureau is not officially involved—yet. I mean, they were in the beginning, involved that is, when we received the NYPD traffic report about the taxi driver who ran into a patrol car because he thought he had an alien from outer space as a passenger. Forwarding the NYPD traffic report to us here at the FBI was only a matter of routine, since it mentioned 'alien.' It came to my attention, and I have to be honest with you, I have been doing a lot of work on this with no official Bureau support." He stopped and looked frustrated. "It's really hard to explain to anyone."

"I know what you mean," Maryellen commiserated. "I know exactly how you feel. I wouldn't be surprised if you threw me right out of here after what I've got to tell you. I fully expect disbelief. In fact, I'm braced for it."

"Well, I wanted to talk to you because you were in the backseat of that taxicab when it ran into the patrol car," the FBI man went on. "It's all in the NYPD traffic report of the accident, that's how I happened to pick up on it. The cabbie, Mr. Patel, says you and an invisible person were discussing space—"

Maryellen cried, "We can't be talking about the same thing, can we? The invisible person was *Targon!* He's the alien from outer space in the accident report! Dr. Dzhugashvili is holding him prisoner in the Bronx!" Her voice rose. "Oh, my God—how did you know?"

The man put down his report and stared at her, confused. "I don't know what I know. Actually, you seem to think I know something, but I thought you came in here tonight because of the message I left on your answering machine. I told you, I've been working on this for a bit now. Yet, it's very difficult to mention aliens visiting Earth to anybody in the midtown New York Bureau. Frankly, it's not the sort of receptive atmosphere one would have in California or Nevada, say, or New Mexico."

"Yes, people here think you're crazy," Maryellen put in. "Believe me, I know exactly how that goes! I was so uptight when I came in here tonight—"

"Actually," Madder interrupted, "I had an interview with your psychiatrist, Dr. Dzhugashvili, when I couldn't get in touch with you. It was not a very rewarding session. He gave me very little information, and acted very bizarre during the entire session."

"Dr. Dzhugashvili," Maryellen burst out, "is behind the whole thing, if you can believe that! Listen, he and that bunch of space freaks in his

Katherine Deauxville

therapy group grabbed Targon on Lexington Avenue just like some Mob kidnapping! It was awful!"

Wolf said quickly, "He was with you at the Crump Tower, the space alien?"

"Of course. Haven't you been listening? We'd been hiding out all weekend—trying to escape these people. But they caught us coming out of the hotel, and the Trekkies and Darth Vader jumped out of the back of an Italian sausage truck with that styrofoam pyramid they sit under for meditation and meetings, and chased us down Lexington and caught up with us and slammed it over us—over Targon, that is. He's the one they wanted, and now they have him! Oh, Agent Madder, you've got to help us! I'm pretty sure he's in the group therapy house on Harvildson Avenue in the Bronx. That's where they keep the pyramid."

He frowned. "I'm having trouble keeping up with all this. The pyramid?"

"Yes, you know, a replica of one of those Egyptian things." Maryellen knew she was sounding somewhat desperate. "The pyramid is supposed to concentrate cosmic power, and it really does have an effect on Targon. He can't stay under it very long. He's really in danger! These people are fanatics! They've captured a real live alien, and they don't want the federal government to take him away until they have a chance to study him and write up reports for Arthur C. Clark and the SFWA."

Agent Madder had been making notes, but he

closed his notebook and put it to one side. "The SFWA?"

"Yes, I looked it up. It's a very large and powerful group—the Science Fiction Writers Association. Dr. Dzhugashvili and the space groupies know if they can deliver a paper and documentation to organizations like that, they will make the history books! They'll stop at nothing. And they might kill Targon if they're not careful. That's why I came to the FBI tonight; you're my last hope!"

"Not so loud," Agent Madder said, looking around. "Actually, I told you before, I'm doing this on my own. I have just as much trouble as you do talking to anyone about aliens from outer space. It's not exactly a great topic here, either, at the midtown office. All you have to do is mention flying saucers, and everyone thinks it's a big joke. But I have to tell you confidentially that I have had for several years now the—er, urgent desire to pursue the subject of aliens. Any kind of aliens, really, but particularly those from outer space who happen to come here to Earth."

"What we have to do," Maryellen said, ignoring his confession, "is get inside that house and locate the pyramid—if they haven't shut it up in the basement or something."

He didn't seem to hear her, either. "I've had a strong motivation to do this ever since I left Colorado. I needed to come to New York, I needed to join the FBI, and I needed to wait for some sign to start my work. It's uncanny. Now," he said in a slow, emphatic voice, "the time has come."

Maryellen watched as Agent Madder pulled open his desk drawer and very deliberately took out a Beretta automatic pistol. He opened his suit jacket and slipped it into his shoulder holster. Then, as if in the grip of a strange mood, he also took out a pair of standard issue handcuffs and put them into a concealed pocket, inside his jacket.

"Are you going to try to get inside the house?" Maryellen wanted to know. "If so, I'm coming with you! Targon needs me. I can't let him down!"

Wolf nodded. "Getting inside that house may be a problem without using a SWAT team, though. And we don't have one of these, naturally. However, I'll work on a plan, try to estimate the amount of resistance. How many people did you say there were in this therapy group?"

"Wait, I have an idea," a voice came. Candy Ruggiero, suddenly stepped out of the shadows. She'd obviously heard every word from her hiding place behind the file cabinets. And she really did seem to want to help.

Wolf looked her over, his eyes glowing. He didn't seem to mind that she'd been lurking behind the files listening to everything.

"We're open to ideas," he said. "That is, if Ms. Caswell doesn't mind."

"I don't mind," Maryellen told them. "As long as her idea gets us into the house on Harvildson Avenue so we can rescue Targon. They've had him for almost twenty-four hours, now. I'm really worried about what we're going to find."

"Then let me tell you what my idea is," Candy said, moving to stand next to Agent Madder. Her hand moved slightly to brush against his, and Maryellen saw the two quiver. "First," the secretary told them, "I go to the front door."

In the house on Harvildson Avenue in the Bronx, Hector Consalvos had spent most of the day constructing a set for picture taking with the help of Jerry and the biggest and most skillful Trekkies who had helped with the removal of the alien from Crump Tower.

The pyramid occupied its usual spot at the far end of the meeting room, and the photography setup was close by—in fact, not more than ten or twelve feet away, so the occupant of the pyramid would not have to be transported any great distance. The setup consisted of a wooden platform about eighteen inches high and a backboard, both draped with a lightweight black cloth. Any object photographed against such a background was sure to have scientific integrity. The therapy group was fortunate enough to have a professional photographer as one of its members.

Despite all this, Hector Consalvos was not happy.

"I haven't checked on his condition for the past eighty minutes," he told Dr. Dzhugashvili, who had brought his black doctor's bag with him for a medical examination of their captive intergalactic traveler. "It's been impossible since breakfast, actually—that was the last feeding. He took the orange juice peacefully enough, but that was followed by this shouting and hostile-sounding singing that he did nearly all morning, and banging on the pyramid from inside. Khafre's Tomb is taking quite a beating. I'm not sure we don't already have some structural damage.

"Have you let him out at all?" Dr. Dzhugashvili wanted to know.

Hector raised his hands in horror. "Out of the pyramid? Perish the thought! We don't dare let him out, at least not until the effect of being inside it has considerably diminished his strength. In fact, we may have to employ drastic measures. Like a little starving. I know no one is in favor of that, but we have to do *some*thing. After his feeding, the alien was feeling so much better he hit Captain Kirk—er, Larry—over the head with a full carton of juice, then would have climbed out of the pyramid if the others hadn't slammed shut the door. Now he's had all afternoon to yell his head off. We haven't fed him anything more, so he is weakening, but we still haven't gotten him subdued enough to be able to reason with him."

Dr. Dzhugashvili gave a cluck of disappointment. "What a pity this space traveler has turned out to be so savage," he murmured. "It was always assumed that any of the extraterrestrials making their way to Earth would be superior beings, cultivated and enlightened—ready, in fact, to enrich our lives. Instead, we seem to have this howling barbarian who won't stop resisting long enough to let us communicate with him. If indeed he *can* communicate." He sighed. "Well, since you say he has been quiet for the past several hours, let us open up the pyramid and see what we can do."

Darth Vader and the Trekkies who had participated in the capture had come to stand around them while they talked. The downstairs meeting room was not crowded, it contained only the members who had actually participated in the operation, and who had been there since early morning. Everyone was still excited. It appeared Dr. Dzugashvili's information had been correct and they really did have a live extraterrestrial trapped in their pyramid.

This was fantastic, earth-shaking news! They told one another it was hard to grasp the enormity of it all, and eventually the story would be on television and in the newspapers. It would be bigger, even, than the first moon landing. But they also agreed that absolute secrecy had to be observed. This group was going to handle its own research, headed by Dr. Dzhugashvili, of course. The doctor would never allow them to be the targets of a federal government takeover like had happened so often in the past!

Hector Consalvos gestured for Vader and the Trekkies to unfasten the latch on the pyramid. "Stand back," he warned. "The alien should be a lot calmer now, but we can't take any chances."

They waited a long minute, then two. Finally, sighing, Dr. Dzhugashvili got down on his hands and knees and peered up into the Styrofoam-and-plaster structure. Then he backed out. He got to his feet, dusting the knees of his trousers with his hands.

"Get him out," he ordered tersely.

"It doesn't look good, does it?" Hector asked.

Darth and the two biggest Trekkies crawled inside. In a few seconds they reappeared, half-shoving, half-dragging a motionless figure in a dull gold, tight-fitting space suit.

Maudie, who was standing at the back of the crowd, rushed forward. "He can father my next baby," she cried. "That's all right with me! I like this one—he doesn't look like any of the others!"

"Please, Maudie," one of the Trekkies said as he moved her out of the way. "Not now."

"Speaking of looks," Hector said worriedly as the others laid the inert figure of the alien on the concrete floor. "He doesn't look as good as he did this morning. He seems considerably dimmer. Like a bad lightbulb."

They could see the space traveler's body glow was nearly extinguished. What remained was not a rich gold color but a pale, almost transparent light that throbbed erratically. The alien's head had fallen to one side and his eyes were closed, his mouth slightly open.

"He's not conscious," one of the Trekkies said. "He doesn't look too healthy to me."

Dr. Dzhugashvili was already on his knees, his black bag open. "His aura is fading. That means something. It must be a vital sign."

"Maybe," Maudie cried, "he shouldn't be inside the pyramid all that much; we know it weakens him. Maybe we could chain him outside here somewhere in a chair. Or even a bed."

Dr. Dzhugashvili was staring at the blood pressure reading he had just taken. "I don't believe this," he muttered. "I don't believe the body temp, either. The figures are totally bizarre. Still, they must be relatively normal for his type. This is a scientific breakthrough—what we have in our hands is a wonderfully diverse life-form! It appears humanoid but it is certainly different in many ways. Gott in Himmel, our discovery will be the sensation of the century!"

"About chaining him outside here," Hector interjected. "Unfortunately, we don't know what powers our alien possesses. For instance, he could be in command of kinetic forces of some sort and start fires, blow up furniture . . . We couldn't handle that. He would certainly escape. Besides, how do we know chains will hold him?"

"We don't," Dr. Dzhugashvili agreed as he got to his feet. "We don't know that chains or any other type of restraints will hold this specimen. Consequently we will have to keep him in the pyramid, feed him a little juice and hope for the best.

"I have called Dr. Lucius Skinner from the Oregon Interstellar Travel Group, and he is flying in tomorrow. Naturally he is wildly excited— I couldn't give him all the details over the telephone, but he could tell that we had made a major discovery. Also I have notified Horace Goldblume of the Geneva Friends of Outer Space Consortium, and he and his assistant will be in from Switzerland tomorrow night, followed by Drusilla de Moreno, the theoretical astrophysicist from CalTech. We have formed a committee and will be contacting our peers to break this marvelously exciting news. When we meet tomorrow night we will make an evaluation of the situation as it pertains to the handling and care of the alien."

The psychiatrist stopped and looked thoughtful. "Perhaps some sort of structure can be fabricated, like a Plexiglas dome, to house him. But how do we know he won't break through that?"

"We need to let him out of the pyramid," Darth Vader said. "Honestly, doc, I don't think it's too good for him, or he wouldn't be so helpless when he's trapped under it. What if he should . . . *die?* Hey, then all we'd have is a corpse to show to those people that are coming tomorrow!"

"A corpse?" the doctor answered. "How do we even know this type of being *dies?* And what sort of stress can they withstand? It is an interesting proposition."

"My cousin has a junkyard," Darth Vader said eagerly. "Let me look around over there and see if he has any Plexiglas domes left over from 1950s construction or something like that. I'll see if I can rig something that will hold him. What the hey, doc—it can't hurt!"

Dr. Dzhugashvili nodded. "Put him back inside the pyramid," he told those around him. As four Trekkies lifted the motionless form of the space traveler he said, "Yes, Jerry, see what you can find. You can start work on it. For the time being, though, we had best keep our alien inside Khafre's pyramid and not feed him for the rest of the day. We want him completely manageable when our illustrious visitors arrive tomorrow night."

Chapter Seventeen

"From my surveillance conducted here several days ago," Wolf Madder told Maryellen, "I can tell you the flow of people in and out is lightest around late afternoon. Then it picks up suddenly at five-thirty, six o'clock—probably when Dzhugashvili's patients get off from work and come here for their meetings. It drops off around eight o'clock, though."

Beside him in the front seat of the FBI car parked on Harvildson Avenue, Candy Ruggiero cuddled the bundle in her arms and spoke to it in a low, affectionate voice.

"Then, this is a good time?" Maryellen asked nervously.

"Well, we can't pick our times, we work with what we can get. But it's not too bad," Wolf assured her. "There are not too many people around tonight, anyway. We got a break when the Doctor left the house half an hour ago, probably to go back to his Manhattan office. According to what we know, that leaves the person known as Hector Consalvos in charge of things. The alien, we hope, is somewhere inside."

"Yes," Maryellen breathed. "Let's hope they've put the pyramid where we can find it, like out in the middle of that big meeting room. But we still don't know how many people are in there."

"No," Wolf agreed. "We don't know how much resistance we're going to meet extracting the alien. But no matter how many there are, Ms. Ruggiero is going to try to help us take care of them."

"Hey. Ms. Ruggiero," Candy said, lifting the squirming bundle from her lap and putting it to her shoulder where she could pat it soothingly, "is *definitely* going to take care of them. While you two go in the back of the house and look for Mr. Targon, I will be creating this distraction at the front door. A big one, you can count on it! You do your job; I'll do mine."

Wolf flashed her a darkly approving smile. "OK, then—let's check the time. It's three minutes to oh-sixteen-hundred. When the minute hand is straight up, we move in."

"Damn," Candy said, struggling to look at her wristwatch and still hold on to the blanket-wrapped body she was holding. "Does that make it four o'clock? Really, I forget. I can never get used to twenty-four-hour time! Oh-sixteen-hundred? Do you start counting the hours after twelve noon, or twelve midnight?"

"Never mind. It doesn't matter," Wolf said, throwing open the door on his side. "Let's go."

Maryellen hurriedly picked up her packages, one a paper bag containing the plastic raincoat, baseball cap, and sunglasses for Targon to make his escape, and the other an insulated nylon beach carryall that held fifteen individual containers of Tropicana orange juice not made from concentrate. She had to run to keep up with Agent Madder and his girlfriend, who were already halfway down the block.

At a nod from the FBI agent, Candy Ruggiero kept on going, headed for the front door, while Madder and Maryellen turned into the driveway that ran along the side of the house to the old-fashioned garage in back.

"Not the kitchen," Agent Madder warned her as they sprinted down the drive, circling a row of large green plastic garbage cans. "There's a smaller window that seems to be a bathroom. We'll go in that way."

The house on Harvildson Avenue had a rather dilapidated back porch. Beyond that were the two kitchen windows and the smaller one Madder had indicated. "Why do people always go in the bathroom window?" Maryellen complained, as the FBI agent gave her a boost up so she could brace her elbows on the windowsill.

The answer for their choice was that the window opened inwards. She found that out as she slid forward on her stomach and just managed to grab the edge of a washbasin before going on to hit the floor with a muffled thud. Madder was right behind her. He navigated the window and washbasin with sleek grace, and landed on his feet. He handed her the bundles of clothing and orange juice.

They could hear the front doorbell ringing loudly and persistently in the other part of the house. "There she is, bless her," Agent Madder said under his breath. "Ms. Ruggiero can hold them for about ten minutes, but that's pushing the envelope. We have to work fast." He shoved Maryellen toward the door. "Let's do it!"

They hurried down a hallway toward what they hoped was the front of the house and the big meeting room that usually held the pyramid. When they came to a door at the end they stopped, and Madder cracked it cautiously.

After peering inside, he drew back. His handsome, expressionless face was taut with tension. "It's the big room and yes, the pyramid is in there," he told Maryellen. She sighed in relief. "There are two guards, a man sitting in front of it reading a comic book, and another wearing a Darth Vader mask."

At that moment they began to hear excited noises at the front of the house. There were loud screams, shouts, and what appeared to be an anguished squealing.

"It's working!" Maryellen whispered. "Ms. Ruggiero's got something started. It sounds like a riot!"

Madder again put his eye to the partly opened door. "The subject reading the comic book has put it down. Now he's going to see what the fuss is all about at the front door. The Darth Vader is staying." He turned to Maryellen. "Are you ready?"

She nodded, eyes shining with excitement. "Yes!" she cried.

Agent Madder flung open the door to the meeting room.

Two people had answered the front door of the house on Harvildson Avenue when Candy rang the doorbell. One was dressed like *Star Trek*'s Captain Kirk, and the other was a large woman built like a wrestler, with a decidedly combative expression.

"Is this the place," Candy asked, "where you go to talk to people about alien abductions? I have to find help because nobody will listen to me, but it's all true! The aliens beamed me up into their flying saucer and had their way with me." She lifted the blanket-wrapped bundle she held in her arms to show them. "But this time I brought the alien baby with me for proof!"

Both Captain Kirk and the big woman were so surprised they stepped backward a bit. Candy instantly took advantage of that and pushed past into a room decorated with blue lights, plastic drapery, and an Indian statue that was also blue.

"Hey," Captain Kirk protested, trying to block her way. "Lady, I think you got the wrong place!"

"Did you say 'alien baby?' " Maudie bellowed, following Candy. "Did you say you were zapped up to a flying saucer and now you have an *alien baby*? That's what happened to me!" She made a lunge for Candy. "Here, lemme see it!"

Katherine Deauxville

Candy screamed, "Don't take my baby away! I'm not giving up my alien baby!" She darted around the side of the blue dancing statue.

Just then a door opened and three more Trekkies dressed as Romulans came in to see what the noise was all about.

"She's got an alien space baby," Captain Kirk shouted to them. "Do something! Call Mr. Consalvos! This woman's been abducted by aliens, and now she says she has their baby!"

"I see it! My God, I see it!" Maudie screamed. "Look at its eyes!"

She caught Candy Ruggiero in front of the Dancing Shiva and grabbed her by the arm. Everyone in the room could see the blue blanket-wrapped bundle Candy held was struggling convulsively.

"Don't squeeze it!" Candy tried to shove the woman away. "My God, let go of me, what are you doing? Idiots—you're going to crush it!"

"Hold her!" Captain Kirk shouted to the Trekkies, indicating Maudie as the woman lurched in her frenzy into festoons of blue-lit plastic sheets, pulling some of them down. But Maudie was past restraining. She had Candy backed up against the wall. "A little baby," she was howling. "A space baby . . . give it to me!" She caught the edge of the blue blanket and tugged.

"Stop! Stop!" Candy shrieked. "You'll hurt him, you . . . you *elephant!*"

It was too late. Maudie had a fierce clutch on the blanket in spite of Captain Kirk's efforts to restrain her. Another frantic pull, and the space baby's blue covering unwrapped with the velocity of a coiled spring, shooting a small body in a silver space suit into the air. Even the three Trekkies screamed.

Meanwhile, in the large meeting room, Agent Madder held the therapy group's guard, Darth Vader, at gunpoint while Maryellen crawled inside the pyramid and tried to drag Targon out of it. He was big and heavy and unresisting—not a good sign. Wolf finally ordered the Vader to help her.

Between them they managed to get Targon out of the Styrofoam pyramid and onto the meeting room floor, at which point Agent Madder promptly ordered the reluctant Dzhugash-vilian to get inside the pyramid himself. He then locked it.

"We have to get some orange juice inside Targon right away," Maryellen whispered. "Good grief, look at him! I think he's semiconscious—if that's what they call it where he comes from. It's a wonder those space freaks didn't kill him, keeping him shut up in that damned pyramid!"

Frantically tearing open a carton of Tropicana, she knelt on the floor, holding Targon in her arms, his head thrown back so that his mouth fell slightly open. "Help me with this, will you please? Hurry—you know we can't get him out of here until he's on his feet! There's no way the two of us can carry him, he's too big. And we'd never get him out of that back bathroom window." She sloshed another carton of orange juice into Targon's partly open mouth. To her joy he swallowed, convulsively. Then his eyelids fluttered. "Look," she almost shrieked. "He's drinking it!"

The FBI agent came to stand over them. "This is the alien?" he said in a strange voice. "You are sure?"

"Of course, I'm sure," she told him. "Look, you can help. Hand me some of these orange juice cartons, will you? The sooner we counteract the cosmic rays in that pyramid that make him so sick, the quicker we can get out of here."

It seemed reasonable enough. But Wolf Madder still stood there, staring down at them, his service Beretta in his hand. "He doesn't look very alien," he said.

"He's been bombarded with anti-matter or something," Maryellen hissed, exasperated. "He explained the whole thing to me. Ordinarily he doesn't look this way. Look, he's trying to get up! Targon, speak to me! Are you all right?"

Targon pulled away from her and sat all the way up. He showed the effects of spending almost twenty-four hours being bombarded by pi-meson particles in the therapy group's pyramid. His long gold hair was dull and hung in rattails. His once glowing features were gray and pinched. The FBI agent standing over him quietly pulled the slide forward in his Beretta automatic. Then he pointed the gun, at arm's length, at Targon's head.

Maryellen watched the movements with amazement. "What are you doing? Good grief, don't point that gun at him, put it away and help me get him up. We have to get out of here!"

Targon looked up, groggily, at the Beretta

poised only inches from his nose. It slowly seemed to register, for he squinted up at Agent Madder and mumbled something.

Maryellen stared in horror at Agent Madder. "Are you crazy?" She realized what was happening, now. For some lunatic reason the FBI agent meant to kill Targon! "Don't shoot him!" She tried to move in between. "It's—he's the alien we came to *rescue*, remember?"

With a backward sweep of his arm, Agent Madder pushed her out of the way. He said something to Targon, and it was not in English, either. It dawned on her they were speaking some language known only to the two of them.

Maryellen didn't wait any longer. With a scream, she hurled herself at the FBI agent's gun hand, hitting his arm. At the same time Targon grabbed for his knees, wound his arms around them, and toppled him. Agent Madder's Beretta went off, burying a bullet in the ceiling. All three of them fell to the floor, fiercely punching and grabbing at one another.

Maryellen heard Targon grunt in pain. Wildly, she jammed her elbow into Wolf Madder's groin, and he yelped.

Suddenly it was over. Wolf was on his back and Targon, gasping for breath, flopped across him, holding him down. Maryellen scrambled for the gun and held it out to Targon.

To her surprise, he shook his head. Maryellen sat back on her heels, holding the gun, while she watched Targon take his index finger and press a spot just above Agent Madder's nose and between his eyebrows, dead center on his forehead.

A little luminous gold spot began to glow under the tip of Targon's finger where it touched the other's skin, then it spread until it was the size of a silver dollar. Agent Madder seemed to relax, as if deeply sleeping.

Targon looked down at him. "He's my youngest brother, Tardek." The glow under his index finger where it pressed against Agent Madder's forehead had spread to his hand. She could see Targon's glowing body aura was coming back.

"Your brother?" Maryellen stared. "You mean he's . . . he's . . ."

"Yes, another Dreian. My brother disappeared some time ago; my parents have been inconsolable. Now I know he was taken, programmed by my enemies, and sent here to Styrex Three to find me when I arrived and kill me. It is a long, well-thought-out plot, apparently."

"Wow, you have some serious enemies," Maryellen said, impressed.

He snorted. "Hah—yes, I have. Now I am sure you will believe me about the danger of rotten bureaucrats." When Targon's finger continued to rest in the center of his brother's forehead, the FBI agent opened his eyes. "Easy, Tardek," his brother told him. "I have accessed your memory banks. Now you know what happened, don't you? Where did you get this body?"

Wolf looked up at him. "Sweet quarks, what happened to you, Targon? You look as mangy as a Nyrockian dog! The body came from somewhere in Colorado, in the west of this country." He grimaced. "I've been here months—years. But you know all that now. Listen, there's this girl—" He lifted his head to look around, and groaned. "Oh, hell, where is Candy?"

In the room in the front of the house with the Dancing Shiva there was mayhem.

"The baby bit me!" Maudie howled. "The space alien baby bit me. Look, my finger is bleeding!"

"Calm, be calm!" Hector Consalvos called. He had just run in from his office. From what the director of the group therapy center could make out of the chaos, a so-called alien space baby that had been brought in by some young woman had just bitten Maudie, then jumped out of the woman's arms and was running around loose.

"Close the doors," Captain Kirk shouted over the uproar. "It's an emergency! Shut the doors to the other part of the house and keep the alien baby in here!"

Hector Consalvos grabbed a nearly hysterical Mr. Spock. "The alien space baby is running around?" he yelled over the noise. "Where is it? What does it look like?"

"Yeah, running on all fours," Mr. Spock screamed back. "You'll see it—it's wearing a little mylar space suit!"

In the meeting room, Agent Madder and Mary-ellen helped Targon to his feet. He was still drinking Tropicana orange juice; she took an empty carton out of his hand and gave him another.

"Oh, please, please," Maryellen moaned. "Let's get out of here. I'm afraid of what these people will do to Targon." She turned to the man she'd known as Wolf Madder. "Is he really your brother? If so, get us out the back way as quickly as possible!"

"Not without Candy," he insisted stubbornly.

Even as he spoke, they could hear the sound of sirens outside. Maryellen started. "What's that?"

"Somebody's called the police. Here," he told her, shifting Targon's arm from his shoulder to hers. "You two go ahead. I'll go back and get Candy. She's done a wonderful job. I'm not leaving without her; I don't give a damn what happens!"

Just then the door to the meeting room flew open. The woman in question burst in, holding in her arms a small struggling body with huge almond-shaped eyes, dressed in a silver space suit.

"Run!" Candy screamed. "The whole crowd is coming!"

Targon took one look at the miniature figure she held and recoiled. "Aaagh!" he snarled. "It's a nasty little Silmurian!"

Maryellen dragged him into the hallway that led to the back of the house. "It's not a . . . whatever you said," she cried. "I'll explain later. Hurry—can't you run a little bit faster?"

Targon couldn't run at all. But they staggered

to the back door, down the steps, and into the driveway in front of the garage. They started toward the street.

Wolf stopped them. From where they were, at the side of the house, they could see two NYPD police cars sitting on Harvildson Avenue, their roof lights revolving and flashing.

"The neighbors probably called the cops after they heard my gun go off." Wolf turned to his brother, Targon. "Ms. Ruggiero and I can go on to our car—we've got our Bureau IDs," he said quietly. "With some fast talk the cops will let us through. I'll go back to the Bureau office and make a few changes. I'll fix everything. However, it'll take a little time and you and Ms. Caswell can't come with me. You'll have to make a run for it. You'd be better off to cut through the hedges and backyards to get out of here."

Targon twisted his mouth. "You'll be in touch, right?" he asked grimly.

His brother nodded. "I'll be right behind you. I'll meet you in the west." The two shook heads.

A few seconds later Maryellen found herself stumbling with Targon through the back areas of Bronx row houses that bordered Harvildson, holding Targon up bodily in the bad stretches. Crossing one backyard they were charged by a Rottweiler, somebody's guard dog, but Targon pointed his finger at it and muttered something, and the dog put its tail between its legs and slunk away. At last they came out on 175th Street.

"I can't believe this," Maryellen gasped, looking around. "We finally got away from that horrible place! What's going to happen to Agent Madder—I mean your brother—and Ms. Ruggiero? They both work for the FBI, but they really put everything right for me. Will we ever see them again?"

"It will work out." Targon was taking deep breaths, trying to get his strength back as he finished the last carton of juice she'd brought. "We will be in touch with them later."

Standing on the sidewalk on 175th Street in front of a dry cleaners, Maryellen helped Targon get into the yellow plastic raincoat, the baseball cap, and a pair of cargo pants she had picked up at the Army-Navy Store when she'd first realized she'd have to rescue him.

"We need a place to go where we can plan our next move," Targon reminded her.

"I have it all figured out," Maryellen said. "For the time being, that is."

Chapter Eighteen

"I thought I'd never catch him," Candy said. She held the little figure in the mylar space suit in her lap as she slipped off the elastic that held the almond-shaped "space eyes" in place. Once free of them, the little dog shook its head gratefully. "All I could think of was, if I lost my sister's Champion Don Hernando of Altavista's Hot Chili Kisses in a group therapy house in the Bronx she would probably put me in jail—if she didn't shoot me first. We pulled it off, but it was a very bad moment when the big fat woman flipped him right out of my arms."

"Don Hernando is a hero," Wolf said. He took his eyes off the approach to the Triborough Bridge long enough to give the Chihuahua an approving look. "He was very convincing as a space baby. In fact, Targon saw him, you may remember, and mistook him for a member of a tribe of professional interstellar assassins, the Silmurians."

"Don Hernando is just a sweetie," Candy declared, holding the miniature dog up to her face and rubbing noses. "He's a little tiger—aren't you, love?—but he's not an interstellar assassin. He'd never hurt anybody in his life."

Wolf grinned. "He bit the fat woman."

"That was different. I'd bite her, too." She smiled. "Ordinarily Don Hernando has the most docile temperament. My sister makes adorable dress-up clothes for him and takes pictures, sometimes she enters them in contests, and he endures the whole thing without a whimper. Any other dog would hate it, I suppose, but not Don Hernando. "Elaine sews for this dog just like he was a Barbie doll! He has matador clothes, an Irish outfit for St. Patrick's Day, a Viking suit with a helmet with horns, a costume like he was George Washington, and even a beautiful little doggie butterfly suit with fairy wings. Last summer my sister made a Whitley Schreiber space alien outfit and bought these big plastic eyes at Halloween. She sewed them onto elastic so they'd fit over his face, and it was perfect. That's what I remembered, that Don Hernando looked just like he'd stepped out of a space ship with those plastic eyes and the rest of the outfit. I thought he'd make a perfect alien space baby to get inside the group therapy house. And he was."

"I have something to tell you," Wolf said.

"About aliens. A lot happened while you were in the front of the house with the little dog, creating a diversion."

"Yes, you and Maryellen must have had a time getting Targon out of that pyramid thing," Candy commiserated. "What happened to the people who were guarding him?"

"One went to the front to see what was happening and was caught up in the action there, and the other one, the big man with the Darth Vader mask, I subdued and locked up in the pyramid so we could secure Targon and escape."

"Wow," Candy said, impressed. "You took on that big Darth Vader guy? I *did* miss a lot. Listen, am I crazy, or wasn't there a gunshot, too?"

"That's what I'm trying to tell you," Wolf said patiently. "A lot happened in there. I may need to go back to the office to clear up a few things. But finding Targon changed a lot of things. We may head west after—"

"Oh, I'm all for that," Candy interrupted, snuggling close to him. "Not going back to the office, though. It's really late, and even if *you* planned to return the car and file a report tonight, *I* think we should take a little time off. God knows it's been an exciting day! Why don't we drop Don Hernando off with his mommy, then go over to my apartment and I'll fix chicken cacciatore for dinner?"

Wolf turned to look down at Candy snuggled up against him as he drove, and he was so entranced he nearly ran off the Triborough Bridge. He pulled back into the lane to a chorus of honking horns and shouted curses.

"Ah, another superb dinner," he said. "I remember, you are a wonderful cook. And tell me, shall we . . . uh, worship the Great Mother Goddess, too, again?"

Candy threw back her head and laughed. "Is that what you call it? That's really cute!" She put her hand on his leg and gave it a loving squeeze. "Yes, we can do that—'Worship the Great Mother Goddess.' You know I'd love to do that. And then you can tell me whatever it is you want to tell me. It sounds important."

Wolf sighed, but he was smiling. "It is. Believe me, it *is*." He supposed he could access the Bureau files from a laptop, and it would be much more fun working from Candy's house.

The elevated part of the train that ran across the East Bronx clicked and swayed through its regular stops going south: St. Lawrence Avenue, Morrison-Sound View avenues, Elder Avenue, at a snail-like pace. Or at least it felt that way to Maryellen; she couldn't wait for the subway cars to go underground. She felt safer that way, although there really wasn't any reason; she and Targon weren't really safe anywhere.

It was bad enough having federal agencies like the CDC and the FBI pursuing them, she thought, but now with the New York City police looking for the suspects in a break-in at the house on Harvildson Avenue . . . It all led her to wonder how much longer any of them—Dr. Dzhugashvili and his Bronx therapy group, Wolf Madder and Candy Ruggiero, even her sister and her husband, Stephen Crump—could keep it secret that there really *was* a space-traveling alien, Targon, on Earth. She hoped that whatever Wolf—er, Targon's brother—was doing, he could calm down the police, the FBI, and the CDC . . . and keep everything covered up. If the truth ever came out, she told herself with a shudder, all hell would break loose. Television, radio, the newspapers, Internet journalists—they would all be in hot pursuit of the story of the century. Maryellen's life would never be the same.

And God knows what being in the spotlight would do to Targon. He would probably never get a body. There weren't any United States laws covering body-snatching for aliens, she thought gloomily, but even if it were medically and legally possible, there were undoubtedly ethical groups who would protest the whole idea.

The train clattered along. It was dark outside, a warm June evening in the sprawling city. Maryellen stared at Targon and herself in the reflecting car windows. It had been a brilliant idea to flee into the subway. They had stopped at a supermarket to replenish Targon's supply of Tropicana—it seemed he could drink a swimming pool full of the stuff—before they took the train, and now he sat with his baseball cap pulled down over his face, long disheveled blond hair visible under it, in the enveloping yellow plastic raincoat and cargo pants, with just the glowing tips of his boots showing. Between his knees rested the large paper supermarket bag full of orange juice cartons. He still looked very strange, but in the New York subway system it was as though he were invisible. Maryellen had noticed none of the passengers had given him a second look. But then in the same car they had with them an elderly woman in full combat fatigues wearing a cowboy hat and carrying a suitcase tied with rope, and a young woman in black motorcycle leathers and knee boots with eyebrow rings, a nose ring, and a tattoo of a sunflower on her forehead.

The subway was good camouflage for Targon. Still, Maryellen worried there was a limit to how long they could stay on it. Theoretically one could ride forever through the greater metropolitan transport system; it covered several hundred miles and four boroughs. However, she also knew that sooner or later they would become weary of shunting back and forth on the subway lines, and get hungry, and be in need of more sleep than they could get in these rattling cars.

At least, Maryellen told herself, they had plenty of money. They might desperately need a plan in their current circumstances, but as soon as they could think of one they had plenty of cash to pay expenses. And plenty more in the bank.

Maryellen couldn't think of what Targon had done to Citicorp's ATM computers without a twinge. She hoped that, like he said, some Chinese banking system somewhere was compensating for the shortfall somehow. As it was, it would be forever on her conscience.

Just to be on the safe side she opened her pocketbook to check the ATM envelope with her cash. They had been through so much in the last few hours, including crawling through a bathroom window at the house on Harvildson Avenue to rescue Targon, that she wanted to make sure it was still there.

Her fingers found the money, but they also found another envelope. She pulled it out and lifted it up to the light in the subway car, but even as she did so Maryellen was remembering where she'd last seen it. And why she'd forgotten it.

It was a thick cream-colored vellum envelope with the crest of Stephen Crump's elegant Crump Tower Hotel. It said on the front, Hospitality Kit. The concierge had handed it to her the day they checked into the President Calvin Coolidge suite. That seemed like a million years ago.

As she opened the envelope's flap and pulled out the contents, she reflected on the hours she'd spent in that hotel room. She would never forget them. The *noksteriani*—ridiculous Targon, thinking he made the stuff up—the strange and wonderful ceremony to the Great Mother Goddess, Targon talking to the hotel computer about conspiracies, making love on the terrace in the shadow of the Manhattan skyscrapers. All the fabulous, tender, exciting moments . . .

The Crump Tower Hotel hospitality pack contained a handful of goodies, presents for its esteemed guests. That wasn't unusual. The advertising world she worked in had practically invented the freebie packets most New York hotels presented the occupants of their most expensive suites. A few complimentary gifts were good public relations. The items in the Crump Tower Hotel kit just happened to be even more expensive and super elegant than most, though about what one would expect from J. Stephen Crump.

She lifted each card and read:

A complimentary dinner for two at Le Cirque, the fabulous French restaurant in Manhattan.

A personalized "small jeweled gift" at Tiffany's on Fifth Avenue.

Two passes for the New York Philharmonic at Lincoln Center, box seats, good at any time.

Champagne and dancing for two to '40s Big Band music at the fabled Rockefeller Center Rainbow Roof.

Complimentary tickets and use of the owner's skybox at Shea Stadium for any New York Mets game.

A five-hour tour for up to sixteen guests around Manhattan aboard a private yacht, good at—

Maryellen stopped. She quickly shuffled back to the engraved card with the pass to the Mets game at Shea.

"What's Shea Stadium?" Targon asked. He held out an individual container of Tropicana Berry Orange with a straw in it, but Maryellen shook her head.

"It's baseball," she said slowly. For once his reading her mind didn't bother her. "Steven has this fabulous owner's skybox at the top of Shea Stadium; I've heard Felicia describe it. He and his guests can watch the game on an enormous television screen—it's almost like a movie theater—while the ball game is on down below on the field. He has stewards to tend bar and serve drinks, even dinner if you want it. There's even a fax machine and a PC. I was thinking—"

"You were thinking," Targon said, switching his carton of Tropicana so that he could lift her hand and kiss her fingers, "that it would be a good place to hide out for the next few hours until we can come up with another plan. And I was thinking it would be a good time to enjoy some *noksteriani*."

"We can't ride the subway forever," Maryellen said. "We've already been out to New Lots Avenue and back, and the next round we'll have to go all the way out to Woodlawn."

"And you are already thinking of sex," he said, smiling.

"I was *not*! I was thinking that several gallons of orange juice have made you look a whole lot better. But still not as good as you looked yesterday." She hesitated. "I really am worried about you. You should have seen how you were when I dragged you out of that pyramid—I didn't think you would live. How do you feel?"

"Hah! You were wondering if making love again would do as much for me as it did before," he said, smiling. And his smile was devastating. "What I say in reply is, yes, I am looking forward very enthusiastically to baseball."

"Good," Maryellen said, abruptly standing up. "Pick up all your stuff, then, because we're going to have to change trains to get to Flushing Meadows."

*   *   *

"Shea Stadium," Targon said as they crossed the parking lot for the baseball field's VIP entrance, "was named for William Alfred Shea, an attorney who was instrumental in acquiring a new baseball team for New York City after the Giants and the Dodgers abandoned it in the 1950s."

"Where do you get all this information?" Maryellen marveled. "And so suddenly? You know the most amazing things about my planet."

"From the Dreian *Styrex Three Tourist Guide and Interesting Places to See* map foldout," he told her. "Thanks to the Great Mother Goddess, I can still access many publications while I am here. Shea was appointed chairman of the Baseball Commission by Mayor Robert Wagner, and first tried to get the Cincinnati Reds or the Philadelphia Phillies to move to New York, but was unsuccessful. He then tried to organize a third major league—the Continental League—in 1958, but it died before a single game was played. Two years later the owners of the National League decided to expand to ten teams, and franchises were awarded to New York and Houston. But there were rumors that New York would be rejected unless it guaranteed construction of a new stadium. So with William Shea prodding him on, Mayor Wagner sent telegrams to the National League owners assuring them the promise would be met. The New York Mets started play in 1962.

"Shea Stadium took $28.5 million to be built and was dedicated on April 17, 1964. It was originally to be called Flushing Meadow Park but was instead named for Shea—which was certainly an improvement. It contains twenty-four ramps and twenty-one escalators and is the noisiest ballpark in the majors because it is in the flight path from LaGuardia Airport. The story goes that when the city scouted stadium sites in 1962, it did so during the winter when flight patterns into LaGuardia were different, so they never measured the aircraft noise. Tonight the Mets are playing the Yankees in an interleague game that started at 7:30 P.M."

They were late, Maryellen saw; the parking lots were full. The Mets–Yankees inter-league game was well underway. She gave the Crump Tower hospitality pass to the guard at the Shea Stadium VIP elevators, and saw him do a double-take as he viewed Targon with his raincoat, Yankees baseball cap, and large paper bag full of Tropicana empties.

"Welcome," the guard said, recovering nicely. Although he did read the hospitality pass one more time. "It's a pleasure to have you as a guest of the Mets and Mr. Stephen Crump. I'll call upstairs and have a steward on duty in your skybox as soon as you arrive." He indicated the elevator. "Please let me let me know any special requests now, so that I can telephone them ahead."

"Yes, that would be a good idea," Maryellen said, following Targon, who was headed for the elevators. "Please have a pitcher of mimosas and . . . uh, something to eat." She'd suddenly realized she was starving.

She quickly stepped into the elevator beside

315

Targon, and the mirrored cage shot them silently to the top of the stadium.

Their private skybox steward, who'd been waiting in the hall in a military-style uniform with NEW YORK METS embroidered over the breast pocket, opened the door and escorted them inside.

The owners' sports lounges at Shea were everything Felicia had told Maryellen they were. In the Crump skybox a pitcher of mimosas and frosted glasses were already waiting for them at a table and chairs by the glass wall that floated over the field. From there they could follow the game, or watch it on the television screen opposite. Perched above the top tier of seats at Shea Stadium was like being in a private jet; at least that was the way Maryellen felt as the steward rushed to pour her and Targon glasses of the mix of champagne and orange juice.

Naturally there were a few drawbacks. The brightly lit baseball field seemed several miles away, but there were binoculars for guests on the bar counter, and the television screen tuned to the game didn't miss a moment of the action. The state-of-the-art system, integrated with a desktop computer, gave the game's instant replay and even freeze-frame enlargements of the action taking place. At the moment the television camera was showing a film clip from a Mets' previous game, looking straight into the face of the Mets' big, handsome, scowling pitcher, Jim Crocker, who'd been acquired from the Colorado Rockies where the nationwide media had crowned him baseball's Bad Boy of the Year.

The scoreboard said it was the top of the fifth inning, Yankees batting. The Mets, the TV announcer was saying, would have a big problem if the Yankees scoring blitz wasn't stopped. It was Mets 6, Yankees 8, and the Mets had already gone to their relief pitchers. Presumably, the controversial Jim Crocker might pitch tonight.

The skybox steward appeared with a large tray of miniature sandwiches, and Maryellen hungrily selected a Reuben and a chicken-and-bacon club. Targon stared at the huge face of Jim Crocker as a film clip from a past Mets game showed the pitcher shouting what appeared to be a string of invectives at two umpires. "This is interesting," he said. "It is called baseball?"

"Well, some people wish Crocker wasn't a part of it," Maryellen told him, her mouth full. "There have been attempts to fine him so much money he'd have to quit, or maybe even somehow put him in jail, but it hasn't happened. The fans used to excuse him for his outbursts against women and his racial slurs—not to mention what he said about New York and New Yorkers before the Colorado Rockies traded him, because he was such a wonderful player. He not only can throw; he's a champion batter, too. But he's been in a *big* slump lately. The sportswriters say it's because of all the criticism and hate mail. He gets booed every time he's on the mound or comes up to bat."

Targon gave her an appraising look. "You are very fond of this game of baseball, then?"

She shook her head. "Not really, but my father is an avid Mets fan, and I suppose I've just grown up with it. Actually, I never was that much interested in sports, any kind of sports—the world of art was always my thing. I really don't know all that much about baseball except that there's pitching and batting and outfielders and infielders, and two halves of each inning . . . things like that."

The steward was at her elbow, and Maryellen wiped her fingers with the Mets' gold-initialed linen napkin he provided and helped herself to two more little sandwiches. "These skyboxes are mind-boggling, aren't they? They're the ultimate in 'conspicuous consumption.' I forget who said that, about conspicuous consumption, that is, but I think they had my brother-in-law in mind. And of course all the other billionaires who buy pieces of baseball teams like the Yankees and the Mets." She sighed. "I suppose I have Stephen to thank again. He doesn't know it, as I'm sure he hardly ever thinks about his hotel's hospitality kits, but he's made it possible for us to be here and wallow in the lap of luxury for several hours until the ball game ends."

On the big screen Orlando Cruz was pitching to Nevin Weiner, the Yankees left fielder. Weiner popped a ball to center field and it was snagged by the Mets' Oscar Saliba for the third out, ending the inning.

Maryellen went to stand beside Targon as the steward filled his glass again. He was looking much better, she saw, due to all the juice he'd had since his rescue. His sparkling aura was returning. And there was definitely more electricity in his laser-blue look. Something twisted inside her.

"We will have to think of something," she said, keeping her voice low so that the steward wouldn't hear. "I . . . I don't want to leave you, in fact I don't think I can, the way I feel about you. That is, not now, not after we . . . well, the truth is, I can't abandon you because you need help! Look what happened in the Bronx. Of course, I'm not in much better shape. My life is in a terrible mess, the Feds are probably still after me, my sister thinks I'm crazy, I have an apartment and work I can't get to, clients who probably want to kill me, the NYPD is—"

"Yes," Targon said suddenly. "You are right. There is work to do if we are to head west."

"Head *west?*" Maryellen could only stare.

"There is an area north of Tonopah, Nevada," Targon said, sitting down at the skybox's computer. "A strip of desert called 'the Dreamworks' or U.S. Government Area 51." He pressed several keys on the computer keyboard and the Mets–Yankees game shrank to a small box on the left-hand corner of the giant screen. "It's a classified area where the most secret units of government security agencies like the FBI, the CIA and the NSA operate their 'black' projects. It's where, it is rumored, your government has sent UFO crews and other extraterrestrials to be studied in secrecy."

"Oh no," Maryellen whispered. "You're not going back to that, are you? Conspiracies, aliens . . . Look, right now we're in a spot; we really need to figure out somewhere safe to go!"

"I am working on that." He turned and said to the small computer screen, which had just lit up, "Is this your serial number—EYY-49-9112-4391? If so, confirm."

Below, in the stadium, a roar went up as the Mets scored two runs on a triple by first baseman Fred MacGraff. The big TV screen showed the score tied at 8, the bottom of the seventh inning.

Targon waited for EYY, but when the stadium's computer continued stubbornly to show only the status of its systems, ROM capacity, and other information, he spoke sternly. "I want to contact MOK4231-74. And stop that," he told it. "No more whining. You can do this, and be quick about it. Merely select a telephone line."

Maryellen saw the steward at the bar was staring at Targon, his mouth open. Before Targon could speak to the computer again she hurried over to explain they wouldn't be needing the man's services, probably for the rest of the evening. If anything came up they would ring the bell to summon him, though, she added. She raised her voice to try to drown out Targon's conversation with the stadium computer. The skybox steward left, still fascinated, looking over his shoulder.

She threw herself into the nearest leather-and-chrome chair and let out her breath in a sigh of relief. Sheesh! They didn't need to scare stadium stewards out of their wits and add to their problems!

Looking up, she saw that Targon seemed to

have contacted MOK4231-74 after considerable bullying of the skybox computer, and was talking to MOK back in the Crump Tower Hotel. From what she could make out of their conversation, MOK had been researching the CIA top-secret files for more information on what the government security agency was doing in the super-classified parts of the Nevada desert around the town of Tonopah.

He's never going to stop, she told herself, trying to be resigned. Furthermore, he'd even told her so. Sub Commander Ur Targon was a trained policeman, an investigator—or part of the military, depending on his later explanation—and this was his profession. Also, Maryellen had to grudgingly admit, she was beginning to believe there might be something to his theory of conspiracy in government spy and law enforcement units after all. If one kept digging long enough, she supposed, something was bound to turn up. And goodness only knew there was enough going on in the FBI and CIA; some startling revelation was in the newspapers or on TV practically every week. Targon's idea of a giant conspiracy dedicated to the memory of J. Edgar Hoover, that all-time master bureaucratic blackmailer, might not be so wacky, after all.

She got up to refill her glass. The small box on the television screen said that it was the top of the ninth inning and that the score was still tied, 8–8, with no outs. Cruz had hit the lead-off Yankee batter with a pitch, and he had taken first base. Next up would be the Yankee catcher, Velton Hodges. The announcer was saying excitedly that Mets Manager Bobby Clarke had gone to the mound to call in his last remaining relief pitcher, Jim Crocker. The stadium was united in its loud disapproval. Both Mets and Yankees fans were howling as the past Rockies star warmed up.

"What is all the noise about?" Targon asked, though he didn't turn from the computer.

"Jim Crocker, the one I told you about, is going to pitch." Maryellen stood in front of the big screen as Crocker proceeded to throw two strikes to the second Yankee batter. On the next pitch, Hodges drove one to the shortstop for the first out.

The next batter, right fielder John May, hit a single to center, putting Yankees on first and second. Allan Wilson came up to bat. Crocker threw a wild pitch and the runners on first and second advanced. Mets fans booed. Tension mounted below in Shea Stadium. In the bleachers it looked like a small riot.

"What on earth?" Maryellen murmured.

The TV camera panned away to show the crowd, which appeared to be in a frenzy, throwing paper cups and cushions down on the field.

"Could I see the game for a moment?" Maryellen asked. "Could I see the *full* screen, and turn up the sound, please?"

Still talking to the computer MOK in Crump Tower, Targon pushed some keys and restored the full-sized Mets–Yankees game. The cacophany of several thousand voices in a packed Shea Stadium hit the Crump skybox lounge with an abruptness that made Maryellen jump and the glasses on the bar rattle.

The announcer screamed that he had never seen New York baseball fans in such an evil mood. Nothing baseball's bad boy Jim Crocker did could possibly please them.

Maryellen watched with fascination as another shower of seat cushions littered the field. Time was taken to clean them up.

Crocker was pitching wildly, there was no doubt about it; even Maryellen could see that. In response the crowd booed so loudly it sounded, even on TV, like a hurricane was scouring Flushing Meadows.

Crocker threw again and the batter connected powerfully, driving the ball right back at him. The pitcher dove for it.

Thirty thousand people and more in Shea Stadium for the inter-league game between the Mets and the Yankees all saw what happened next, captured by a half-dozen network television cameras, radio announcers, and a legion of newspaper and wire service sports page photographers. As Crocker reached for the baseball, it slipped through his hands and hit him squarely on the chin.

Although there really was no way the sound could possibly carry all the way from Shea Stadium's pitcher's mound, it almost seemed there was an audible *crack* that those watching on television could hear. The air seemed to ring with it.

Wilson made it to first base, but probably no

one saw him. All eyes were on Jim Crocker as he toppled over like a felled oak tree.

"Good grief," Maryellen whispered. She put her hands to her mouth in horror as teammates, umpires, and coaches ran to the motionless man stretched out on the mound. "I hope he isn't badly injured. He looks so—"

Her voice trailed away; she was unable to say the word. But there was an awful finality in the way the pitcher lay sprawled in the center of the field.

On the other side of the skybox Targon had abruptly stopped talking to MOK in the Crump Tower Hotel. He sat perfectly still. Then he said, without turning to look, "Crocker's neck is broken. A freak accident. He's dead."

"My God, how do you know?" Maryellen couldn't believe that. "Maybe he's just knocked cold. Oh, this can't be happening, not out in front of thousands of people!" Actually there was now such a crowd on the pitcher's mound it was impossible to tell what was going on. An eerie hush had settled over the packed stadium. "Look, here comes the ambulance!"

Targon stood. "I have only a few seconds," he said.

"What?" Maryellen turned to see him poised by the huge plate-glass window that hung over the baseball diamond several hundred feet below. Not one but two ambulances had screeched out onto the infield and an NYPD patrol car had materialized, the police trying to keep the Mets and Yankees fans in the stands.

Something cold gripped her heart. "What are you doing?" she cried.

She saw a flash of blinding white light like some prankster in the bleachers catching the night game lights in a mirror. Then, before her very eyes, Targon disappeared.

Chapter Nineteen

"Poor son of a gun," the Mets' catcher said, as he bent over the inert body of Jim Crocker that the medics had placed on the ambulance stretcher. "Hey, I wished him dead a lotta times, but I swear I didn't mean it." His voice cracked. "I mean, not like this! Right down the middle of a game. Jeez, he saw it coming!"

"I get no pulse," the Mets' doctor said. He shook his head, then placed Crocker's limp hand back on his chest and looked around. "It's really too bad."

The anxious faces of the Mets' pitching coach and first- and third-base coaches looked down at the inert man on the ambulance stretcher, along with the umpires and the Mets' trainer and manager, who had come running from the dugout. Two New York uniformed policemen crouched beside the ambulance medics, who were vainly checking vital signs.

"What a waste, to die so young," the team doctor murmured. "What was Crocker's age? Twenty-nine? Thirty?"

The small crowd on the pitcher's mound made a wordless noise of regret. *Yes, it was too bad.* Around them the stadium was still eerily quiet.

"Sorry, I hafta do this," one of the ambulance medics said, putting a blood pressure sleeve around the fallen pitcher's left arm. "Gotta do everything by the book, no matter what, guys."

"He never knew what hit him." The Mets' manager was a short gray-haired man who hadn't loved the newly acquired pitcher, either. "That's the way to go, though—short and sweet. Crocker always lucked out. Otherwise we had a bet he was such a stinker he probably was gonna get killed by the fans."

"Ouch," the ambulance medic said. "What the hey—I just got shocked!" He looked down at the blood pressure equipment, which had a bright blue phosphorescence that faded even as he watched. "Jeez, how about that? What is there out here to shock me?"

At that moment the Mets' pitcher sat straight up on the stretcher.

"Get that thing off of me," Crocker snapped. He tore the blood pressure sleeve from his arm and tossed it at the doctor. "Now, let's engage in this primitive pastime and get it over with. Tell me, am I supposed to throw the baseball, or try to hit it?"

327

For a moment the group bending over him was too stunned to move or speak.

"No, it can't be," the doctor whispered. "I examined him myself, and I tell you this man is not alive."

But the Mets and Yankee fans filling Shea Stadium plainly saw Jim Crocker haul himself from the stretcher and stand. While thousands watched he flexed his shoulder muscles, then rotated his right—his pitching—arm, to try it out.

Slowly, after long seconds, the crowd's strange silence gave way to a vast, disbelieving murmur. It gained momentum and volume and then peevishly swelled to a roar.

Faker! more than thirty thousand voices accused. *Get on with the game, Crocker!*

Paper cups, seat cushions, and all sorts of debris again rained down on the baseball field. The chant began in the reserved seats and rippled upward, then flowed out to the bleachers as it grew louder, accompanied by boos and catcalls. "Crocker, you're not hurt, you bum" they called. "Send him back to the minors!"

"Sweet quarks," Jim Crocker said, brushing the front of his Mets uniform with careful, exploratory hands. "I gather from what I'm hearing we can't just walk off the field, so obviously we must continue." He looked around. "Come, are we going to do something for these howling idiots who bought tickets, or not?"

The faces of the Mets coaches, umpires, and medical people around him were still frozen with shock. Then the doctor cried, "Wait, if Crocker isn't dead, he has at least a concussion!

I believe his neck is broken. I mean, stop everything! He's in no condition to play."

The umpires were scowling. "Crocker," the head umpire yelled. "What did you just pull? Is this another of your antics? Like some kind of trick to have a time-out called, or what?"

"*Throw the bum out,*" the Shea Stadium fans were howling.

"I—I can't believe you're in any condition now to pitch," the Mets trainer stammered. "Crocker, I saw you myself! You—you—were sort of . . . well, *dead!*"

"He *is* dead," the doctor insisted. "I'm sure he had a broken neck." He looked as if he were going to cry. "Actually, I can't explain any of this. It's humiliating."

The pitching coach stepped between them. "Hey, let him play," he shouted. "It's the top of the ninth and we haven't got anybody else. For God's sake, Crocker's our last relief pitcher!"

Crocker crossed his arms over his chest. The uproar in the stands was deafening. "Look," he said. "I haven't got a lot of time to devote to this; I have other things to do. Do you want me to start throwing baseballs? If so, tell me where."

They stared at him.

"He can't play," the manager moaned. "His brain is damaged from that hit on the head. He's talking funny. He doesn't even know what he's doing."

"Crocker's brain was always damaged," the pitching coach hissed. "So what else is new? Jeez, let him play! We all gotta go home sometime tonight."

329

"You gotta be kidding," the head umpire said, shaking his head. When the others didn't say anything, only stared at him, he shrugged. "Okay, I give up."

With the others trailing him the home plate umpire walked away from the pitcher's mound, then stopped and turned to face the crowd. Forcefully, dramatically, he threw his arms wide.

"Play ball!" he roared.

High above the field in the Crump's skybox, Maryellen slumped in the big black leather chair before the television set and watched the new Jim Crocker take the mound against the Yankees.

The network sports announcer had screamed himself hoarse describing the truly incredible events that had taken place during the last part of the evening. In fact, he was so overwhelmed he kept repeating one phrase over and over, "Ladies and gentlemen, we are watching history being made," without, apparently, realizing what he was saying. The first time he'd said it was when everybody assumed from what they were seeing that Mets pitcher Jim Crocker was dead. At the very least the man appeared severely injured.

Now, miraculously, Crocker had risen from the ambulance stretcher, tried out his arm, then walked back to the mound. The crowd couldn't believe its eyes, and neither could the Mets broadcaster; he'd yelled himself silly along with the thousands gathered below.

But Targon was Jim Crocker now, Maryellen

was thinking. She was just as stunned as everyone else. It had all happened so suddenly—although she remembered he had warned her he might do it at any time—that she could hardly believe it.

Yes, but Jim Crocker?

The whole idea left Maryellen at a loss.

Crocker was good-looking enough, she had to admit, studying him as he stood alone on the mound while the pitching coach explained something to him—no doubt where to throw the baseball.

Actually, Crocker fit Targon's exacting body standards better than most. Six-feet-three-inches, nicely muscled and with the powerful, athletic grace that distinguished nearly all major league ball players, he also had unruly blond, slightly waving hair that he kept close-cropped in the current style, a straight, rather longish nose, and handsome features that actually had more of the seethingly macho look of Antonio Banderas than movie star Brad Pitt. Crocker's famous trademark, a bad-tempered glower, didn't seem to have made the transition, though: The frown on his face now seemed only one of concentration.

Maryellen held her breath as she watched the pitcher's wind-up. She might not know much about baseball but the motion, even to her, seemed a little wobbly—as though Targon didn't know where to put his feet. But the baseball left his hand at what must have been, she realized, awed, near the speed of sound. The Yankees hitter missed the ball completely—he just stood

there, still expectantly staring at the infield—
and it knocked the Mets catcher flat on his back.
The plate umpire ran forward to see if he was
all right.

The Shea Stadium fans came to their feet,
howling. The bases were now loaded, the score
still tied at 8 with one out. In front of the dugout,
the Mets manager demonstrated that he was
having a nervous breakdown.

On the TV screen the network announcer
croaked, "Baseball fans, you have just seen history made here today. League bad boy Crocker,
who just did some of the worst pitching ever
seen here in Shea Stadium, was then knocked
cold by a hard line drive up the middle at the top
of the ninth. For a few minutes it looked pretty
bad, but hey, we found out this kid is indestruc-
tible! Crocker's come back with the most amazing pitch ever seen in this part of the woods. And
he just did it again! Did anybody clock that?" he
asked someone off camera. "Folks, the umpire
is signaling Yankee Rodney Samuels is *out*—
looks like Rodney never even saw it!"

To the accompaniment of the sound of a New
York baseball crowd gone berserk, Crocker repeated his dazzling "light" ball as the Mets announcer was now calling it, to strike out the last
Yankee hitter. The score was still tied, a regular
cliffhanger, the broadcaster declared with what
was left of his voice. The ball game was now at
the bottom of the ninth, and the Mets were up.
The whole world was waiting to see if Jim
Crocker was going to perform spectacularly as a
hitter or, after that dazzling spell of pitching at

the top of the inning, he was going to revert to his well-publicized problems and screw up.

Yes, but where was all this taking them? Mary-ellen wondered.

She was watching Targon and feeling so tense she was gnawing at her fingernails. Targon was Jim Crocker now, a baseball star. Yet he'd been talking about going west, to Nevada, to continue what he regarded as his professional duty to un-cover terrible conspiracies buried in the federal government bureaus of the FBI and CIA.

From what he'd said, Maryellen supposed she was going with him. She hadn't thought it over much, but she definitely wanted to go; he was the biggest and most exciting thing that had ever happened to her in her whole life. She knew now she was in love with him. On the other hand, the situation was wildly complicated. For starters, how was Targon, now Jim Crocker, going to get out of Shea Stadium after the ball game? How would they make their getaway?

She hadn't, Maryellen realized, the slightest idea.

Down in the dugout, the Mets' manager was now a state of collapse. He could barely look up as the cause of all his anxiety, Jim Crocker, ap-proached him for instructions. He was the first batter up.

"You're too sick to play," the manager said, covering his eyes with his hand. "I know it, don't tell me. Getting hit in the head made you sud-denly spastic."

The big Crocker frowned down at him. "Pull yourself together if you can; I'm perfectly fine. I

333

merely need you to tell me what to do. Now, as I understand it, in this inning you want me to hit the ball when the man on other team throws it to me. Is that correct?"

The manager, as the Mets' trainer bent over him, could only shudder. The trainer put his arm over the manager's shoulders and the rest of the Met team gathered around.

"Crocker, it's the bottom of the ninth in a tie game," the trainer yelled over the mayhem. "You remember that much? You gotta hit the ball, that's all. Sheesh, Crocker, we *win* if you do. Think of it, our team will *win*—and we really need one right now!"

They could see Crocker thinking it over. "You're right," he shouted back. "It's getting late, and I need to get out of here—I have someone waiting for me." He paused. "Just how far do I have to hit your baseball?"

The other Met ballplayers looked stricken. It couldn't be worse, their faces said; Crocker was obviously out of what was left of his mind.

But the manager slowly lifted his head. "Out of the ballpark," he whispered to the trainer. "Tell this moron to hit it as far as he can—whatever. Out of the ballpark."

Crocker had heard him. "That sounds reasonable. Tell me, do you want it to go to the right or to the left? Or straight down the middle?"

The manager screamed. Four Mets players rushed to hold him up.

"Anything, anything," the trainer said hurriedly. He escorted Crocker away from the dugout and in the direction of the bright lights at home plate. The stands were reverberating with the roar of thousands of fans. It was hard to even think. "Just hit it as far as you can, Crocker," he yelled in his ear. "Understand?"

"That's a different concept," the pitcher responded. He leaned on his bat and looked in the direction of the pitcher's mound. "Actually, your phrase 'as far as you can' would encompass other parameters difficult to estimate under these circumstances. Let's stick with your original 'out of the ballpark.' It's simpler."

"Oh, God," the trainer moaned. He hurried away, leaving Jim Crocker, the Mets batter, alone at the plate.

Above them, in Stephen Crump's skybox, Maryellen jumped to her feet. She couldn't sit still any longer in front of the TV, she was filled with too much excitement and anxiety. Targon was down on the field, batting. He was the Mets' last best hope to win the game. A win, she gathered from what the network announcer was shrieking, of which the Mets were in desperate need. And Targon knew nothing at all about baseball. Or, at least, practically nothing.

From all the howling going on, the Shea Stadium fans were not in a friendly mood. To Maryellen's ears, it sounded like the Coliseum crowds must have sounded waiting for the hungry lions to appear. And Targon, Maryellen realized, was now an earthbound Jim Crocker, subject to the laws of gravity and everything else to be found on "Styrex Three." That included, she thought with a kind of horror, the fury of thoroughly ticked-off New York City baseball fans.

It was too late to do anything about it even if she could. The television camera showed Jim Crocker already at bat. He swung at the Yankee pitcher's first throw, a low ball that looked impossible to connect with, a sucker ball. But his bat met it with a resounding *thwack!* the TV microphones picked up perfectly. Then the cameras quickly panned to the dark sky and bright lights over Shea Stadium.

For a few seconds it seemed there was a bright speck like a baseball high over Flushing Meadows and the borough of Queens that seemed to be intent on joining the stars. Then it disappeared. Another TV camera immediately adjusted to a position over the left-field stands and began to search again, although uncertainly. Shea Stadium erupted in an avalanche of noise.

Behind the fence in center field, just to the right of the 410 marker, the Mets' Magic Top Hat began to move. The hat, which actually resembled a black kettle rather than any haberdashery item, opened up so that a red Big Apple, representing New York City, popped out of the top. This festive visual effect occurred only when a Met hit a home run. The maddened crowd hardly noticed.

"Baseball fans," the television announcer wheezed. "Once again, we've seen history made here tonight in this game between the Mets and the Yankees! Believe me, fellow sports fans, I guarantee you there's been nothing like it in the entire annals of baseball! The Mets' Jim Crocker has returned to his former championship style of ball-playing and knocked that ball out of the park—a move so dazzling none of us here are sure what we've seen exactly!"

Maryellen looked around for her purse and the other things they had brought into the sky-box with them: the duffel for Targon's change of clothes, the bag with the Tropicana empties. Nothing she couldn't leave behind, she decided quickly.

But she hesitated.

There *was* something between her and Targon, wasn't there? She wasn't just imagining it. Did Targon really need or want her? If so, he hadn't really put it into so many words. She could be deluding herself. . . . Still, she'd risked her life to crawl through that bathroom window of the house on Harvildson Avenue to help rescue him; she'd knocked his brother's hand away when he seemed about to put a bullet through Targon's head; she'd done a whole lot of things no person in their right mind would have done unless they were madly in love! Did he understand that? And did he feel the same?

He seemed to. Certainly the way they'd made love was a once-in-a-lifetime, earth-shaking experience—even, she was sure, for someone from outer space.

Maryellen didn't know what the future held for her, but for good or bad, Targon was part of it. She saw that now. All the rest, she thought, breathing a little prayer, just had to fall into place.

337

On television the announcer was sobbing, "Yes, it's true, baseball fans, listen to me. The Mets' Jim Crocker, the Bad Boy of Baseball, just won a white-knuckle game for the home team tonight. After all the trash talk, after all the hate! But many of us here are asking ourselves, Where did that ball go? The answer may be that NASA has something on its radar screens that shows a New York City baseball team, the Mets, has just put a ball in orbit! This has to be the most astounding home run in sports history! Hey, hey! Here comes the crowd!"

The television screen quickly turned to a horde of ticket holders surging over the barriers and onto the Shea Stadium baseball field in spite of the struggles of police to hold them back.

"This doesn't look too good," the announcer croaked. "The fans have got the Yankees pitcher Michael Martinez pinned down in center field. No, the crowd is picking him up and hoisting Martinez to their shoulders—in spite of the fact he threw the ball that Jim Crocker just batted out of the stadium for the winning run! And where is Crocker? Last time he was seen, he was coming back to home plate. Hey, if the Mets manager is on his toes, he'll get Crocker off the field right away! With the mood of the Yankees fans in Shea Stadium—"

Maryellen didn't wait to hear any more. Grabbing her pocketbook, she ran out into the corridor and to the nearest elevator. She was in such a hurry she punched the wrong floor. Instead of 'Players Area' where she hoped to find the Mets dressing room, the elevator let her out onto the reserved section, where the hallways were packed with people. She pushed through the jam up the ramp, toward the seats to the left of home plate, only to be grabbed by a uniformed Reserved Section guard.

"I want to see Jim Crocker," Maryellen screamed.

"Yeah, lady," the guard bellowed back. "So does everybody else in the stadium!"

"Well, let me go with them," she told him.

He shook his head. "You gotta have a ticket."

Maryellen had a sudden brainstorm. While the crowd jostled her, knocking her up against the burly guard's chest and stomach, she found the envelope with the Citicorp cash and pulled out several hundred dollar bills.

"How much is a ticket?" she yelled, waving them in front of his face.

"I'll see you down to the fence," the guard shouted, neatly snagging the hundreds.

It was a fight to get there, even with the stadium guard running interference. Hundreds, perhaps thousands of people were flowing over the reserved sections, the barriers, and onto the baseball diamond. Several NYPD patrol cars had been brought onto the field, but the fans had rushed to them and were rocking one, trying to turn it over. Oblivious to the carnage, the Shea Stadium loudspeakers were blaring the Mets' closing music, "Take Me Out to the Ball Game."

"Here," the guard shouted. "Look for Crocker around here."

He picked Maryellen up and shoved her over a fence and onto a cement projection overhanging the field. She suddenly found that she was looking down from the top of the dugout onto a group of embattled Mets players who, with the manager, the trainer, and a couple of umpires in their midst, were trying to fight their way into the underground exit and dressing rooms.

Maryellen waved both her arms. "Where's Jim Crocker?" she screamed. "I'm looking for Jim Crocker!"

"Hey, who ain't?" someone in the crowd yelled.

None of the Mets players answered her, they were too busy making their getaway. But the trainer paused and held up his hands and helped Maryellen climb down from the dugout roof.

"You looking for Crocker?" the trainer roared in her ear. "You his girlfriend? Hey, no offense! Believe me, I'm glad for Crocker that he finally got a girl who will talk to him." He pointed. "Okay, the last time I saw him he was over there by home plate. The crowd got to him first as they came over the fence."

"Oh no," Maryellen cried. She threw herself into the press of bodies. After a few feet she came upon a knot of Yankees fans seemingly piled on top of someone lying on the ground. She knew who it was instantly.

Maryellen told herself later that she must have completely lost her head. Because no one, man or woman—and especially a woman not terribly physical, only five-feet-seven inches tall and weighing 119 pounds—unhesitatingly throws herself on five or six New York City Yankees fans mauling a fallen Mets player on his back in the Shea Stadium infield.

"Get off him!" Maryellen yelled, charging at them. She didn't have anything to swing except her pocketbook, and she didn't want to use that as it was full of Citicorp money. Instead, she took off her shoe.

The rest, as the Mets network announcer would say, was history. Her black kid dress pump had a medium heel that made a punishing weapon. Coming from behind and screaming wildly, Maryellen hammered home a respectable number of hard blows before the Shea Stadium baseball lovers gave up and scrambled off into the crowd.

She helped pull Targon to his knees. "I knew you were in trouble," Maryellen shrieked, "I just *knew* it was going to be a big change for you, this Jim Crocker thing! Look what's happened!"

"Come along," he told her, seizing her by the hand and pulling her with him. "By the Pearls of the Great Mother Goddess, I'm not sorry to leave. I have had enough of Styrex Three baseball."

"Oh no! Your eye is bleeding!" Actually, he also had a sizable reddish-purple lump on his forehead. "Through the dugout," she panted, pulling at Targon as two more fans in Yankees souvenir baseball caps tried to jump them and punch him out.

There were still several Mets players standing around inside the dugout, watching the riot taking place at third base. The trainer held out his hand and helped Maryellen down into it, then hurried them to the rear entrance. He handed Targon a duffel bag.

"I got these together for you, Crocker," the man told him, also giving him a ring of car keys as he steered them toward the elevator. "I think you oughta get out of here fast—before you get killed. Pick up your Humvee in the players area—it's right where you left it."

"I want to thank you," Maryellen began, breathlessly. "Of everybody here—"

She meant to say that of everybody she'd encountered at Shea Stadium, the Mets trainer was the nicest so far, but he had started back down the underground tunnel to the dugout.

Five minutes, later Maryellen and Targon were sprinting across the Mets players parking lot.

"Where are we going?" Maryellen cried. She was out of breath and her heart was pounding. He was taking her with him, she was pretty sure of that now, but he hadn't said where.

He turned to look at her. "Las Vegas. Secret Area-51, north of there. Away from all of this. I have to accomplish my mission. My brother will join us as soon as he can. I'm not going to do this alone."

"Wait—I'm going to Las Vegas? 'Us'? Did you say that?"

"Yes. Las Vegas. With me." They skidded to a stop. "Sweet Quarks. What is that thing?" he nodded to the Humvee that suddenly came into view. It was customized with paintings of full-flame rocket engines along its sides.

"I don't know that I *want* to go to Las Vegas,"

Maryellen began. But then she cried, "Oh, ye gods. I might have known Crocker's dratted Humvee would look something like this! Here, give me the car key ring; the door lock release is on it."

He did so, then, before she could click the door open, he whirled, and pulled her into his arms.

"We can't stop now," Maryellen cried, struggling. "What are you doing? We're on the lam— you know what that is, don't you? It means we can't waste any time, we've got to *leave!*"

"We are pausing so that I can tell you that you are wonderful," he said, his eyes glowing. "Attacking those baseball fans when they had me on the ground, that was a very brave thing to do. And very effective, too."

"Well, I knew you weren't used to the whole . . . you know, Jim Crocker thing yet," Maryellen said, blushing. She wasn't accustomed to being praised for beating people over the head with the heel of a shoe. "I was afraid those thugs would have you at a disadvantage. They did rough you up a little, anyway."

"It is nothing," he murmured, planting a kiss on the tip of her nose. "You were very bold and courageous. My father, the military police commander, will approve of you greatly. So will my entire family."

With that, he lowered his head and kissed her passionately, lingeringly. It was a sensational kiss; this time the Mets parking lot erupted in pyrotechnical effects that left them both glowing, sparking a little, and dazed. The magic, if anything, was better than ever.

"Good grief," Maryellen burst out when she could get her breath. "That was fantastic. *We're* fantastic! Wait! you look different, a little," she said, gazing into his face. "You're changing. What is it?"

He kissed her again, softly. "Jim Crocker is from now on a 'greatly reformed character' as you say here on Styrex Three. Besides, it occurs to me to tell you that Crocker was not the baseball player that people thought they knew, but a Ka-Zorokian."

"You mean—"

He shrugged. "They cause a lot of trouble, the Ka-Zorokian criminal element I told you about. No matter," he told her, "Jim Crocker's future will be much improved. I think he will leave New York and retire from baseball before these New York City fans catch up with him. As you said, baseball fans are 'weird.' They are entirely too enthusiastic about their sport."

Maryellen shuddered. "I think you've got something there." She finally got the doors to the Humvee open. Targon slid in behind the wheel and looked at the dashboard. "I gather one has to have a certificate to operate this odd machine?"

"A driver's license, yes," she sighed. "You probably have one somewhere in your wallet, probably in the duffel, but can we please hurry? Oh good, there's a car phone in the Humvee! Now I can call Felicia and say goodbye, let her know I'm all right. She's been so good to me—

and the federal government did tear up her apartment. All because of me."

She saw Targon sitting still, staring out the windshield. "Here," she told him, motioning him to move over. "Let me drive."

"Listen a moment." He put his hand on the steering wheel. "I have something to say to you. This question you've been asking yourself over and over since I kissed you. My answer is *elorison-a-nexo*. In Styrex Three language it means I love you, you also love me—which is excellent—and we will travel to the west together this year to begin our investigations at the secret Area 51-of the federal government. I understand the American West is a good place to raise children."

Maryellen could only stare at him. "Elorison-a . . . What you said," she whispered, her heart pounding, "means all of *that?*"

"Yes, and also," he said as Maryellen and he changed seats. She inserted and turned the key in the ignition and started the Humvee. "The first baby will arrive a few days after an ancient Styrex Three holiday that is called St. Valentine's Day. This is an unprecedented event and will be greeted with much excitement on Dreia. A Styrex-Three baby has never happened before."

For a moment she sat still, staring through the windshield at the outlines of a brightly lit Shea Stadium. A few Mets players had started to straggle across the parking lot.

"And just how do you know I'm pregnant?" she managed, finally. "You know you love me and I love you, and all of what you just said—and you know I'm *pregnant?*"

He looked at her with some surprise. "Naturally. The Great Mother Goddess always lets the male know first, so that he can surround his love partner with tenderness, protection, and the things she will come to crave. In your case, according to our Styrex Three guidebook, they are garlic dill pickles, halavah, watermelon, anchovies, and coconut cream pie."

They rode in silence for a long while, headed west. As they entered the Brooklyn-Queens Expressway, Maryellen was thinking: *Love, tenderness, protection, and garlic dill pickles.* It sounded perfect. She sighed with happiness.

"There ought to be a sign around here for the Verrazano-Narrows Bridge," she said. "Remember the George Washington Bridge? Well, this one is even prettier."

THE
STAR
King
SUSAN GRANT

Careening out of control in her fighter jet is only the start of the wildest ride of Jasmine's life; spinning wildly in an airplane is nothing like the loss of equilibrium she feels when she lands. There, in a half-dream, Jas sees a man more powerfully compelling than any she's ever encountered. Though his words are foreign, his touch is familiar, baffling her mind even as he touches her soul. But who is he? Is he, too, a downed pilot? Is that why he lies in the desert sand beneath a starry Arabian sky? The answers burn in his mysterious golden eyes, in his thoughts that become hers as he holds out his hand and requests her aid. This man has crossed many miles to find her, to offer her a heaven that she might otherwise never know, and love is only one of the many gifts of . . . the Star King.

___52413-9 $5.50 US/$6.50 CAN

Catherine Spangler

SHADOWER

Sabin has been in every hellhole in the galaxy. In his line of work, hives of scum and villainy are nothing to fear. But Giza's is different, and the bronze-haired beauty at the bar is something special. Not only can she sweep a man off his feet, she can break his legs—and steal his heart. And though Moriah isn't what Sabin had come for, she is suddenly all he desires.

The man is a menace, what with his dark good looks and overwhelming masculinity. Worse, Sabin is a shadower, a bounty hunter, which means he is only one step removed from the law. He is dangerous to a smuggler like Moriah, to her freedom. Yet he draws her as a moth to a flame, and even as she pledges to stay cool, her senses catch fire. Then, in his arms, Moriah realizes that this bounty hunter is different. His touch is gentle, and his kiss sweet. And his love leads to a fantastic freedom she's never known.

___52424-4 $5.50 US/$6.50 CAN

Aphrodite's Kiss
Julie Kenner

Crazy as it sounds, on her twenty-fifth birthday Zoe has the chance to become a superhero. But x-ray vision and the ability to fly are only two things to consider. There is also her newfound heightened sensitivity. If she can hardly eat a chocolate bar without convulsing in ecstasy, how is she to give herself the birthday gift she's really set her heart on— George Taylor? The handsome P.I.'s dark exterior hides a truly sweet center, and Zoe feels certain that his mere touch will send her spiraling into oblivion. But the man is looking for an average Jane no matter what he claims. He can never love a superhero-to-be—can he? Zoe has to know. With her super powers, she can only see through his clothing; to strip bare the workings of his heart, she'll have to rely on something a little more potent.

___52438-4 $5.99 US/$6.99 CAN

Aphrodite's Passion

JULIE KENNER

Available April 2002!

FROM
LOVE ✦ SPELL

Aphrodite's Passion

JULIE KENNER

Aphrodite's Girdle is missing, and Hale knows the artifact will take all his superpowers to retrieve. The mortal who's found and donned it—one Tracy Tannin, the descendent of a goddess of the silver screen—wasn't exactly popular before the belt. Now everyone wants her. But the golden girdle can only be recovered through honest means, which means there is no chance for Hale to simply become invisible and whisk it away. (Although, watching Tracy, he finds himself imagining other garments he'd like to remove.) Maybe he should convince her she is as desirable as he sees her. Only then will she realize she is worth loving no matter what she is wearing—or what she isn't.

___52474-0 $5.99 US/$7.99 CAN

Dorchester Publishing Co., Inc.
P.O. Box 6640
Wayne, PA 19087-8640

Please add $2.50 for shipping and handling for the first book and $0.75 for each additional book. NY and PA residents, add appropriate sales tax. No cash, stamps, or C.O.D.s. All Canadian orders require $5.00 for shipping and handling and must be paid in U.S. dollars. Prices and availability subject to change. **Payment must accompany all orders.**

Name _____

Address_____

City_____ State_____ Zip _____

E-mail _____

I have enclosed $_____in payment for the checked book(s).
 ❑Please send me a free catalog.
                    CHECK OUT OUR WEBSITE at www.dorchesterpub.com!